Secrets of Two Sisters

by

Debbie G. Brownfield

SECRETS OF TWO SISTERS

Printing history: 1st edition, 1st printing/ November 2013
1st edition, 2nd printing/April 2014

ISBN-13: 978-0615921617 (Debbie G.\Brownfield)
ISBN-10: 0615921612

Published by   CreateSpace
                    7290 Investment Drive, Suite B
                    North Charleston, SC 29418

PRINTED IN THE UNITED STATES OF AMERICA

Acknowledgments

I am so grateful to those who have proven to be true friends. The following people have provided unending encouragement and support:

Natalie, who owns the coolest kids' bookstore; Brenda, Amy M., my sister, and Gabby, who all listen to my ideas, critique my manuscripts, and challenge my writing; my brothers who are very critical proofreaders, Don and Mary Ella for their unstinting encouragement; Ralph and Carolyn for unlimited use of their library; Becky M. and Teresa S. for financial help and encouraging words; Chuck for his invaluable assistance with various technical details; the Flowertown Writers and the Summerville Writers' Guild, and the gang at Catalyst for keeping life REAL, week after week!

Jessica King and Mark Melcher have helped with their awesome photography and cheerful attitudes in spite of several attempts to get it right! Chip Googe always comes through with work on the covers, and the support personnel at SmartDraw have been wonderfully helpful with the family trees.

In *Secret Agendas* and *A Secret Place*

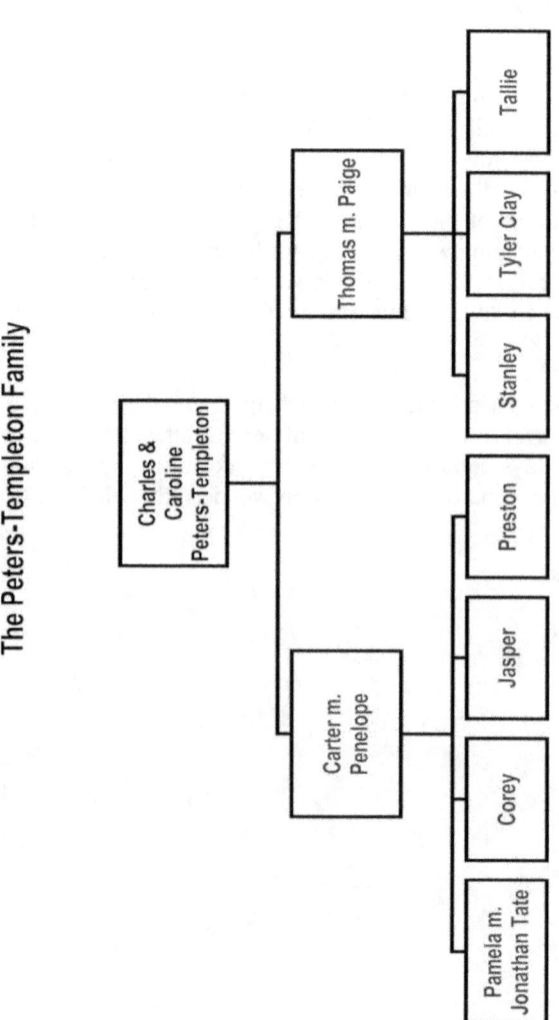

The Peters-Templeton Family

Charles & Caroline Peters-Templeton

Carter m. Penelope

Thomas m. Paige

Pamela m. Jonathan Tate

Corey

Jasper

Preston

Stanley

Tyler Clay

Tallie

In *Secrets of the Enemy & Secret Agendas*

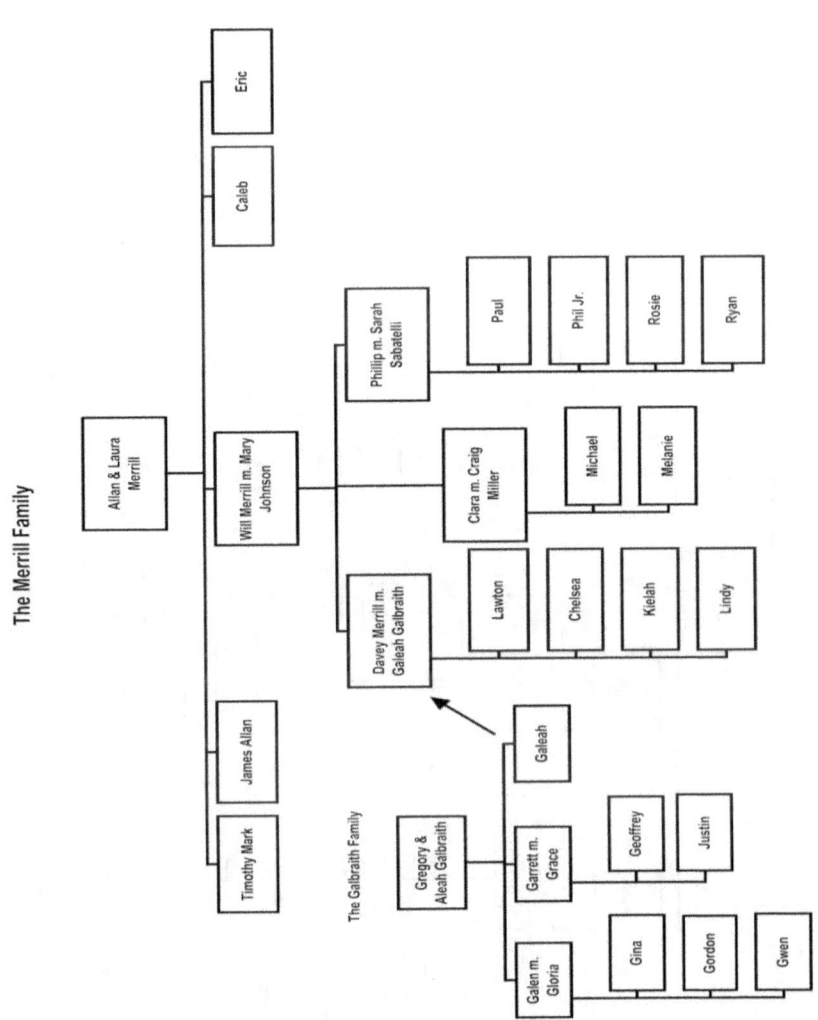

In *Secrets of Two Sisters, Secrets of the Enemy, Secret Agendas, & A Secret Place*

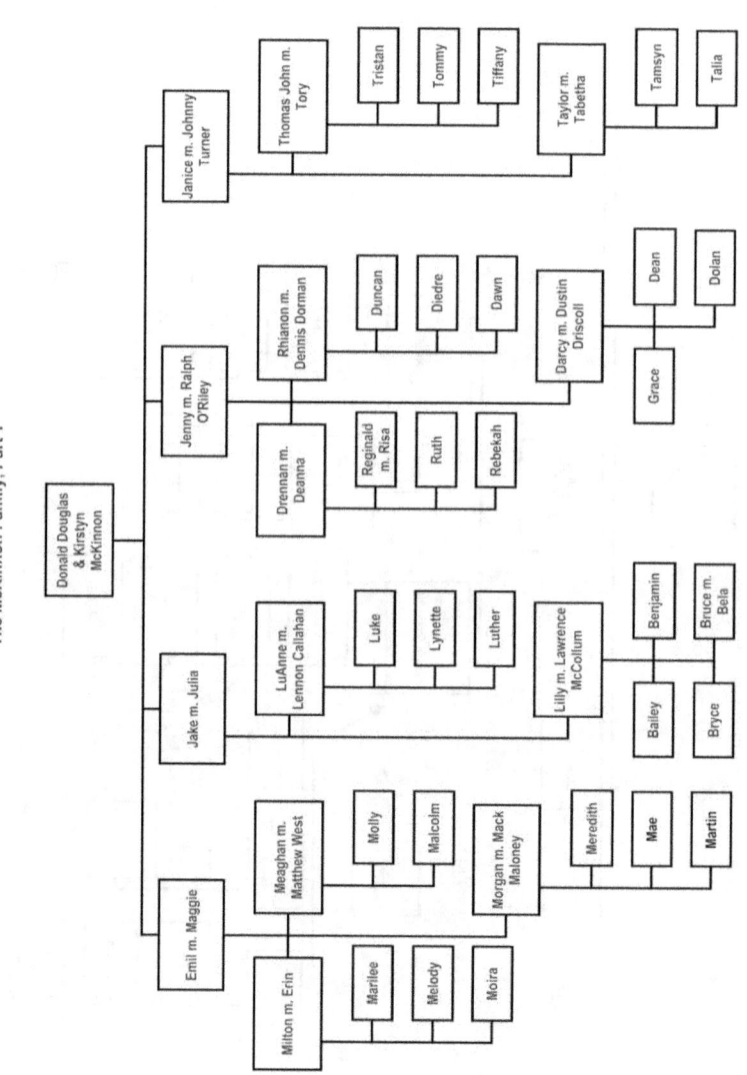

The McKinnon Family, Part 1

The McKinnon Family, Part 2

In *Secrets of the Enemy*

The Dumotte Family

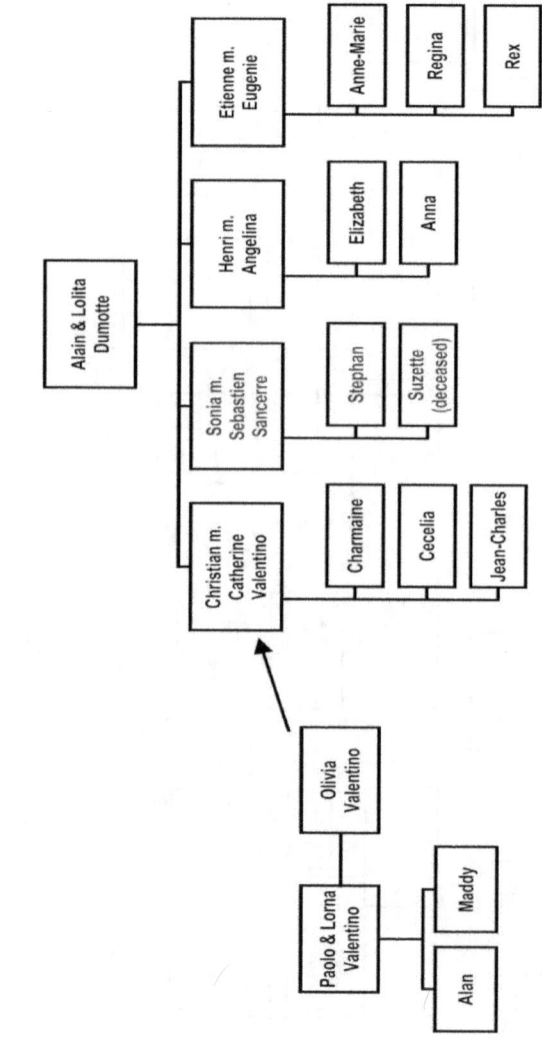

In *Secrets of the Enemy* and *Secrets of Two Sisters*

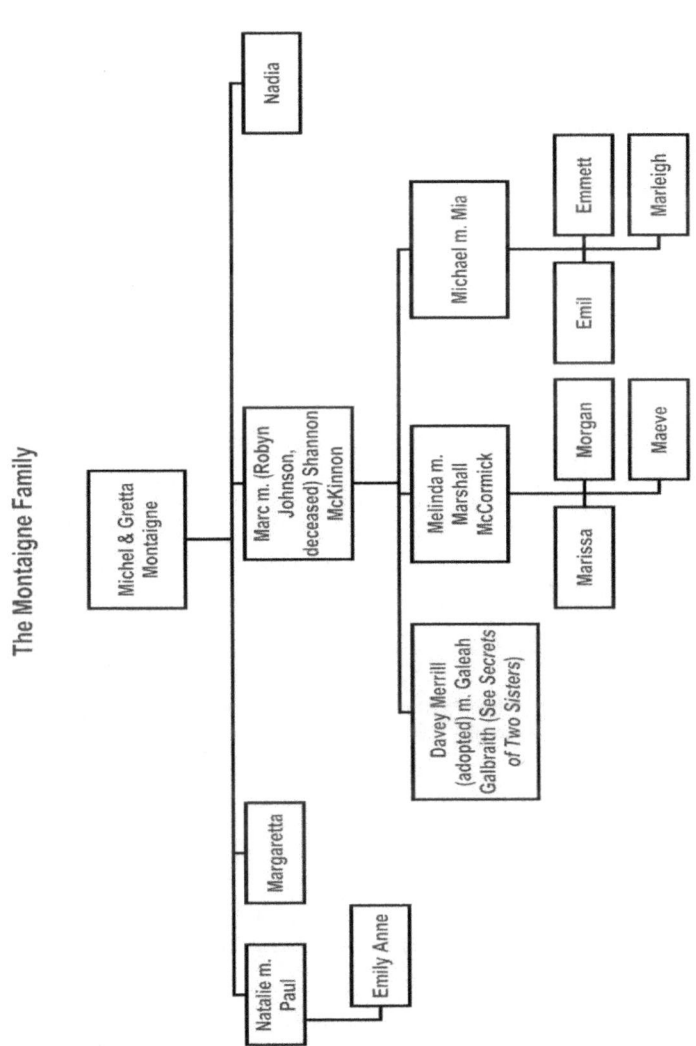

The Montaigne Family

Michel & Gretta Montaigne

Natalie m. Paul

Margaretta

Emily Anne

Marc m. (Robyn Johnson, deceased) Shannon McKinnon

Nadia

Davey Merrill (adopted) m. Galeah Galbraith (See Secrets of Two Sisters)

Melinda m. Marshall McCormick

Michael m. Mia

Marissa

Morgan

Maeve

Emil

Emmett

Marleigh

Chapter One

As I waited impatiently for Davey, I thought about how this culminating moment had begun in a convent with a news clipping, a body, and a box containing the brief shining moments of a young mother's life. Well, actually, it had begun earlier than that, but this was a secret I hoped would never have to be revealed.

Rosalie came through the office door and into the great room with its magnificent view of the lake and great ceiling timbers of oak and gave me a thumbs-up sign. "He's really coming! They just called, and they are on their way."

She came to the chair where I sat and gave me a quick hug. "Now don't you get too uptight. You want to look your best for your young man." She gave me a roguish wink that contrasted with the angelic look of her delicate face and shining cloud of blond hair.

Rosalie had become a great friend during my treatments at the Hope Cancer Treatment Center. Her tireless energy had unearthed the whereabouts of my Davey after several years of fruitless wondering.

And now he was on his way.

"Would you like anything before he gets here, Mary?"

"No, I'll just sit here and reminisce a bit," I said patting her hand. "I know you'd like to look around more."

She gave me another hug and strolled to the terrace and the gardens beyond.

I gazed out the window overlooking the lake. I didn't mind being left alone with such a view. It rested me, yet the pageantry of the changing seasons was like a kaleidoscope of color. The far hills were a dusky blue today and the pale willow green of the leaves by the little stream . . . reminded me of the green in the basement of this place when I had taken the records of Robyn Montaigne.

*****

Although I outwardly looked composed, my heart pounded in cut time as I walked from the end stairwell of the convent in Lucerne, California where I had cloistered myself.

What I hoped to accomplish, while not rank disobedience, would certainly not be approved if discovered. Last night the remains of a young woman from France had arrived overnight air to be held in the holding room located in the basement until family could be found to grant her spirit eternal rest.

We called it the holding room. It was really a morgue, but that word sounded so final and lifeless. In spite of the debilitating disappointments I had experienced the last several years of my life, I still believed in the goodness of God and that the spirit lives after death.

Why I still believed that at that time in my life I don't know. I still hadn't worked through the guilt, anger, and bitterness of my experiences. Instead I had submerged my feelings beneath a mask of calm acceptance.

Normally I avoided this area of the basement; I couldn't abide being around the lifeless bodies awaiting burial. But Allee de Lamente Paris, France? There couldn't possibly be a connection.

Just as I was about to open the door to the holding room, a group of noisy twelve-year old girls burst into the hallway. They had been practicing a play and were thirsty. Unfortunately, a small kitchen was next door to the holding room.

"What are you doing?" asked Nancy, a blonde, with protruding blue eyes and a keen perception of anything out of the ordinary.

"Taking care of some business," I replied noncommittally. Then before she could ask me what business, I asked her some questions. Perhaps if I took the empathy approach, I could avoid her curiosity.

"I'll bet you girls are thirsty after all your hard work. Will the play be ready in time?"

"We have two more weeks until our first performance, and if Margaret here would learn her lines..." suggested Nancy in a needling tone.

Margaret, a petite child with long, dark, lustrous hair hung her head. She was a little slow, but once she learned something, she never forgot. Although I gave music lessons to the girls who showed a proclivity, it was Sister Anne who was helping them produce dramatic plays. And here she is, I thought with relief.

"Come along, girls," she called as she bustled down the long hall that ran the entire length of the basement. Her round face was red and her body rocked back and forth as she marched swiftly to keep pace with her charges.

Nancy and her friends disappeared into the kitchen. Anne winked at me and asked, "Was Nancy insulting Margaret again? That child has got to learn the grace of kindness or she will never realize her potential." She winked again and followed the girls through the doorway.

Anne optimistically found the good in every person, young and old, and in spite of her flyaway appearance, she was universally liked for her cheerful acceptance of situations and people.

Now was my chance. I slipped into the mausoleum and shut the door softly behind me. My eyes adjusted to the muted light playing through the four small square windows placed three inches down from the ceiling on the opposite wall.

It was a large, rectangular room with a huge table in the middle, and a sink area filled with dissecting equipment along the wall closest to the door on my immediate left. The block wall with the windows was bare except for four large anatomy charts showing nerves, muscles, and organs of the body.

The long wall opposite the windowed wall was lined with caskets and interment equipment, but it was to the far wall on my right lined with vaults holding dead bodies that my mind was riveted. I knew the body from France was in one of those vaults.

The undertaker who serviced our convent would arrive in two hours. How would one go about finding the right vault? I didn't want to have to examine every vault, not to mention my distaste at looking into lifeless faces of the deceased. Although not large, our convent acreage contained the burial grounds of the entire area and was used frequently by others in this community located in the California mountains. I swallowed down the lump in my throat, told my stomach to behave, and walked softly across the tiled floor.

I decided to begin on the left and work across the eight rows of three. Gingerly I pulled on the cold metal handle of the first vault. It slid out soundlessly, but heavily.

Oh no! I'd have to pull back the sheet to look at the face. Steeling my taut nerves, I pulled it back and saw the face of old Mr. Peters. I pulled the sheet up quickly and crossed myself. The next one was empty. The third one gave a little groan as I opened it.

I jumped and looked toward the door. Anyone passing by in the hall might hear the noise and investigate. And then there was the group of girls. Hopefully, they were being too noisy. I slowly pulled back the sheet and then sucked in my breath!

It was true! I knew this woman whose body had been shipped back from France. Robyn had passed away and in the prime of her life at the age of thirty-one. I caught sight of cardboard then and pulled the drawer out further to investigate. The vault groaned again.

A rustling noise on the other side of the door caught my attention. I pushed lightly on the drawer—fortunately it did not groan going back in—and dashed quickly but quietly to the nearest empty casket.

"Miss Anne! Do you believe in ghosts?! We heard someone groaning in there," announced Nancy. The other girls giggled nervously.

"Nonsense!" said Anne. "Anyone who has the misfortune of being placed in that room is well and truly dead. Come along girls. We need to walk through the second act again." I heard her voice cadence lower as she walked down the hall.

"I'll bet it's that nosy nun, Miss Mary," said Nancy.

"She's not nosy, she's nice," said Margaret. "You're just jealous 'cause you can't take music lessons."

"Am not!"

"Are too!"

With relief I heard their voices fade. At least Margaret knew how to stand up to Nancy sometimes, I thought wryly. And it was nice to have someone, even a child, defend me.

Five minutes later I ventured from behind the casket and pulled open the drawer again. It was easier this time. I knew what to expect. The cardboard was really three small boxes piled on top of the torso and legs of the deceased. I wanted to examine them, but what if someone came?

I decided to pull them all out and take them up to my room. The undertaker likely wouldn't know of them anyway and would not miss them. I pulled them out, covered Robyn's face, and shut the drawer. Carefully I opened the top of each to see if they were worth the effort it would take to conceal them on the way to my room.

The first box contained a six-inch stack of papers and files. I could easily conceal the stack with my habit if I discarded the box. The second and third boxes contained what looked like family memorabilia. My heart stopped, then beat painfully when I saw a small box with Christmas paper on it.

It couldn't be! I opened it and with shaking fingers pulled out tissue paper surrounding four glass-blown ornaments. The sound of my sob shattered the silence and shocked me.

Hastily I shoved every thing back into the boxes. I placed all the boxes beside the door and carefully opened it. No one was in sight. Quickly I gathered the files and papers from the first box and began the journey to my room on the third floor. I saw no one.

When I returned to the holding room, I decided to dispose of the box in the kitchen. Quickly I took it next door and put it in the capacious trash can. It sank nearly to the bottom. Good! More trash would cover it before it was emptied. I looked at the cups in the sink and longed for some water myself, but I had work to do.

"What are you doing?" a young voice demanded.

I swung around to see Nancy glaring at me, curiosity etched on her face.

"I was looking at the mess you all left for me to clean up," I retorted.

"Are you going to wash dishes? I'll help."

"Aren't you supposed to be practicing?"

"We're all done for the day, so I guess you're stuck with me," she announced gleefully.

Frantically my mind returned to the two boxes. I at least had to get the one with the ornaments up to my room. But I didn't need Miss Nosy suspecting anything.

"All right," I muttered.

We ran water and began washing. Nancy kept up a lively chatter about the play and her starring role in it while she dried the glasses and put them away. We were nearly done when Anne heaved through the doorway.

"There you are, Nancy. You shouldn't wander around, dear, and keep your aunt waiting for you," she scolded gently.

"But I've been helping Miss Mary clean up," she protested righteously. When Miss Anne said nothing, she added, "What's she doing down here, anyway? I bet she knows something about the ghost next door."

I flushed and glanced nervously at Anne, but she was already out the door. Her "Come along, dear," floated back to us.

Nancy looked at me triumphantly, and then ran after her. That little brat! Had she seen anything after all? Or was she just suspicious?

My nerves tautened, but I turned resolutely from watching them to the stairwell and once again opened the door to the holding room. I clasped the box with the ornaments firmly in my arms with the black sleeves billowing around it. Again, I encountered no one.

Only ten minutes until the undertaker arrived. I ran down the three flights of stairs, hoping I would see no one who would question my lack of sedateness. I quickly scooped up the third small box, closed the door gently but firmly, and climbed the stairs one last time.

As I began on the flight to the third floor, I heard a door clang open beneath me. Cautiously I peered over the railing. It was Miss Sebastiani and the undertaker! I heard low murmurs of their conversation, and then another door clanged. I was home free! I made it to my room and closed the door.

I fished a small box from the closet in my room for the papers and then placed it on the bed. The three small boxes of various shapes stood on my bed like the three gifts of the magi. Though far less ornate, they were infinitely precious to me.

Chapter Two

It was four o'clock and since it was my turn to help with dinner preparations, I had less than an hour to peruse the boxes. But first I had to find a good hiding place.

The one small suitcase I had brought with me was under my bed. I pulled it out and opened it. The box with the papers fit easily, as well as the first box. But the second box, the one with the Christmas ornaments, was about a half an inch too tall to allow the suitcase to close with ease.

I carefully took the ornaments out and placed them beside the box. Mashing down on the corners of the box might help. Yes! It worked! The suitcase was closed with everything inside when I heard a knock at my door.

Quickly I shoved the suitcase under my bed. Looking wildly around, I saw nothing out of place. Who could it be? Had I been spotted on my way up the stairs or along the hall?

But it was only Sister Anne. She pulled the chair out from my desk and sat down heavily.

"Those kids sure do tire me out," she said. She began a monologue on the potential of "her kids" as well as a few of their endearing faults. Normally I listened eagerly because she had a real rapport with them and a keen insight into the motivations behind their behaviors. We shared many of the same students, she in drama and I in music. But today as she droned on, all I could think of was the information I would find about Robyn and her family.

When she paused, I nodded and tried to be attentive. I really did feel guilty. Sister Anne was the one person who had accepted me as her friend without reservations upon my inauspicious entry into convent life. How much did she guess about my true background? Probably not much.

I had kept to myself the first year almost entirely. Sister Anne's kindliness had helped to ease the desperate loneliness and betrayal I felt. Her pithy commentary on convent life had given me the glimmer of hope and humor necessary to deal with life's bitter blows.

Now, three years later, the calm of my exterior was beginning to melt slowly, slowly down into my heart like snow when the temperature is barely above freezing, and I had begun to feel more at peace within my soul. Until now.

"Don't you have K.P. duty?" She winked at me. "That's what we always called it when I was a girl and at camp. If you want, I'll walk with you down to the kitchens and help. I've got nothing better to do. But don't let Mother Sebastiani hear it. She'll say that prayers are more important than our daily bread."

As I agreed to her plan, I looked longingly at the suitcase under my bed. Now Robyn and her life would have to wait until tomorrow. I had evening prayers and an early bedtime. At least it seemed early to me. My father's strict schedule had still allowed us to stay up until eleven every evening.

Reluctantly I followed Anne down the stairs to the kitchens. They were located on the southern end of the convent. Because of their large size and the arrangement of the windows, the sun shone into the rooms most of the time. It was early fall, and I let the warmth of the sun and the cooling tang of the wine-like air sweep over my hot face.

Imperceptibly I relaxed. I had always loved the fall season. It reminded me of the grape vineyards surrounding the area where I had grown up with their large purple-red leaves on brown vines, the smell of spicy cookies baked by my mother, exciting, blood-pulsing basketball games, and long walks with Will in the woods . . . no! I slammed shut the door emphatically on the memories of the only man I had ever loved.

Anne returned to the table, by which I was standing with a large sack of potatoes. "Guess what we get to do?! Don't you just love peeling potatoes?" She was full of joking good humor. Belatedly, I collected potato peelers and we began working.

While Anne droned on, my mind wandered again, this time to Robyn and her family. The shock of losing her was lessening. I began wondering about her family. What had happened to Marc? And what about Davey? That was the deep ache that I had been holding back for the last twelve hours. What had happened to Davey? I closed my eyes and let the anguish roll over me.

A hand clutched my arm. Anne's face looked at me with alarm. "What's wrong, Mary? Are you ill?"

I shook my head mutely.

"Then what's wrong? You've been acting withdrawn all day. Is there anything I can do to help you?"

I hesitated and looked around. We were sitting on stools at the far end of a large butcher block table. I could see two sisters helping the cooks. One was preparing roasts to go into the ovens and another was kneading bread for tomorrow morning's breakfast.

Chatting merrily, they were working at opposite ends of the long white counter, the one with the overhead shelf in the middle that ran the entire length. One cook was washing a few dishes, and the other was at another service counter checking off a list, probably of supplies needed from the local stores.

She stood now and walked toward us. "Very good," she said when she saw the bowl of white potatoes in the standing water. "Keep up the good work, girls." She disappeared around the corner toward the supply room.

Should I unload my guilty conscience and anguish on this kind and humorous woman who had befriended me at a time when I desperately needed a friend? Almost, I allowed myself that luxury.

"I-I . . . think I'm homesick," I said nervously. Then in a rush, "I've always loved the autumn season: the weather, the leaves changing from greens to golds, reds, plums, wines. It's all so beautiful here just like it was where I grew up. My Mom always baked spicy cookies in the fall, and when I walked into this kitchen, it, well, it overwhelmed me for a minute. I'll be all right."

Anne looked at me commiseratingly. "That still happens to me sometimes, too. I came here straight out of high school, you know. My Mom died when I was fourteen, and I just went wild for a while with the parties, the boys, the drugs and the booze. My Aunt Linda and Uncle Bill tried to

help, but I simply saw what they were doing as interference."
She sighed. "I'm afraid I wasn't very nice to them."

"Well, anyway, one weekend when I was sixteen, we all went boating on the lake. By Saturday afternoon we were all stoned or drunk or both. My boyfriend, Jeff, was a daredevil, and he dared his best friend Phil to climb this tower. It was circular, made of brick, about sixty feet high, and close to the base was an electrical system.

They started to climb. Jeff was goofing off and waving at all of us down below, his blond hair lifting the breeze. Phil was right below him. Jeff slipped on one of the spikes and fell down into the electrical enclosure." She swallowed. "He landed on the wires and was fried. But what happened to Phil was worse." She swallowed again.

"I shouldn't tell you all of this," she said. "It's really awful."

"Go ahead," I breathed.

"Phil slipped and his chin got hooked on one of the spikes in the tower. It nearly ripped his head off his neck."
A stone hit the bottom of my stomach and another smaller one lodged in my throat. What an awful thing to have to see. It was obviously still a vivid memory for Anne.

"Anne, I'm so sorry."

"It's still hard to talk about with anyone. But you are so easy to talk to. I don't think I've told anyone here about that. They'd probably kick me out if they knew how many quarts and kilos I've had."

Looking around the peaceful kitchen controlled the too-real images in our minds.

"It's hard to believe what we've been through when we become immersed here at this tranquil place. Maybe that's when we chose to come here," I offered tentatively.

"Yes," said Anne. "I made my peace with my aunt and uncle and graduated from high school with honors. Can you believe it?" She shook her head in disbelief. "But I had had enough. I began going to mass after Jeff died, and that's when I decided to become a nun if they'd have me. This place is like a rest stop for me while I get my bearings and heal, but then I want to go to a place in an inner city and work with teens who are messed up like I was."

"That's beautiful, Anne," I said.

She turned a knowing look on me. "There's something about you, Mary, that needs healing, too." She touched my hand in reassurance. "But I won't pry. If you ever want to talk about it, I'll listen."

Chapter Three

It was Sunday afternoon when I finally had the time to myself to look through the boxes from Robyn's coffin. I pulled the suitcase out from under the bed and opened it. Leaving it on the floor would enable me to close and shove it quickly back if I was interrupted. That would be unlikely. Sunday afternoons were supposed to be spent individually in quiet meditation. A twinge of guilt pierced through me at my disobedience, but I quickly dispelled it.

I opened the first box and pulled out the sheaf of papers. The top yellow envelope was marked birth certificates. Taking a deep breath, I opened it and pulled out four parchment-like papers. The first one was for Robyn Jennifer Johnson born August 4, 1937 in Santa Rosa, California. I knew all about that one.

The next one was for Marc Paul Montaigne born July 1, 1936 in Paris, France. Why was this here? Marc should have it in his possession. Questions without answers.

As I lifted Marc's birth certificate and saw the one underneath, I sucked in a quick breath, feeling a familiar clench of my gut.

I had seen the next birth certificate. It was on fancy parchment from Mercy Hospital with a blue ribbon border and baby shoes and rattles in each corner.

Slowly I expelled my breath and read David William Merrill born September 3, 1960 in Santa Rosa, California. I couldn't bear to look any longer. Quickly I turned to the last page and examined it curiously. Elyssa Mary Montaigne born May 25, 1963 in Paris, France.

So, Robyn had given birth to a little girl. How special! Elyssa Mary after me! I knew without being told that she had named her little girl after me! A wave of forgiveness washed over me. I held the certificates tightly to me and sobbed.

This would never do; someone might hear me. I quickly buried my face in my pillow and cried. Feelings of relief and regret, blessedness and bitterness billowed over me like rough waves over a jetty of rocks.

Goodness! If Robyn had had a little girl, where was she now? Was she a lost child like Davey? I sat up quickly to continue my investigations. The next manila envelope had stains on it. Were they water stains? Maybe tear stains?

I pulled out parchment papers again and saw the words "Death Certificate" at the top. The first page recorded the facts: Elyssa Mary Montaigne born May 25, 1963 and deceased June 14, 1964. The other pages were church bulletins giving a human touch to the tragic event.

Only two years ago. Poor Robyn and Marc. Quickly scanning the document, I came to "Cause of Death: Pneumonia complicated by heart disease." Had they known of the heart problems before Elyssa had come down with pneumonia? Had Robyn been able to be there for her little girl? Had she been able to get medical attention for her? Frustration welled up. So many questions and no answers.

The next manila envelope contained bank statements, receipts for utility payments, paper with budgets written out in Robyn's handwriting, and more loose receipts. That made sense. Robyn had always been meticulous about keeping her financial affairs in order. It was a good thing, too. Marc with his artistic temperament hadn't handled that type of perfectionism very well.

I examined the loose receipts curiously: I was so hungry for a knowledge of how Robyn had lived. What had her life in France been like?

I began to sort through the receipts, placing them in piles according to vendors and types of purchases. Prima's must have been a grocery store that she had frequented. Rielley's seemed to be a department store of some sort. If there were no answers anywhere else, perhaps I could piece together a portion of her life through grocery receipts. It seemed so pitifully inadequate.

Then a thought blazed into my mind like a wild fire out of control on the California hillsides: you at least knew Robyn. You knew her favorite food, her musical laugh, her sense of humor, her organizational skills. You knew the essence of her.

How fortunate, and yet I longed to know more. And that longing would plunge me into the dark horror of the life Robyn had endured, and show me at last why she had been willing to follow the man she loved to another continent and a new life.

To truly know someone, you must be willing to travel through their life with them, vicariously enduring their pain until that pain becomes so entwined around your heart that it is your own.

Slowly I stood and stared out my small convent window, but I didn't see the blue-green mountains in the distance or the closer tall golden-white oat grass under California oaks. Instead I saw a baby boy with tiny but long fingers and fine dark hair. Where was Davey? I pulled some rubber bands from my desk and put them around the receipts. Then I stuffed them in the manila envelope and looked at the rest of the loose papers.

Most of them were play bills from the operas in which Marc had performed. I found his name on play bills for *Rigoletto, La Boheme, Andrea Chenier, Pagliacci, Tosca,* and many more. For being so young, he had already had a prolific career. It was a thrill seeing his name listed as the tenor. I had always admired his voice, and in this bittersweet moment, it was hard to believe that I had hated him so at one time.

Beneath the playbills were half-sized envelopes with cards inside. I pulled one card out of the protective envelope. It was report card of Davey's! My hand trembled, and I felt like laughing and crying at the same time.

The name of the school, Saint Exepery, was printed in the top left-hand corner. Underneath was Davey's name, David Merrill, and the grade and age, Kindergarten. He had been five years old! When I went to replace it in the envelope, the bottom kept sticking. When I put my hand in the bottom, there was a small piece of cardboard. I pulled it out and discovered a small one-inch by two-inch picture.

It was of Davey! Such a solemn little face he had with the dark hair and big blue eyes I had memorized from his infancy. The tears flowed in earnest now, and I was uncaring. I kissed the picture over and over.

At last, I calmed down, but the emotional storm had worn me out. I carefully looked over the few remaining envelopes from the first box. The report cards and pictures continued through the third grade.

I studied each photo carefully for clues to the personality of the little boy. I would guess that he was a rather sober child; there was never a full-fledged smile in any of the pictures, only a slight grin in three of them. He was probably a pleasant but serious child.

If only there was some other way to learn of his personality and his life. But I could handle no more. I carefully packed everything away except for the pictures. Those I carefully taped to an index card. I turned on the lamp and cuddled in my blanket. Davey's face grinned at me as I fell into a heavy, dreamless sleep.

Chapter Four

My duties and activities at the convent kept me busy most of the next week. When I had first talked to Mother Sebastiani about entering, she had not been the implacable, spiritually superior person I had expected to encounter. Instead she was very gracious and interested in me and my talents.

It was almost as if she had been informed about me and my intentions before I arrived. But that would have been impossible; Robyn was the only one with whom I had ever discussed entering this convent, and in spite of our differences, I always knew I could trust her implicitly.

My talents in music had particularly interested Mother Sebastiani. She asked about the musical activities in which I had been engaged in high school and my three years of college. I told her about playing the tenor saxophone in my high school band for three years and in the jazz band for two years; about playing the piano for the school's elite singing group, Santa Rosa Singers; even about playing the piano for the Holy Word Baptist Church.

She didn't flinch or blink an eye as I had expected at the last part. In college I had turned to the symphonic band and had developed an appreciation for classical music. This love, this appetite for classical music had surprised me. I guess it developed because I had been deprived of it for most of my growing up years. Also, some of it was similar to the church music I had played.

I was always surprised to find a familiar melody or harmony line haunting the pages of the music I played in the symphony. This love developed into a passion and became an almost supernatural spiritual force in my life.

I felt so close to God when I was playing in the symphony. It was as if the ambivalence I had felt during my teenage years between the church and my father's strict authoritarianism and the music I so loved, had been refined and purged, so that all that was left was this deep passion for the music.

Robyn had been musically inclined too, but in the vocal area. She had helped me to secure a position in the symphonic band in college. It was there, during one of the yearly operatic performances, that she had realized just how much in love she was with Marc Paul Montaigne, the brilliant tenor from France.

I had never seen her so happy in the long time I had known her. I had seen many people fall in love during college, but Robyn was absolutely radiant. She married on the twentieth of May, three weeks after school was out at the end of my freshman year. I would never forget that year.

Again, I slammed the door of my mind on the bittersweet memories from the past. Mother Sebastiani had given me the job of giving instrumental and piano lessons to children from the surrounding Lake area.

The first year I taught music lessons only three afternoons each week. The rest of the week I helped in the kitchen making breads, rolls, pastries, and desserts. But word of cheap music lessons had spread quickly, and the heavenly smells of rising yeast, cinnamon, nutmeg, and fruits such as apples, plums, peaches, apricots, pears, and of course, grapes became sweet memories.

Instead, I listened to raucous oboes, clarinets, and saxophones, or tinny trumpets and trombones. I enjoyed the silvery sounds of the flutes, and the mellow tones of the french horn. And there was always the piano. My training in music education had given me just enough knowledge to teach the violin, viola and cello for about a year and a half.

When my students graduated from my care, I sent them to a retired strings teacher from Vienna, Franz Glasser. He and his wife, Fiona, were retired college professors. They had fallen love with the Lake District in northern California during their vacation time and had bought a home lodged precariously above the lake along a winding mountain road about two miles from the convent.

Because I spent five hours every afternoon giving these lessons, I think Mother Sebastiani took pity on me and only had me assigned to help in the kitchen two Saturdays a month.

I missed spending time there. Working with the smooth, elastic dough, kneading and punching, punching and kneading it, had helped to eliminate the pent-up frustrations I felt about my life. I had usually ended up spending Saturday afternoons there during this past year whether I was assigned to do it or not. The kitchen staff could always use an extra pair of hands.

The fog I had deliberately enveloped around my mind had been dissipating in spite of my efforts to keep it firmly tacked in place. The appearance of Robyn's body in the holding room had swept out the last bit of the mists, and now raw emotions were beginning to show. Unfortunately, the more deeply wounds are covered, the less they heal. They need air and time to scab over properly so that true healing can take place.

The same questions that had plagued my mind five and eight years earlier began their disjointed merry-go-round journeys again. Even the music that filled my afternoons began to sound like broken organ chords in accompaniment to my thoughts.

Morning prayers and meditation were an agony as the questions once again surfaced after the cessation sleep brought. By evening vespers, spectres and disjointed scenes from the last eight years haunted my spirit until I wanted to scream out the truth. But what was the truth? I was still blind to it, deliberately blind. The mind has a wonderful propensity for blocking the truth until it can be faced in all its raw realities.

The one thing that calmed my overwrought nerves was the card with the pictures of Davey. For some reason, the questions ceased at night when I could hold his pictures in my hand. My battered brain could relax into a trouble-free sleep.

I had considered examining the contents of the other two boxes into the late hours of the night, but I was afraid that the light from my window would cause more questions to be asked, questions I would not be able to answer.

It was Sunday afternoon again before I had free time to examine the boxes. Once more I pulled out the battered brown suitcase and opened the lid carefully. The small box of Christmas ornaments begged to be handled although I remembered them well enough.

But wait! As I unwrapped them from their carefully constructed cocoons of tissue, I noticed that to each one had been added names in gold paint with the artistic flourishes of an artist: "Marc," "Robyn," "David," and "Elyssa." Such a cozy little family group.

Bitterness flooded me and my mouth twisted in a distorted grimace of anger and, was that hate? Yes. I finally acknowledged the emotion that I had suppressed for so long. I hated Robyn for what she had done to me. I hated that she had taken the most precious thing in the world from me. Tears of rage ran frantically down my cheeks.

I clenched my hands into fists and beat into the pillow. I tensed my whole body until I felt like a corked bottle ready to explode.

It was so unfair. I wanted to crush the blown-glass ornaments into tiny slivers of pain, but they were all I had left of that wonderfully carefree afternoon Robyn and I had spent together shortly after the summer she had met Marc.

I had been intoxicated with the freedom of my first year away from home and college, and Robyn had been a graduate assistant. We had shopped for Christmas presents until late afternoon. Our last stop was a tiny shop with a wide selection of ornaments.

"Ooh, look at these beautiful notes." Robyn held up an exquisite pair of eighth notes made of crystal and gold with a tiny gold filigree chain for hanging on the tree.

"I like this saxophone better," I said. It was all gold tones with a gold ribbon at the top. The keys, however, were inlaid with what looked like mother of pearl. It was exquisite.

"You know, we really should each get an ornament in remembrance of this special day," said Robyn. "It's been so relaxing and fun. You don't get many like this while you're in college."

"Well, I certainly don't have much money left," I admitted ruefully.

"Neither do I. Maybe, though, we can pool our money together and buy a set; you know, matching ornaments or something like that."

"We'll have to find something we both like, but that shouldn't be too hard," I said enthusiastically. "How much do you have?"

"Five ninety-eight, but I want to save some for a cup of coffee on the way home," said Robyn.

"I have six dollars and twenty-seven cents. I guess I'll splurge, too, and get an iced tea," I said.

"Okay, let's start looking. We both like music," said Robyn.

We searched, but everything we both liked was too expensive for our pocketbooks. We decided to go for a simple but elegant style.

"These are pretty," I said hesitantly, holding up some blown-glass balls etched with gold glitter.

"Nah," we said together.

"Ooh, I see them," said Robyn. She pulled out a set of four white frosted cone-shaped ornaments, twisted, with flecks of gold embedded in the glass. They were truly originals and beautiful in a very unique way.

We bought the ornaments, giggling like giddy high-school children, and in truth, we were just children at the time, or at least I was. Robyn had already been pulled into an abyss of fear from which I had been protected.

Looking back, I could sense but not explain the abandonment with which she threw herself into the joyful fun of that afternoon. It was certainly puzzling in one so composed and unruffled as she. But I was young and immature and totally absorbed into my little world, as I perceived it.

I'm glad, glad that I had perceived no inkling of the painful pleasure that would all too soon conspire to end the safe world I had inhabited and bring me into life with its sharp realities.

But for that one afternoon, we had known joy and happiness. The ornaments at least gave me that brief, shining moment. They also reminded me of Will.

Chapter Five

Will was the golden boy, tall with blonde curly hair, brown eyes and a long Roman nose set in his narrow face. He smiled easily, and loved to tease. He had been my boyfriend since tenth grade, and the semester away at college had not changed our relationship.

The Merrill family had moved down from the Portland, Oregon area in August, so Will was one of the few new faces in high school my tenth grade year. All the girls were crazy about him. Even the senior girls, more subtle than the freshmen in initiating conversation and sending coy glances, were entranced.

When it was discovered that Will was an exceptional basketball player, there was even more of a fuss. I watched the adulation from afar. How would I, plain Mary Johnson, ever attract the attention of such a superstar? I refused to throw myself at him in such an obvious way as the other girls were doing.

Once he caught me watching him when Ashley Lynn, the tenth grade beauty queen, was talking to him animatedly. He pretended to be listening to what she was saying, but when the bell rang, he looked absently around. When he caught my glance, he smiled ruefully in a self-mocking way and took his seat.

It was that weekend I discovered Will's second love, and we became friends. I wasn't allowed to have a job yet. My dad was very strict, and ruled our household with a somewhat draconian harshness. To escape, I often went hiking in the hills that surrounded Santa Rosa.

One of my favorite places was called Bald Eagle Knob. The crag of rocks protruded out over a small valley with a meandering stream. Because of its isolation, I could spend many undisturbed hours sitting in the lap of the rocks. It was my thinking place where I could be alone and yet not alone, for there was always nature and her beauty to contemplate.

But the way there was usually treacherous and overgrown, with the danger of rattlers always present. The first part of the way was easy. I just followed some old logging roads.

On this early Saturday afternoon, the sun shone warmly, and the air held just a tinge of early October chill in the mountains. I breathed in the purifying pine scent, and knew that whatever was wrong in my family, somehow it would work its way out.

It was too bad that Mom had to stay at home when I could tell that she, too, longed to get out and away for awhile. She had been red-eyed this morning, and had given my sister too-ready consent to spend the night at a friend's house, although with strict instructions to be in church, and on time, too, so that Dad wouldn't be mad again the next day.

Putting away thoughts of guilt, I took the faint path that cut off to the right of the logging road where I was walking. It led into a dell that, after the rains in the spring, became a vernal pool with exquisite and short-lived ferns and delicate flowers. I jumped over a small stream in the middle of the dell. It was fed by a spring halfway up the mountain on my right. I turned slightly to the left and looked up the path.

Right before it grew steep and disappeared into the manzanita scrub, a huge pine tree, scarred and twisted by a bold streak of lightning down one side, stood sentinel. Around its base a small copse of young pines was growing. About twenty feet tall, the tips gleamed in the sun with the fluorescent greenness as of new growth. Slowly and silently I stepped into the copse and entered my own enchanted fairy cathedral.

The sunlight filtered through the lacy pine boughs, and the air was a mite cooler. The ground was nearly six inches deep with pine straw from many ages. I always felt safe and cherished within this copse, as if God's hands totally surrounded me and provided protection from all evils.

During the summer when it was hot and I needed to think, I would come here and lie on the cushion of pine needles, cooling off in this quiet place. But today, with the wine of autumn in the air, I wanted to sit in the warm sun.

Backing out of the copse, I headed up the steep path that angled to the left and wound around the mountain to Bald Eagle Knob. The silver-green leaves on the manzanita lay nearly flat, a good indication that there would be no rain in the near future.

Underneath the smooth, but twisted red branches, I kept a wary eye on any movement that would indicate a snake. I hated them. But with only a few scratches from the low-growing scrub, I made it to the Knob.

The Knob was really an outcropping of rock close to the top of the mountain, but was located on the opposite side of where the spring-fed brook meandered and where the pine copse cathedral grew. The path approached from the top and then wound across and down the mountainside into thick woods.

Carefully climbing down so I wouldn't pitch into the valley below, I seated myself into a scooped out piece of the rock, perfect for sitting in, and let my legs dangle down against the rocky face. Leaning back against the rocks I had just scrambled over, I watched an eagle gliding on the wind currents in the cerulean sky.

My mind relaxed and drifted, and I wondered what it must be like to be a bird. What would I see in the valley far below? Its perspective must be so much keener than the perspective that we as human peons must have on life; that is, if a bird could have the kind of brain people have. Did a bird just enjoy the feel of the wind rushing along its wings, or was everything cut and dried, only the instinct of survival, of searching out and finding the next meal, the most important thing in its brain?

The sound of a snapping twig on the path above interrupted my reverie. I twisted quickly around, and on the path coming the opposite direction from which I had come, was Will Merrill.

Between the glare of the sun and his golden hair, I was nearly blinded, but I could barely discern a green T-shirt, camouflage pants and boots. He was holding a gun; I deduced that he must like to hunt.

His face wore a happy grin as he made his way carefully down to the outcropping of rock where I was sitting. My stomach fluttered, and my hands became clammy. What would I say to him?

"What's your name?" he asked. "I've seen you in my Math and English classes, but I don't know your name."

"Mary. Mary Johnson. And you are Will Merrill. Everyone knows that."

"Yeah, that's part of being the new kid in town, I guess."

"So what are you doing up here? I mean, I didn't think anyone knew how to get up here to Bald Eagle Knob."

"Is that what this place is called?" he asked. Then he leaned over the protrusion of rocks. I gasped in alarm. It looked like he was going to pitch right over on his head into the valley and the trees below us.

"See that house way down there with the white fence by the road? That's the house where my family just moved. We live out in the sticks, I guess, compared to most of the kids in school, but I like it 'cause I like to hunt. There's plenty of hunting around here."

"Anyway, when I was mowing out back with the tractor this morning, I saw what I thought might be a trail. It sure winds around a lot, and there are several interesting looking forks, but one of them comes here." He stopped for a moment and looked at me consideringly. "How did you get way up here?"

I was tempted to tease him and say "I hiked," but I didn't know him very well. "You must come past my house on the way home from school every day. We live in the yellow house, the second to the last one on Timmons Road before you come up all those hairpins and into this little valley here."

"That's a pretty steep road to hike." He looked at me admiringly.

"I'm in pretty good shape," I said with asperity. "Besides, I know a few shortcuts. I came in from the opposite direction you came," I said, indicating the trail behind me to the right. "I didn't know there was a trail down behind your house. I've never gone that far."

He had been leaning against the rock, carefully balancing his gun across his knees. Moving restlessly, he squatted and rubbed his backside.

"This is a mite uncomfortable. You want to see something I discovered a ways back there?" He pointed down the trail from where he had come.

"Sure." I moved to scramble up, but Will held his hand out to me. I took it, pretending nonchalance, but inside I felt trembly again. He released my hand and took the lead.

"I'd better go ahead," he said, "since I know the way."

I followed him silently, wondering where he was leading me, but too entranced with the awe of walking with the wonder boy of our high school to question his motives too deeply.

As the trail wound down from Bald Eagle, we entered the shade of tall pines. The sound of the birds calling to each other was muted under the quiet canopy of old pines, and the sound of our footsteps was merely a faint "pad-pad" due to the pine needles and soft dirt.

Will soon stopped at the base of a small platform about twenty feet high with a short and shaky ladder leading up to it. I looked at it dubiously. Will interpreted my glance.

"You go up first. I'll catch you if you fall."

I looked at him questioningly again, but with a wither-thou-goest-I-will-go attitude, I began the ascent. Will came up directly behind me. We situated ourselves side by side on the small platform with our legs dangling down over the front. I took a breath and looked around.

It was breathtaking! The stand was situated ten yards from an intersection of three different paths. Though trees still towered above us, the view was commanding; surely no one could come along without us noticing them first.

Will asked me about my family. I answered hesitantly; my tongue seemed to get tangled up with the words I wanted to say, so he began to tell me about his family. He had four brothers, two who were in their early thirties, living in Charleston, South Carolina, and two who were younger and still lived at home.

Caleb was twelve and took life seriously. He loved building electrically- and battery-powered toys and was experimenting with his friend, Andrew, on a small robot they had developed together. Will spoke with admiration of his brother's brains, and I could tell he admired Caleb tremendously.

The youngest brother, Eric, was a whirlwind of energy, enthusiasm, and inquisitiveness. At seven, he could get into more trouble in twenty-four hours than any other child in the elementary school. His reputation had begun when he had climbed a tall pine tree on the playground to "see what a squirrel was doing." When he had fallen down, still holding onto the tree, he had skinned his stomach royally and had also broken his ankle.

A cast had not stopped the irrepressible child. He simply became the Master of Ceremonies on the playground and had turned the place into his own three-ring circus.

By this time I was laughing, and the nervousness I felt had disappeared. I was even bold enough to ask him about his accent. Not only did he have a slight accent, but his word choice was often peculiar and sounded different to me.

He grinned when I asked. "Mary, you have finally met a real southern gentleman," he teased. "I was born in Charleston, South Carolina and we lived there until, when I was ten, we moved to Portland, Oregon. Portland was nice, but there's nothing like the Old South with the Spanish moss hanging from gnarled oak trees and alligator eyes watching you from the water." He broke off and turned his head slightly to see my reaction.

I was watching him admiringly. I could tell he knew, too, but I refused to feel embarrassed. Still watching my face, he reached for my hand, turned it over and kissed it. Faraway, a bell sounded.

Will reached for his gun. "That's my Mom's dinner bell," he said. "It's time we were going."

I snapped from calm bemusement to sudden fear. "Oh, no! My Dad. If I'm late for dinner, I'll be in so much trouble."

"Don't worry. We'll stop by the house, and I'll tell Mom I'm walking you home."

My alarm increased. "No! I mean, if my Dad sees you, I'll <u>really</u> get in trouble."

"Well, how about if I walk you just to the end of the hairpins?"

"I know a faster way. I don't mind walking by myself."

"Tell you what. I'll give my Mom a signal, and then I'll walk part way with you. You can show me your shortcuts."

"All right," I assented.

He shot his gun into the air twice to signal his Mom. We walked for the most part in silence. After helping me over a log, Will held my hand the rest of the way. I was filled with elation and apprehension all at the same time. He liked me! I could tell he liked me!

When we got to the last hairpin, Will asked, "Why don't we meet here next Saturday, too? It will be fun to talk to someone about what's going on at school and get the inside scoop about everything."

"Sure," I said. "But I don't know what time I'll be able to come."

"I'll just wait around the outside of the house until you come. Then you can meet my Mom. She's the best."

Chapter Six

School had never been so interesting before. Though Will didn't attempt to sit by me that week or even talk to me except for "Hi!" and "Have a great afternoon!," he smiled at me often.

When Ashley Lynn tried to flirt with him in Math class, he looked over at me and smiled. When Ms. Simpson shared a funny joke with us in English class, he looked back to laugh about it with me.

During the day I lived in a dreamy aura of bliss; each evening I became more and more concerned about what to wear the next day and especially what to wear on Saturday. I even tried my hair in different styles, but finally decided that leaving it the same would be best. After all, Will seemed to like it just the way it was.

My sister quickly guessed that I "had a crush" on someone, but I was not ready to talk about Will to anyone. I overheard my Mom telling Mrs. Pratt from church that I was "going through a stage."

My Dad? Well, I avoided my father as much as possible. He acted very affectionately toward my sister, but he seemed to avoid me. I always felt guilty because I knew I should love my father. Well, of course, I loved my father. But I didn't like to be around him. My feelings weren't hurt in the least when he ignored me.

Between his harshness and his rejection, I should have felt unloved and embittered, but instead, I only felt relief. And my Mom's meek and gentle spirit was very soothing. I could always find love and comfort from her when I needed it.

Friday evening I was filled with anticipation and dread, but I knew better than to let my Dad even guess my state of mind, so after I had helped Mom with the dinner dishes, I sat meekly in the living room reading a book.

Saturday morning I awoke to the smell of bacon, eggs, and pancakes. This was the usual fare for weekends when Dad didn't have to work. He insisted on a full breakfast with everyone present. Though my sister, my Mom and I didn't eat nearly as much as he did, he worked steadily through each food group, swallowing it all down with great glasses of milk and orange juice.

My sister and I helped Mom with the dishes and had our usual tussle over splitting up the house chores. I ended up with dusting. I hated dusting and vowed that I would never keep knick-knacks around to collect dust when I had a home of my own.

This morning, different than all the rest, I breezed through this abominable chore in forty-five minutes; it usually took me two hours. My next job was to clean the bathrooms.

Then I began straightening my room, taking the time to put away all of the clothes I had tried on and scattered around throughout the week. I chose to wear jeans—they were the only practical thing to wear hiking—with a dark blue sweater I had received for Christmas the year before.

Checking to see if the coast was clear, I headed to the bathroom and quickly washed. I spent some time on my face, but finally made a moue of frustration at the girl in the mirror and went downstairs to find Mom. She was surprised I had finished my chores so quickly, but assented readily to my request to go hiking.

Will was waiting for me by the white fence that surrounded the place where his family lived. He led me up the gravel driveway and onto the front porch of their large, yellow farmhouse.

His mother, obviously informed about me, came from the kitchen area as we entered the front door, wiping her hands on the apron she was removing from around her waist. She ran a hand through her short graying brown hair before extending the other one and grasping mine firmly.

"You must be Mary," she said. "Will has told us about how you met up the hill in back. It's so nice that he has a friend at school."

I slanted a grin up at Will. We weren't exactly friends at school, but I let it pass. "It's nice to meet you," I said to his Mom rather awkwardly.

"Come on into the kitchen. I'm doing some baking, and I'll pack up a snack for you two to take up the hill. I know how hungry boys can get." Her laugh followed her as she headed to the back of the house toward the kitchen. Will stood aside and motioned for me to precede him. What nice manners, I thought.

Mrs. Merrill was very talkative and laughed easily. She asked me about my classes and teachers; she was excited when I told her that I played the tenor sax.

"Oh how neat!" she exclaimed. "I played the alto sax for three years in high school and all four years of college. You'll have to bring yours up here some time and we can play together."

"Yes, you should hear Mom honking on that thing," teased Will with a straight face.

She swatted him with a towel on the backside, and he jumped aside laughing.

Watching them laugh and joke together like good friends was a revelation to me. Our family was so, so *distant* and *unfriendly* in our interactions with each other somehow compared to this family, but I hadn't known the Merrills long enough to explain the difference.

"There you go," said Mom Merrill as she snapped down the lid of a small picnic basket and handed it to Will. "Now you make sure he shares some of it with you," she said with a roguish wink at me.

Mom Merrill watched us out the back door and past the shed filled with farming equipment, waving her dishtowel when we turned to wave where the trail disappeared into the tall pines.

We walked silently side by side under the cool pines. Will grinned down at me and I smiled back up at him. He reached for my hand and began swinging it gently back and forth. This sweet communication needed no words. After the long week of anticipation, I relaxed in the quietness of the woods. I had been so keyed up all week; I felt that now I could finally relax.

How strange! Last time I had been so awkward and nervous with Will, but his glances during the long week at school and his actions today had reassured me that he really did like me.

The path forked and Will urged me to the right down toward the river instead of left up the mountain. I lifted an eyebrow in question.

"I thought we'd eat down by the river," he explained. "I've been doing some scouting around this week after school and basketball practice. There are some beaut places around here."

His words gave me a thrill of pleasure. Had he been looking forward to this date all week, thinking about me as much as I had been thinking of him? Had he been looking for a special place for us? Again I felt reassured and relaxed in the pleasure of his company.

The path wound around the base of several mountains, crossed the road, and continued toward the river. Much of the riverfront was within easy access from the road, but there were still quite a few spots that required a strenuous walk and scrambling around some rocks; these places also afforded privacy.

Will had chosen a spot well off the beaten path known as Rattlesnake Rock. I had been there once as a girl, but with all the other easily accessible areas along the river, few people ever came here.

Oak and cottonwood trees lined one bank and provided cool shade from the often-blistering California sun during the summer months. This gave way to a rocky area known as The Cliffs because they provided great diving surfaces and deep pools in which to plunge.

Crossing over to the other side of the river was a sandy beach area and a rather barren expanse of rocks where the rattlesnakes sunned sinuously in the summer sun. Most people chose to stay on the side with the oaks and cottonwoods.

Will began to spread out a small blanket while I stood still and let the ambience of the place overtake my senses. The russet, burgundy, and goldenrod leaves of the oaks and cottonwoods contrasted with the deep green of the pines higher up the hill.

I could smell the bouquet of fall on the rill of the small breeze that rustled the leaves and created currents to ride upon for the great birds of prey wheeling over some tiny carcass up the mountainside.

The sunlight danced on the waters, highlighting the silver froth that hit the rocks, bouncing off the myriad shades and tints of blue as the river sang along, and glinting off the emerald green and gray of the mysterious depths below The Cliffs.

Covertly I studied Will as he smoothed the blanket and unpacked the hamper his mother had packed. His blue plaid shirt, open at the neck, revealed fine golden hairs a shade darker than those on his head. The jeans he wore emphasized his long, thick legs.

Suddenly my sixteen-year-old mind and body was filled with sweet, wild urgings. I longed to run my hands up and down those long legs and finger the hairs on his chest. Panicked that he would be able to read my licentious thoughts, I turned again toward the river and let out a smothered scream. Not more than four feet away a snake was slithering across the sand toward the river, but too close to my toes.

Will whirled around. "Take it easy and don't move," he said calmly. "Darn, I wish I had brought my gun," he muttered. He reached down for a large rock, then aiming carefully, he heaved it onto the rattler, pinning it there close to the head. Pulling up his pant leg, he pulled a knife from his brown hiking boot.

He glanced up at me, and noting the panic still on my face, he gave me a reassuring nod and told me to look toward the river. I heard the scrape of metal against granite and a small, then a great splash in the river.

When I looked around, the snake was gone.

Will came toward me then and pulled me into a long hug. It was at that moment that I fell deeply and irrevocably in love with Will Merrill. I knew that here was someone whom I could trust: with my feelings, my body, my life.

Not only was he gentle and caring, humorous and fun, but he was strong and courageous. Fear would never tear him from me. Only a great sense of duty and responsibility.

That afternoon cemented the beginning of a great friendship and a great love. We sat companionably side by side and munched on the delicious lunch of ham sandwiches, chips, apples, homemade oatmeal cookies, and tea.

Our conversation was not only of people, but of great events and elevating ideas. When Will's hunger was sated and the hamper repacked, he stretched out full-length on the blanket. I followed his example, and our conversation continued along nonsensical lines: the shape of the clouds, the what-ifs about home, and school and life.

We rarely touched. Will told me later that he knew I would be his girl forever, but his Mom and Dad had candidly told him to make sure he took a relationship slow.

Before we left, he plucked a blade of grass and fashioned a ring out of it for me to wear. It was the outward sign of what had happened to both of us that day.

I still have that ring, brown and dried, but in a hidden place of honor in my small jewelry chest.

Chapter Seven

Will began walking me to and from classes and carrying my books "like a true southern gentleman," as he would say.

The first time he joined us for lunch, the small group of friends I sat with were in such awe that they would hardly speak to him. But I saw him weave his southern spell on them, and ours soon became the most animated table in the lunch room, especially when other members of the basketball team and cheerleaders started dropping by to speak to Will.

My sense of the absurd was tickled to suddenly see the wallflowers in our high school rubbing elbows with the more popular members.

My sister was quietly envious. Dad had thrown insanely jealous temper tantrums over any boy that even looked at her in church. The only way she could date a boy was on the sly.

I was close enough in age to pity her, so I never used my knowledge of her dating life to tell on her as some siblings would. Dad, however, would inevitably find out, and then all hell would break loose in our house.

It would start out with an ominously quiet dinner. My mother would nervously wait on Dad, filling his plate with seconds before he asked and jumping to serve him his after-dinner coffee the second he was finished eating.

Waiting for the right psychological moment when we were all on edge, he would demand to speak to my sister in "the bedroom," the one he supposedly shared with Mom, although she spent many hours on the couch in the living room.

My Mom always turned up the radio loud or drew me outside for a walk if the weather permitted. I never knew until years later what actually transpired in that room; my sister would emerge white-faced and looking as if she no longer cared to live. And, of course, she would break up with her boyfriend.

Sometimes my sister would watch me at school when I was walking with Will, and a look of almost despair and then determination would pass over her face. These momentary glimpses into the soul of my sister dimmed my happiness, but only momentarily.

If I had known what a supreme sacrifice she was making for me, maybe I would have been able to share her pain, been more sympathetic, but I was caught up in the bliss of a first and true love.

Outside of school, the only time I was able to see Will without Dad finding out, was on Saturdays.

They became our favorite days, and I fell in love with every member of his family. His mother was so jolly and fun, and his younger brothers began to come to me, telling me of their trials and triumphs in the schoolyard and also at home.

Mrs. Merrill told me that I was the sister they had never had. I loved spending time in their rambunctious, rollicking household.

Mr. Merrill was much quieter than the rest of his family, but the perpetual twinkle in his eyes clearly expressed his enjoyment of his family. The first time I saw him put his arms around his wife, rub his face against hers, and kiss her, I nearly left the room embarrassed. I had never seen my father act that way with my mother.

Instinctively I watched for Will's reaction to this display of affection. He grinned at them and kept dicing the cucumbers for the salad for dinner. Obviously this behavior was not unusual, but I gulped and went quivery inside imagining Will doing the same to me.

"Stop, Dear," protested Mom Merrill lovingly. "You're embarrassing our guest."

Dad Merrill winked at me. "Don't be silly, Love," he said, continuing to hold her in a tight hug. "Mary probably sees this at her house, too."

I never had, but I wasn't going to let them know. Will slanted a glance at me where I was seated at the table playing checkers with Caleb. His slight grin indicated that his thoughts ran parallel to mine. The frisson I felt compelled me to jump up and offer to set the dinner table.

The stormy November weather had kept us inside this afternoon. We had played board games with Will's brothers: Chinese checkers, chutes and ladders, and regular checkers.

Caleb beat Will three times at checkers. Clearly his mind was not on the game, so Caleb had disgustedly sent his brother to the kitchen, carried the game to the table, and begun showing me the "best" way to beat an opponent. Now he gave up in complete disgust with us both.

My sister and I had told mother about Will two weeks before. Since Dad was working late at the office, my mother had assured me over the phone that she didn't mind me eating dinner at Will's house as long as I was home by eight, long before my father was expected home. It was relatively easy to tell my mother about Will.

It was going to be much more difficult to tell my Dad.

And that's what Will and I argued about on the way home. He wanted to come home and meet my family. I had met his family the second week we had known each other, but he had never met mine.

It was our first argument, and I was crushed because my family wasn't something I could change. There was no way he could understand what my family was like, I thought with a sigh. But I had to try.

"My parents aren't like your parents," I began haltingly. Will patiently waited for me to continue in the quietness of his Dad's car. The only sound was the hiss of the tires on the wet pavement and the rain hitting the roof. He drove very slowly to prolong our time together, and I was grateful for his time and his patience.

I rubbed my left wrist, a habit I had when I wanted very passionately to say something, but didn't quite know the right words. "My Dad never tells my mother he loves her, never even touches her, not the way your Dad did with your Mom this afternoon."

I continued to grope for the right words. "Mom is quiet, not jolly like your Mom. She cries a lot. She thinks I don't know, but I can always tell. I don't know why. She doesn't seem sick or anything." I stopped, unable to explain my dread that Mom was dying of some terrible disease.

Will digested this information then asked, "What is your Dad like?"

"He," I hesitated then decided to speak my bald feelings. "He's a selfish pig. Don't get me wrong. I love my Dad, but he doesn't seem to care about any of our feelings, and he has to have everything his own way. Sometimes he makes me feel like I hate him for what he does to our family. Is it really possible to love and hate someone at the same time? I do."

Now that the dam had broken, I couldn't seem to hold back the ugly flow of words.

"He makes my sister's life miserable, especially when he finds out that she likes someone. It's like he has to always be in complete control of everything in our family, and no one can have a life without him knowing all about it and approving it first. Every time my sister gets a boyfriend, he makes them break up."

I swallowed the lump in my throat and continued. "He rarely speaks to me unless I do something he doesn't like, but then, I've never had a boyfriend before either. Now do you see why I don't want you to meet him yet? He'll send you packing if he finds out," I ended in despair.

I buried my face in my hands and began crying quietly. The thought of losing Will was more than I could endure.

I felt the car ease over onto a grassy area beside a prune orchard. Will's arms circled my shoulders, and he held me tight against him.

"I'm sorry, Mary, I didn't know. Don't cry. Please don't cry. I guess I've been pressuring you about it because I want you to be able to come to my games. I thought maybe your parents would come and bring you, but it looks like that's out of the picture."

He ran his fingers through his short curls, stared ahead for a few minutes, and then lifted my chin with his hand. He used his thumb to dab at some of the tears, and I felt comforted.

"I'll let you decide when to tell your Dad; just don't let it be a year from now," he tried to joke. He put his arms around me in a hug again, rubbed his face against mine just as his father had done earlier in the day to his mother, and lifting his face, lowered his lips gently to mine.

His lips were soft and moist and tender. It was brief, that first kiss, but it soothed my spirit, and gave me courage to consider facing my Dad.

Chapter Eight

As it turned out, I was able to attend one of Will's big games before Dad found out about him. The first week in December Dad always had to fly to company headquarters in Los Angeles for "debriefing and special training" as he liked to call it, in deference to his military background.

This was an annual event, one looked forward to by the whole family. Dad would come home in a jollier mood, and during that one week he was gone, it seemed as if the rest of us could be ourselves.

Even Mom would let down and chase us around the kitchen, snapping at us with a towel when we began pilfering the cookies she was baking. She never did this when Dad was home.

Will's big game against Montgomery occurred the same weekend that Dad was away, so Mom agreed to let us travel with the Merrills in their big white Ford station wagon to see the game. I had never before been allowed to attend a game, and the assault on my senses was nearly overwhelming, but immensely exciting.

The cacophony of bouncing basketballs, squeaky tennis shoes, excited conversation, and cheering seemed deafening in the small gym. Cheerleaders in red and grey undulated across the floor on the opposite side of the gym in front of the middle section of bleachers.

On our side, orange and black were the predominant colors. Large orange signs in black lettering hung on the wall above the bleachers with slogans deriding the Montgomery Vikings or praising the Santa Rosa Panthers.

As we filed into some seats four rows above and behind the team, Will's eyes sought mine, and a delighted smile filled his face. I hadn't seen him much today. The team had traveled here on the bus, leaving before the final bell had rung for the day.

Of course I was prejudiced, but I still thought he looked particularly virile and handsome in the white basketball uniform with orange trimming the arms and legs and emblazoning his number, seven.

The air inside the gym was stifling with the smell of sweating bodies and cheap perfume, but the doors opened frequently bringing with it the pungent odor of wet pines and cigarette smoke.

Although I had removed the black jacket that matched the black skirt I had worn for the occasion, the coolness of the outside air was a welcome touch on my flushed face.

Will's team was called from the bench to the court. I watched admiringly how he handled the ball. His body and the ball seemed one as he dribbled down the court and executed a perfect, left-handed layup.

Watching him and the other players warm up was a pleasure, and when the game began, he was like greased lightning on the court.

No move seemed too difficult for him. His energy inspired the team. Pulling ahead of the Montgomery Vikings, they kept Montgomery on the defensive the whole first half.

At half time, the teams disappeared into the locker rooms. I was disappointed, expecting to make more eye contact with Will. Mom Merrill gave me some money. Eric and Caleb began hopping around me energetically like bunnies. Obviously they knew what was coming.

"Could you go with these two munchkins of mine to get something at the concession stand in the lobby?" she asked. "Your sister can stay here and talk to me. And don't forget to get something for yourself, too," she added.

I protested, but she insisted, and I found myself waiting behind twenty other people while Eric and Caleb kept up a lively discussion of what I should buy with my share of the money.

"She should just get some Neccos; then she can have some money left over to buy a pop," asserted Eric.

"Maybe she doesn't want to eat anything, dummy. It's hot in the gym. Maybe she just wants a drink."

"Am not a dummy. She'll get more if she does it my way," said the irrepressible Eric. "You gonna get some Neccos, Mary?" he asked.

"Maybe. I haven't decided yet," I answered, trying to politely suppress the argument. The line moved along nicely. When it was my turn, I couldn't decide, but finally bought some penny candy and a drink. There. That should satisfy both of Will's little brothers who seemed to think I needed both their help and their approval in making my selection.

When we returned to the gym, the teams were just returning from the locker rooms. Again I caught Will's eye, and he winked. I went shivery all over. Mom Merrill caught his wink and my reaction and grinned.

What a neat mother Will has, I thought. Not at all possessive of her son like my father was with my sister and me, and so sort of understanding of all of us kids.

The second half of the game heated up. Montgomery came back with determination to beat the Panthers. They quickly scored two points, then intercepted a pass from Frank Woods and scored another two points.

Will reacted with a driving dribble into the key and an easy lay-up. We were still ahead, but when the Vikings followed up with three more baskets, the score was only six points away from being tied.

"Come on, team! We can do this!" shouted Will. He made a pass to Larry Larson. Larry neatly passed it behind his back to Terrence King who slam-dunked it.

Montgomery pounded it down the court for two points, and then tried to intercept, but fouled instead. After the rebound, Will kept a tight control of the ball until the end of the third quarter.

By this time, with the aid of Mr. Merrill's shouted instructions to Will and the other team members, I was able to follow the game with some understanding of what was happening.

At the opening of the fourth quarter, Montgomery was still down by six points. Will fired it to Terrence, but it was intercepted by Montgomery's Willie Morgan.

Slowly they were gaining on us, and I began to get nervous. Sweat was pouring off Will's body. Was he nervous too? In spite of the sweat, he looked as calm and in control as an old weather-beaten, experienced sailor at the helm.

When the game tied a few minutes later, the gym erupted with noise. Both sides wanted desperately to win the privilege of going to the playoffs. No one sat now. Standing with the rest of the crowd, I nervously watched the rest of the game, wishing I knew more of what was happening.

With one minute remaining in the game, Larry made a desperate attempt at a basket, but instead received a penalty. Montgomery pulled ahead two points. At the rebound, Montgomery's Dave Solomon got tangled up with Will. The ref called a foul on him, and the ball was Will's in a one-and-one free throw.

With twenty seconds left, and all the pressure on him, Will made the first basket. Without a miracle we would tie at best; even I could see that. Will missed the next basket, but Larry Larson timed the rebound perfectly and tipped it back into the net. We won by one point!

The jubilant fans swept the court. Joining them, I found Will and was embraced in an exuberant bear hug. He kept his arm linked through mine during all of the congratulations until his teammates crowded around him and carried him off to the locker room.

Will elected to join us on the ride home. I later found out that normally the players all rode together back to the school. How he finagled it, I never found out, but I was so glad that he did. We sat in the very back of the wagon; Caleb, Eric and my sister sat in the middle seat and of course Mom Merrill and Mr. Merrill sat in the front.

Will pulled us close together, and sat holding my hand in his lap. He had to discuss every point of the game on the way home, but I didn't mind. I was in heaven listening to his voice, enjoying his scent and the closeness of our bodies.

Little did I know that this was the beginning of a deliverance for my sister, this association with the Merrill family.

I would not understand until after her death how difficult it was for her to be around Will and me, but how necessary it would be to give her the courage to do what she had to do, inadvertently returning to me the things I would come to desire most.

Chapter Nine

"Where are you going to college?" I overheard Mom Merrill ask my sister.

"I was thinking of the Conservatory in San Francisco. It has an excellent music program: they even bring in young artists every year from other countries as part of an exchange program to help teach and keep us abreast of national trends in music."

"That sounds good. What are you going to do with that kind of training? You always need to plan a career even if you get married and don't need to use it."

Mom Merrill eyed her knowingly and continued.

"You're so pretty, you'll probably get married right out of college, but even then, more and more wives have their own full-time careers, and I predict that in a few years in the 60's, even more women will begin working, holding down a full-time job."

My sister flushed, but answered, "I'd like to teach music in an elementary school when I graduate," she paused and then added cynically, "if my father will ever allow it."

"Nonsense," said Mom Merrill. "Once you move out, your father doesn't have any more say over what you do."

"I hope that's true, I do hope so," said my sister. "If you only knew." She stopped.

"Tell me, child," said Mom Merrill.

My sister glanced over my way. I kept my head down, but I'm sure she knew I was listening. "I can't. But thank you for letting me talk. It's a relief to know there are some sane adults in this world. Now, let me show you the recipes Mom sent over."

It was the Saturday before Christmas. Mom and Mom Merrill were swapping recipes through us, and because of it, my Dad had come to know about Will's family without much fuss. He still had yet to find out that Will and I were actually dating, but maybe it would be easier this way.

Will entered with an armload of wood for the fireplace, stomping his boots off on the oval braided rug at the back door.

How cute he looked with his blonde hair curling up and around the edge of the Giants baseball hat he wore! I enjoyed learning new things about him, and one of the things I had learned most recently was that his hair, naturally curly, would begin curling with the slightest bit of moisture in the air.

He gave me his one thousand-watt grin and, kicking off his boots, strode to the fireplace near where I was sitting, stacking the wood in an orderly pile. He checked the fire, added another log, and then sat beside me.

"What are you doing?"

"Looking at your Mom's recipe collection."

He grabbed the notebook from my hands, rifling through the pages. "Hey, these are some of my favorites. I didn't know Mom had done this."

"There are probably a lot of things about your Mom that you don't know," I commented wryly.

Will's glance shifted to the window. Raindrops hit against it in a musical symphony, conducted by the wind with periods of crashing crescendos and intermittent whole rests or sustained long tones. Wisps of fog drifted by as clouds touched the earth with ethereal gentleness.

"Do you still want to go hiking with me today?" he asked plaintively.

I could tell he wanted some action, but was unsure of my reaction to the weather. "Of course," I answered.

I watched his face light up with my response, and I couldn't help laughing at him. He was so like a little boy sometimes!

"What's so funny?" he asked suspiciously.

"You. You are!" I gasped between giggles. "You want to go so badly, but you didn't know if I would go with you. It was so cute." My giggles turned to laughter again.

Will looked sheepish, and then reacted typically with action. Diving over the arm of the couch, he began tickling me until I rolled to the floor and begged for mercy. My sister and Mom Merrill looked on from their seats at the dining room table through the wide door and just shook their heads.

"Children," I heard my sister mutter.

Will let me up, and we scrambled into jackets, scarves and gloves. "We'll be back in an hour or two," he announced.

The fog created an enchanted but muddy fairyland. We walked hand in hand up the path in back of the house, past the deer stand we had climbed the day we had met, and then single file to Bald Eagle.

The rocks, slippery with the rain, were no place to sit, but we lingered a few moments, hands clasped, looking down into the valley. It was difficult to distinguish Will's house through the curling, writhing fog that wafted through, around, and above the pines.

Continuing on, we made our way to the Cathedral, the copse of smaller pine trees surrounding the scarred and twisted one standing sentinel by the small stream. Only it wasn't a small stream any more. It was a raging mountain stream about eight feet wide and three feet deep.

"Want to cross?" Will asked grinning at me.

"How?"

"Well, we could go up to the Cathedral and pull off our shoes and socks and wade. It can't be too deep."

A spirit of adventure filled me. "All right," I agreed.

We entered the copse. Gingerly I sat down beside Will. The thick bed of pine needles was not too wet. I pulled off my shoes and socks and rolled up my pant legs. Looking up at Will, I surprised a look of longing and desire on his face. Without speaking he pulled me closer, leaned over and put his lips on mine.

The intensity of his passion surprised me, but I didn't resist as he gently chewed on my lower lip and teased it down and open so he could slip his tongue slowly inside my mouth. He seemed to be tasting nectar as he continued to run his tongue over my lips, exploring my mouth.

Groaning, he pulled me closer and his actions intensified. Wave upon wave of desire shook me. Having never experienced such passion before, I didn't even think of resisting.

With a shuddering sigh, Will released me. He lay back on the pine needles, eyes closed. I watched his face, too caught up in the emotion of the moment to really think about what was happening. Later, when my world was black with loneliness and loss, I would dream and think about those few moments and my first taste of passion.

Slowly Will opened his eyes and smiled at me. He had a dreamy look in his eyes that I didn't understand at the time, but his smile was enough for me. He stood up and pulled me to my feet. Without a word we exited the Cathedral and began to cross the tumbling brook.

The water was cold, but Will's passion had so warmed me that I didn't feel it except to note how refreshing it felt as it rushed against my legs trying, as a small child might, to knock me down. Although I had rolled my pant legs above my knees, they still got wet. On the other side, we leaned against a rock and put our shoes and socks back on our feet.

"You want to climb to the very top of a mountain?" Will asked. I think we have time."

"Great," I responded. I didn't want to return yet. I was too excited, and my sister would surely suspect something.

Walking along the old logging trail, Will finally came to the place for which he was looking. It was a much smaller stream, just a trickle down the mountainside.

"Let's follow this up. It shouldn't be too difficult. Careful of that boulder there."

We ascended the mountain cautiously, passing bright green lichen on fallen logs and strange orange mushroom halves growing at the base of trees.

All the wood, fallen and living, was a sodden dark brown-black from the rain, except for the manzanita and the madrone which glowed a dark red-brown in contrast. The rain had slowed to an unsteady drip-drip, but the fog was denser, weaving in and out of the trees like silent specters in this enchanted forest.

At last we reached the top. We stood in a small clearing about six feet in diameter. A perimeter of trees surrounded this area already descending like so many stairs down the mountain.

From our vantage point, the clouds were below us blocking out any view we might have had. It gave us an eerie closed in feeling, and the silence on the mountaintop was truly deafening. It was as if we inhabited a lonely land all to ourselves, unpopulated by any other human or animal life.

Will squeezed my hand and we raised our arms, hands still clasped and circled around looking all around us. Then he placed his lips on mine again. Immediately I opened my lips to him. The mountain spun us around and around in a sea of sensation.

Will groaned. "Mary, you're like an intoxicating elixir." He rested his face on my hair for an instant. Then pulling his thoughts together asked, "Will I be able to see you on Christmas Day?"

"I don't know. My Dad might not allow it. I just don't know." I sighed.

"Well then, there's probably no better time to give you this than now." He pulled a small package from his jacket pocket.

I held it mutely.

"Go ahead and open it," he prodded.

I opened the package carefully and pulled a small box out. Opening the lid, I exclaimed with delight over a heart-shaped silver charm with a small red stone at the left side. The thin, delicate chain gleamed palely in the white light of the clouds that began to swirl around us.

Will glanced around us. "We'd better start back home, or we'll get lost out here in this fog."

I gave him a quick impetuous hug. "Can you carry this in your pocket for safe-keeping?" I asked. "I don't dare put it on; it might get lost out here."

"Sure," Will said.

We tried to make our way slowly down the mountainside, but first Will slipped, and then I slipped. Our jeans muddied, we decided to continue the quick way down. Sliding down on our backsides over rocks and twigs, I knew I would certainly feel it the next day, but it was such fun.

Once safely on the logging road, we looked at each other: we were both covered with mud from the hips down.

I giggled first, our eyes met, and we began laughing uncontrollably. Linking arms, we sang Christmas carols in between fits of laughter all the way back to his house.

Chapter Ten

Two important events occurred after Christmas. First, my father found out about Will. It happened right after the New Year and before school began again.

I was looking forward to seeing Will as usual on Saturday, but my Dad, in an unusually expansive mood, had planned to visit a vineyard in Napa, partially owned by one of his business associates. He wanted the whole family to come since we had been invited to dine at an elegant restaurant with the associate and his family.

"But I usually see Will on Saturday," I said when the subject came up at the dinner table. My sister gave me a "how-could-you-be-so-dumb" look, and my mother's movements at the kitchen counter seemed to freeze. My Dad calmly kept eating.

"Who's Will?" he asked between bites.

Trying to recover, I said carefully, "Will Merrill. Mrs. Merrill and Mom have been exchanging recipes, so we've been going over there on Saturdays."

"And Will?" He was as pugnacious as a bulldog.

"Will is the oldest son at home. He has two older brothers in South Carolina and two younger brothers who live here." I didn't know if I was giving too much information or not, so I shut my mouth. Mom sat down at the table, and my sister followed the exchange with painfully intent interest.

"Is he your boyfriend?" Talk about cutting to the chase.

I decided there was no point in beating around the bush. "Y-yes." I swallowed hard, realizing that I would have to take whatever consequences occurred from my answer.

We all waited tensely for a response, but Dad calmly continued eating. Several minutes later he said, "Guess you'll have to change your plans for this Saturday."

And that was that. Although we waited for him to explode with anger that evening and even the next several days, no explosion occurred.

The only change I noticed was my Dad watching me in the evening hours while I was doing my homework or practicing piano. The glint in his eye was one I could not interpret, but it so unnerved me that I began doing much of my homework in the privacy of my bedroom.

My sister's reaction was one of anger and then deep depression.

"I can't believe Dad is going to let you have a boyfriend after all those he's chased away from me. It just isn't fair."

I sympathized with her. Dad was sure weird. But when she slipped into a fog of depression, Mom and I were both worried about her. This was her senior year, her last hurrah before college. Even with the ambivalence that occurs when closing a chapter in your life and beginning a new one, her sadness was too deep and unalleviated.

Though I often saw her smiling and joking with her friends in the cafeteria, there always seemed to be that sadness lurking in her eyes. Watching her covertly on weekends, I noticed the cloud that seemed to be hanging over her was dispelled whenever she spent time with Mom Merrill.

We went to the vineyard restaurant in Napa Valley and met the business associate and his family. Mr. Stanley was a tall, muscular man with a balding head and a black mustache.

He exuded charisma and even made my Mom blush when he brought her hand to his lips "in salutation of her beauty." His evening clothes did not quite hide his paunchy belly, but with his old-world manners and charm, it went unnoticed.

Mrs. Stanley was petite with an exotic oriental look, accentuated by the mandarin collared red silk evening dress she wore. Her beautiful mane of raven black hair flowed well past her waist, giving her a young, rather than a sophisticated look.

I expected her to act either withdrawn or snobbish toward my mother; instead she talked simply and quietly of everyday household things, putting my mother entirely at ease.

The three younger Stanleys were as well-bred and well-mannered as their parents. Ten-year old Jessica wore a simple white dress with a pale blue sash, but it was Phillip and Paul who put my sister and me in awe.

They both looked like young gods with wavy black hair and classic features. Phillip, the oldest at twenty-three, was fostering a beard. We learned over dinner that he was the business manager for his Dad. Paul, two years younger, was still attending Cal State University.

To my surprise, I enjoyed dinner. It was obvious that Dad, in an inept way was trying to encourage Phillip's attentiveness toward my sister. Did he have any such horrid designs for me? I didn't think so.

Paul was nearly out of college, too old for a sixteen-year old. But it was fun talking to him and Jessica. She was both smart and funny, and we found ourselves laughing several times at her humorous remarks.

Phillip and my sister were seated to my right and the adults were seated to my left. I could tell that she enjoyed the conversation and attentiveness Phillip was giving her. But as the meal progressed, she noticed my father's eyes on her, and she became somewhat subdued and withdrawn. Darn it Dad! I thought. Why can't you ever just leave her alone?

Phillip continued to call my sister and even came several times to visit her. Dad seemed to accept it, to have planned it.

Phillip even came with us over to the Merrills one Saturday. Mom Merrill approved of him unequivocally, and he seemed to really enjoy their household much as we did, although it must have been a totally different atmosphere than the one to which he was accustomed.

His attention seemed to help lift my sister out of her depression although I could still sense in her a deep-seated despondency at times.

The second thing that happened was not really in the nature of an event, but rather a matter of ongoing puzzlement for me. Will was even more attentive in the ensuing months, and yet he didn't again kiss me as he had done that day we hiked in the storm.

I felt so confused. Had I done something wrong? Did he really still care for me? Maybe he had changed his mind and now only saw me as a really good friend. I was still so new to the dating scene that I had little confidence and needed reassurance.

We continued to see each other in school and on Saturdays, but my mind was in a muddle. It was a difficult time. I became jealous when Will talked to other girls, but at least I was smart enough not to show it.

As May came, Will was making plans to work as a camp counselor, and I was growing more and more despondent. Two Saturdays before he left, we climbed to Bald Eagle and talked.

We leaned back and watched the eagles in silence for a while. Finally, Will took my hand in his.

"I'm going to miss you this summer."

I didn't say anything. How could I tell him all my fears and really make him understand. But Will wasn't about to let anything come between us, especially when he would be absent for most of the summer.

"Mary, I know something is bothering you. Can you tell me about it?"

I did so appreciate his directness. "Yes, but you're going to think I'm ... well I'd rather not say."

"Try me."

"Remember that day right before Christmas when we went hiking in the rain up to the top of the mountain?"

"Remember it! I'll never forget it!"

"Remember what we did before and also on top of the mountain?"

"Well, I gave you a gift and we kissed…."

"Right," I interrupted. "I feel so stupid saying this, Will." I started to cry, but plunged ahead. "Why haven't you kissed me since then? I keep wondering if I've done something wrong or maybe you see me as just a friend but don't know how to tell me…."

"Mary, Mary, don't cry, Mary. This may be the wrong time to tell you this, but I love you. Every day I find new things that I love about you. After I kissed you up on the mountain, I had to talk to my Dad."

"Talk to your Dad?" I was horrified.

"I had to, Mary. It was so hard for me to stop when I did. I wanted to make wild, passionate love to you. You just don't understand how difficult it's been."

He ran his hand through his golden curls. Then he turned and looked deep into my eyes. His own were nearly black with his seriousness. He brushed a strand of hair from the wetness on my cheek.

Overwhelmed with the wondrous relief at his words, the tears began to flow quietly down my cheeks again.

"Oh, Will!" I sobbed.

I buried my face in his shoulder while intense, wild sobs ripped through me. He held me, rocking me back and forth until I quieted down. I looked up trying to smile and explain how relieved I felt.

"I was so afraid, Will," I said.

"You mean you've been carrying this around inside of you since way back then?" He was amazed.

"Yes. It's been awful. I was jealous whenever another girl even looked at you," I said, smiling rather shyly up at him.

"We still have to talk about this some more," Will said. He swallowed. "I've never had feelings like this before for anyone, and I wanted to get a more ... well, a more adult perspective on things."

I nodded, silently willing him to continue.

"So I talked to my Dad, and boy, was that hard. But he gave me some good pointers on how to keep things under control. The bottom line is that if I want our relationship to be long-term, and I do, then I have to look at where I want our physical relationship to be from now until we get married. The more physically involved we get, the more difficult it will be to stop, so the easiest thing, actually it's the hardest thing, is to not get too involved physically, especially when we have two more years of high school to go."

He looked at me to see how I was handling this revelation. I nodded slowly. It made sense.

"I know most people don't believe this; they just think you should act how you feel. I'd love to do that, but I think I would lose my self-respect if I caused anything to happen to you, like, uh, you getting pregnant or something."

I blushed. I couldn't help it. But Will was looking down at his hands, thank goodness, and didn't see. He continued.

"Besides, Dad said the relationships that last the longest are the ones in which the guy and girl are best friends. It's better to build our friendship right now than to get involved in a physical relationship."

It was the longest speech I had ever heard Will make and one that didn't come naturally to him. That he had been so frank with me in spite of his embarrassment showed me how much he really did care for me. His words gave me plenty of thinking to do, but now he was waiting for me to respond.

"Thank you, Will," I said softly. "Your Dad is right, and I'm glad you can talk to him about things like that."

I wanted to ask if it would be all right to kiss once in a while, like right now, but I didn't have the courage. If it were to happen, it would have to be initiated by him anyway; he was so much taller than I.

And he did. He lowered his mouth slowly, tantalizingly to mine, and kissed me, first gently, and then with greater passion. The blue of the spring sky seemed to burst through me as he kissed my cheeks, my closed eyes, and my mouth again, stopping briefly to nibble on my ear lobe before claiming my lips again as a hungry man who had missed several months of meals.

With a final lingering kiss, he squeezed me tight, and said, "There. That'll have to last us for several months!"

In spite of the separation looming like a gloomy forest before me, my spirit was lighter and freer than it had been for several months. Unknowingly, Will's frankness set the tone for our relationship and forged our friendship into a strong and sure thing that even time and pain never broke for me.

Chapter Eleven

The long, hot summer ended, and Will finally returned from camp. I wanted to run to him when I first saw him on my doorstep with a bouquet of flowers in his hand, but I felt awkward and shy, as if around a stranger.

Maybe it was because this was a formal date, not just seeing him in his home with his family or going for a hike in the woods.

We went to a nice restaurant. Will had spent very little of his small earnings from camp, so he wanted to take me somewhere special. He looked so nice in his khaki pants and plaid shirt. I wore a dark green skirt and a gauzy blouse for the occasion with a string of fake pearls my sister loaned me.

Conversation centered on the latest gossip of Santa Rosa such as who was dating whom and the latest information about the space program. Will had been awed and excited when the United States had launched the first man-made satellite in March.

Now it seemed that America was really entering the Space Age with the beginning of a space organization called NASA in July. Even up at camp, Will had heard the news, firing his imagination to even greater heights.

"Maybe when I go to college, I can get a degree in engineering and eventually work on spaceships at NASA," he said, his eyes glowing.

When that topic was exhausted and Will had returned from his own space orbit, I asked about the camp, how it was laid out, who all the staff members were, and about some of the activities.

I knew most of the answers already, but I wanted to watch Will talk, to get to know him all over again. He was taller, his hair was even more golden, and he had a gorgeous tan.

Dinner was finally over, and we drove around for a while, past prune orchards and hops fields, then down highway twelve toward Sonoma. Will swung the car around and parked under some large live oak trees, their limbs spreading a curtain of privacy over us.

We were above the city now, and we could see the lights blinking on one by one as the sun slunk behind the hills, taking its punishing heat with it and tingeing the sky a rosy color that faded slowly into a pale golden color.

Finally only a shimmering aqua blue was left on the horizon that gradually changed to light, medium, teal and royal blue, until above us the stars poked their faces out of a velvety midnight blue. A faint delta breeze flowed in through the open windows, slowly dissipating the heat of a Californian summer.

Neither of us seemed inclined to talk. It is difficult to discuss feelings when you've been separated from someone for a length of time, but we held hands and tried to grasp the fleeting meaning of unspoken words.

At last I gave up trying to think of a way to tell Will how much I had missed him and how much he still meant to me. Instead, I scooched even closer to him, and with a sigh, leaned my head against his arm.

He began moving his thumb in a circular motion on the back of my hand. It was an action that I found, curiously, to be both comforting and stimulating. Somehow, it seemed to release the curious restraint we had been feeling.

"I'm so glad to be back home. I missed Mom and Dad, Eric and Caleb. But most of all I missed you." Now he turned and faced me directly, leaning his elbow against the steering wheel, but placing his left hand lightly on my shoulder.

"Most of all, though, I was afraid something would happen between us; your Dad would spirit you away or you would meet someone else."

I sat up straight and looked incredulously into his eyes. He was serious. Why in the world would he think that I would meet someone else? He was the one who was so popular.

Then it struck me: just because he was popular, why would he have different fears than anyone else? It was a revelation that bolstered my self-confidence and taught me to look at situations from different perspectives.

"No. There's no one else."

"What about this Stanley guy I keep hearing about?"

"Stanley? Oh, you mean Phillip and Paul. Phillip comes to see my sister once in a while, and I think they correspond, but Paul? Paul's too old for me. I don't know where you heard about them, anyway."

"Just a girl at camp trying to make me jealous, I guess."

"Who?" I demanded.

"Sylvia Strickland. I think she's a good friend of Ashley Lynn's."

"Well that explains a lot. Ashley Lynn has always had a crush on you."

"I didn't know that." Will sounded aghast.

Boys were so dumb sometimes, especially where girls were concerned. I shook my head in amazement. Not a very gregarious letter writer myself, Will's letters had been even briefer. Now I knew why. Since I knew the truth, I decided to play with it a little.

"I can't believe you would even think I would write you and then dally with someone else in your absence."

Will actually blushed slightly. "I'm sorry, Mary. I guess I let my fears run away with me." He ran his hand through his golden hair.

"Prove it." I was feeling more in control and even audacious now.

"Mary," Will groaned. "Don't tempt me just now." He slid his left hand behind my head, tilting my head upward and claiming my lips. The intensity of his passion warned me that he was fully aroused. When he suddenly broke it off and started the car, I didn't question his love this time.

School started, and my sister left for college, though she continued to return home on most weekends. My Dad seemed to shrivel all of sudden and become a crabbed old man. As I look back, I can see how Mom caught the brunt of his venom, but at the time I was too caught up in the new world that was opening to me.

How many times did I trot off to some activity or another without any conscious knowledge of the cost to the rest of my family? And did my busyness save me from a deeper evil that I was unwilling and unable to face?

Now that I was an upperclassman, I became more involved in the many activities available, and I remember eleventh grade as the year of an endless round of activities as I grew more confident socially.

Cheerleading was not my style, but I ran for the office of Junior Class Treasurer and won. That automatically involved me in Student Council, the School Improvement Committee, and the various Class Days when we decorated halls and team lockers before big games.

I grew musically as well. I switched from concert band to jazz band. I tried to get into the marching band on the chance that I might be asked to join the select ensemble that played for basketball games, but I asked too late in the year.

Marching band practice had begun on August first in the empty school parking lot. I consoled myself with the thought that I hadn't had to swelter in the heat, and maybe I could go with the Merrills to more of Will's games this year.

And I did. Mom Merrill made sure I was included in all their plans to attend the games. I never tired of the pulse-pounding, invigorating excitement, and yelled myself hoarse more than several times.

For Christmas that year I bought Will a shirt in his favorite color of forest green. Bought at an expensive department store, it nearly depleted the stash of money I had been saving since October, but I think he liked it much more than the cheap cologne I had bought him the year before as a last minute, desperation gift.

We decided that hiking to the top of the mountain—we called it Cloudy Heights as it was nearly always above the clouds in the winter time—should be a tradition for us every Christmas.

Like the early part of eleventh grade, Christmas was a socially hectic time. In addition to the Christmas music at school, I had music to learn for our church Christmas program in addition to preludes, offertories, and other special music.

Then were the parties, drop-ins, and last minute shopping expeditions with my sister who arrived home from college full of expectations of sisterly excursions with time for long chats.

College had cracked open the door of resignation to a quiet life of familial devotion and revealed a world of exciting and obtainable possibilities finally available to her. She was anxious to share these new things with me, but I was so busy involving myself in school and church activities, I didn't see the hurt my busyness caused her.

Fortunately, Mom Merrill was there to pick up the slack for me. Subconsciously I had buried myself in a maelstrom of activity to avoid the realization that my family, as I had known it, was shattering into millions of tiny fragments.

My parents were so immersed in their own problems that they seemed glad to have me busy. If I had paused for a moment to really meditate on the change in my Dad from a dictatorial machinator to a silent, self-absorbed man, I would have been terribly worried.

But I was too busy being the social butterfly and girlfriend of one of the most popular boys in school. It was a heady experience for a heretofore unknown wallflower.

Prom, was the last big social event of eleventh grade. Held on Friday evening, over one hundred juniors and seniors attended, dancing until one in the morning under the blue and silver streamers which decorated the ballroom of the Old Towne Hotel, and then bowling until five when we congregated at Denny's for breakfast.

The numbers had diminished by then, and we were a more subdued crowd. Will drove slowly to Janet's house where I was supposedly spending the night.

Dad had broken his well-maintained wall of self-absorption and had told me in no uncertain terms that no daughter of his would attend such a heathen event as a prom. It wasn't what a Scripturally separated Baptist should do.

That evening when Mom came to my bedroom to say good night, she had begun reminiscing about the prom she and Dad had attended. What a hypocrite Dad was, I thought, and I determined that I would somehow go.

I snuggled closer to Will on the seat of his Dad's new Edsel Villager. I was tired, but my mind was alert, and I was enjoying every minute playing the grownup lady in my white, satin sheath with diamond-sequined sleeves. Will was extraordinarily handsome in the black tux his Mom had rented for him for the evening. The loosened cravat and bow tie along with the faint stubble on his jaw added to his rakish good looks.

He drove in a leisurely fashion with his left arm resting along the window of the car, his thumb hooked at the side of the steering wheel and his right arm draped comfortably around my shoulders. One of Sinatra's new songs played softly on the radio, and a lone bird awakened somewhere near the road to query the morning star as it hung huge and glistening in the aqua velvet sky.

"I could drive like this forever," Will said quietly.

"Me too. The world is so beautiful this time of the morning. How come I've never seen it before?"

"I have," Will asserted.

I looked questioningly at him. "When?"

"Oh, several times when I've been hunting. There's nothing like watching the sun come up in the woods."

"I'll have to see it with you sometime," I said, eager to share the experience with him.

"You're doing it right now." I felt rather than heard Will chuckle as he said it. He slowly eased the car over by the side of the road, turning off the engine.

We sat in silence, absorbing the stillness of the quietude before dawn. A mountain range loomed before us, grayish-black in the gloaming before first light. The brilliance of the morning star began receding as the dawn, like a silent magician, flung a silken scarf of pale blue, then peach, then rosy pink across the sky above the mountains. Will broke the silence.

"Do you realize how much you've grown this year, Mary?"

"What do you mean?"

"When I first met you, you were so quiet and shy, but you had a sparkle in your eye, and I knew you would be worth knowing. You kept surprising me last year by what you said and did, and now this year, you've become so much more confident and outgoing socially. It's been fun watching you, but you've sure been keeping busy, almost too busy for me!"

I considered his words. He was proud of me; that I could tell, but maybe it would be good to slow down some. I thought of my sister's hurt when I had been too busy to spend time with her at Christmas. I also remembered my Mom's worn and sometimes haggard face and times when she had seemed utterly worn out.

"Are you telling me I need to be less busy?" I asked point blank.

Will looked somewhat uncomfortable. "No-o-o, not exactly. I guess what I'm trying to say is that I admire the way you've changed, but just make sure you take the time with the people you're around; time to understand them, time to make them feel special. You can start with me," he said in a wheedling tone. "You can make me feel special before I drop you off at Janet's house."

"Like how?" I asked, teasing him.

"Oh, I bet you can think of a few ways," he said.
He seemed to be daring me to take the initiative. Sliding my hands along his arms, I locked gazes with his. Slowly I removed the bow tie from around his neck, fiddled

with unbuttoning the first three buttons of his shirt until he drew his breath in harshly.

My hands moved up to his face, and I traced the outline of his lips as lightly as I could with my fingertips teasing him to respond, but he still held himself rigidly in check.

Holding my palm against his cheek with one hand, I fumbled at the next two buttons on his shirt with the other while I continued to watch his eyes. His eyes darkened with intensifying passion, and a thrill of awe shot through me that I had the power to elicit such a response from him.

When I splayed my hands across his bare chest, moving them slowly around to his back to pull him toward me, his iron control broke and he lowered his lips to mine, kissing me passionately. But I wasn't through seducing him.

The freedom he had given me to make the advances was like an elixir emboldening me. I traced my tongue around his lips and flicked it against his tongue several times until he groaned with pleasure and his body shuddered. Gradually, the passion diminished. I didn't want it to ever end, but we both knew it must.

"Did I do a good job of making you feel special?" I asked demurely.

Will's response was only a growl as he buttoned his shirt and started the car.

Chapter Twelve

My sister did not come home that summer, so I did not have an opportunity to make up for the slight I had shown her at Christmas. Thanks to Mom Merrill, however, I was given the opportunity of working at camp with Will.

Related to their church, it was called Keystone, and was located in the low Sierras. Formerly a hunting lodge with several smaller cabins scattered around it, the churches had contributed money and time to build several more cabins, a large bathroom and shower facility, and a sandlot for volleyball.

I was surprised to learn that Janet, also a member of Will's church, was on the staff as well. Janet and I, along with the other female staffer, Becky, stayed in a small cabin up on the hill near the bathrooms. Will occupied another small cabin with the other two male staffers, Steve and Al.

Our staff leader was Sharon Keyes; she was a young college grad, loads of fun, and her Daddy had owned Keystone before it was sold to the church denomination. Her Daddy also owned a great deal of the land around the camp and in the small valley below the camp.

Arriving Saturday morning, we discovered a gargantuan task ahead of us, or at least it seemed gargantuan to me. We were to beat out all the mattresses on the bunk beds, sweep and mop each cabin, and clean the bathrooms until they were spotless. Since he had been on the staff the year before, Will quickly became the unofficial leader.

"Okay, guys, here's how we do it so we can have the evening free." We all formed a circle around him. "We guys will go from cabin to cabin hauling out the mattresses and beating them. When we're finished with a cabin, you girls go in and sweep and mop it. Then we'll all work on the bathrooms: guys do the guys' side and you girls do the girls' side." He looked at his watch. Even with stopping for lunch, I'd say we'll be done by four."

And he was right. I had never worked so hard before, but with Will's inspiration, and chatter and song to lighten the work, our group quickly became a dynamic work force.

I was responsible for sweeping the cabins while Janet and Becky came behind me with mops and hot water. Janet and Becky, working together, quickly established a routine and a rapport. I was content to listen to their talk as I worked sometimes in the cabin they were in, and sometimes by myself in the cabin the boys had just vacated.

It was a hot afternoon in spite of the tall pines, and soon the boys were working without shirts. I admired Will's muscles moving in rhythmic beauty as he pounded enthusiastically with a broom on the mattresses Steve and Al brought from the cabins. A deep contentment filled me as I gazed around on the beauty of the camp, listened to the lazy drone of insects, and inhaled the scent of pine on the warm air.

When we finished the cabins and started on the bathrooms, the fun really began! I already knew Janet, a tall, willowy girl with curly blondish-brown hair. Becky was petite and pretty with thin, silky dark hair and a smooth olive complexion. She had a beautiful smile, but was impishly ready for any fun that came along.

After sanitizing the five shower stalls, we held a whispered consultation. We could hear the boys cleaning the shower stalls next door, so we decided to turn on all the cold water in the showers at once and deluge them with hot.

It worked! Before we could stop laughing, a hose nozzle came snaking into a corner of the screenless window and the entire vanity area of the ladies room was decorated with droplets of water. Calling a truce, Janet went outdoors and retrieved the hose. We hosed down the cement floors, finishing what the boys had started for us.

When the bathroom was spotless, we went to our cabin to change, but before we got there, Will called to us to change into our swimsuits. We went down to the river for a refreshing swim. Sharon and her brother Jim brought a cooler of food, and after an hour of vigorous swimming, we were ready for the pop and the hot dogs roasted over driftwood collected from the edge of the river.

We ended the evening with roasted marshmallows over the embers and stories from Jim and Sharon about the people who lived around the camp and down in the valley.

And that was only the beginning of the fun that summer. Sharon took us horseback riding all over the La Sierra's, clawing up mountains at a forty-five degree angle along trails her Dad had made with a small bobcat tractor. These machine-made trails created breaks to help reduce fire hazards.

We also spent time swimming in many wildly beautiful spots along the Russian River, picking blackberries along the canals used to transport water to fields laden with California's rich bounty of produce, and even playing volleyball, calling the score in Spanish with the Mexican workers during the long twilit Saturday evenings after their work week was finished.

One Saturday we worked hard all afternoon after the campers had left, beating out mattresses and cleaning the bathrooms. As we were finishing, we heard the welcome sound of neighing horses.

The sun warmed the scent of the pines around us, and the lazy drone of bees promised a welcome break from the work. We scattered to our respective cabins to change: first bathing suits and then sleeveless shirts and shorts. We never knew where Sharon would take us, so it was best to be prepared!

I had a black horse named Samantha. She was calm and sweet-natured, a perfect mount for me since I had not done much riding before this summer. We took some trails that I'm sure only Sharon and her family knew about over the mountains and down into the valley to the Keye's ranch house.

The boys took the horses to the stables, and Sharon handed bowls to us girls with instructions to get some blackberries for some blackberry ice cream after dinner.

We headed toward a spot were the canals crossed over a section of the river. It was cooler in the shade of the blackberry vines that hung from the canals; other vines grew along the river, so we were sure to find some large, juicy berries.

The canals were five-foot wide cement pipes that had been cut in half and dragged into place. They were about four feet deep, but Sharon had warned us not to try to walk in them because at times the current was very swift.

Sure enough, we found some huge, delicious berries; they were at least an inch long. We stripped the ripened black-purple berries from the bushes that grew along the river path, but couldn't find a path through the tangle of vines with their prickery thorns, and those thorns seemed to sting sharper the closer we tried to get to the water.

"Ouch," Becky exclaimed as she tried to get in closer.

Janet shaded her eyes from the sun and gazed longingly at the vines that hung from the canal over the river. "Aren't those the hugest we've seen yet?" she asked of no one in particular.

I followed her gaze. They were! Clusters of two-inch berries hung down over the river. We both moved as close to the canal as we dared, leaving Becky to extricate herself from the thorns clutching at her thin, cotton, eyelet blouse. A small breeze ran a delicate touch across the hanging vines, tantalizing us.

Janet, who was at least five inches taller than me, reached as high as she could, but the berries remained two inches from her fingertips. "Here," she said. "Let me climb on your shoulders and try to reach them."

I was dubious. "How about if you just put your legs around my waist? That should put you up high enough," I said. "If you climb on my shoulders, I'm afraid I'll get top-heavy, and you'll fall."

For some reason, picturing this sent us into laughter. Once we had recovered our breaths, Janet climbed up on my back. It was hard to steer her directly under the berries with my head bent down from the awkward position I was in. Becky had finally extricated herself and began supervising, telling me where to go. It was hard work, but Janet was finally getting some of the juiciest berries.

"Uh-oh. I think we should stop. We've got an audience," Becky hissed. Janet turned her head to look up toward the Keyes' house just as I moved. It was enough to send us both off balance. We landed in a tangle of arms and legs and berries on top of Becky.

Then we heard the stifled laughter. A group of five to six Mexican workers was gathered on the lawn under the shade of tall maple trees, watching and laughing at us.

I could feel myself going red, but as we straightened ourselves and anxiously examined the damage to the berries, the glances of the men changed. They could sense our anxiety from the thirty-yard distance, and after a quick discussion in Spanish, they moved languidly toward us.

Using gestures, they indicated their willingness to pick the berries for us. This was novel. Six Mexican men picking berries for three white girls.

They stripped to the waist and jumped into the middle of the bushes. We watched, fascinated by the fact that the thorns didn't seem to bother them a bit. The fine display of bronzed six-packs engaged our attention as well. Becky found a large maple leaf and began fanning herself. I noticed that she used it to flirt, using those large dark eyes of hers.

Janet, the most phlegmatic of us girls, began a running commentary of encouraging and complimentary words. The men flashed grins at us. They probably could understand the English Janet was saying though they could not speak English well enough to communicate.

They finished their task in ten minutes, returning to us with ten overflowing buckets of berries. We gave our thanks as they escorted us up the river path to the wide, green lawn by side of the Keyes' garage.

Sharon emerged from the side door and her eyes grew wide with surprise. She questioned the men in Spanish. They gave a laughing explanation and asked a question. She communicated a few minutes more with them, then turned to us and said, "They have a surprise for you all after supper."

Will, Steve, and Al returned, and Sharon put us all to work grilling hamburgers, hot dogs, and corn on the cob for our supper. Her Mom and ten-year old sister, Susan, brought out a huge fruit salad and some tea and we soon all sat at the picnic table on the back open patio, contentedly enjoying the food and the feel of the breeze on the warm air of evening.

The sun slanted her six o'clock rays through the languidly moving leaves of the maples, burnishing their edges with gold and resting her fingers on Will's already golden head.

I longed to wind my fingers in his hair, too, but physical contact between staff members was forbidden in front of campers. Our only private times together were very brief and rare. I hoped that maybe sometime this weekend we could spend the luxury of a whole hour together by ourselves.

We had only two more weeks left before returning to Santa Rosa. But I had learned so much more about Will this summer, I mused.

His leadership qualities had developed, and I had also noticed his tactfulness with others, from the shyest nine-year old camper to the middle-aged counselors, to old Mr. Tate who showed up every day at four with his water truck to spray down the fine dust that rose from the road, lacing the plants, bushes, trees, and anything else unfortunate to be standing by when a vehicle moved anywhere around the camp. My musings were interrupted when a penny was dropped into my lap. "A penny for them," Janet said quietly.

"Actually, I already know who you're thinking about. If you two want any time by yourselves, you'd better not be broadcasting it with your eyes," she said.

Janet knew my predicament and was entirely sympathetic. Sharon was a dear, but she was a stickler for obeying the rules, and even enforced them when no campers were around. It was probably because she felt so responsible being in college and not too much older than we were.

We were just taking the leftover food into the kitchen and finishing up the dishes when the young Mexican men who had helped us earlier showed up with a volleyball.

Sharon called for the boys to help her wheel two poles cemented into the middle of two tires out of the garage and to hang a net between the two poles. We hurried to finish the dishes so we could join the boys playing volleyball.

"Dos y quatro," called out Pedro, and we watched as he served the ball over the net. Al set it up to Steve who in turn, spiked it over the net. Their competitive spirits were in full force, but they let us join them anyway.

Janet, Becky and I, challenged to play our best, ended up wearing ourselves out early, but the boys played until dusk, determined to beat the Mexican men who were only slightly older than they were.

Sharon had started an ice cream freezer, so in spite of aching muscles, we each cranked for five minutes. After my turn, I leaned a lawn chair back into a reclining position and let my mind drift. I was nearly asleep when a stream of cold water splashed down over one shoulder. Bounding out of the chair, I saw Steve doubled over in laughter. Janet and Becky were laughing, too.

I chased Steve around for a few minutes. Looking daggers at him, I said, "You'd better watch out: I'll get you back before the week is over."

Returning from helping Sharon put away the poles and net, Will advised Steve, "You'd better be careful. When she looks like that, she really means it!"

Will and I finally had some time to spend together on the way back to camp. We were all too tired to hike back, so Sharon took us back in her Dad's truck.

We elected to ride in back. Steve, Al and Janet rode with us, and I could have hugged Janet for keeping Steve and Al entertained so that Will and I could cuddle. We didn't talk much, but it was comforting to be held.

"I miss you," Will whispered in my ear as the truck wound around and up the final mountain toward camp. He positioned himself behind me so I could lean my head against his chest. His long legs stretched on either side of mine, and I felt surrounded by his love. He twisted his fingers between mine and bent his head to hear my reply.

"I miss you, too. Pretend I'm kissing you, okay?"

"How?"

"You want a full description?"

"You bet."

"Well…" This was a little embarrassing. I had never put my lovemaking with him into words, but if he wanted me to do so, I was willing to try.

"We start with our lips slightly parted, and we're just kind of tasting each other." Boy, this was difficult. "Then we grow more passionate, and…" I just couldn't continue.

Will's arms tightened convulsively around me. Just then the truck slid to a stop. We were at camp. Will bent his head and quickly kissed me on the lips. I scooted forward so he could stand up before Sharon got out of the front seat.

Two days later I got my revenge on Steve. He had decided to stay up late the night before and wouldn't get up to help us serve breakfast. I shared my plan with Janet and Becky. They thought it was a superb idea.

Giggling, I filled a pitcher with cold water and made my way toward the staff boys' cabin. Steve was snuggled in his sleeping bag with one arm and his head protruding.

"Good morning, Stevie," I said in a syrupy voice. He grunted. I paused a moment, debating the quickest way to escape after the dirty deed. I decided a quick dash of the pitcher and a quick sprint toward the door was the best way to accomplish my goal.

The water splashed out onto his head, and he sat up gasping. I ran, but he didn't pursue. Will clued me in on the reason later, but Becky, Janet and I laughed every time we saw him for the next few days.

Two weeks later Will, Janet and I were home in Santa Rosa eagerly awaiting our final year in high school.

Chapter Thirteen

The first thing I noticed when I returned home from camp was my mother's frailty. Her skin seemed translucent and her spirit wistful. My father's rage exploding around her contrasted strongly with this frailty, but she also seemed to be detached from his selfish outbursts.

It was as if her emotions were no longer engaged with our household. She existed on an emotional plane far above ours where she basked in another light and where she had found calm and peace. She was radiant, but her radiance frightened me; it was so ethereal, so otherworldly.

My father, on the other hand, had shrunk both in body and in temperament. His face, dour with selfishness, was pleated with wrinkles, and his lips almost never curved upward. He seethed inwardly with uncontrolled passions. This was expressed most often in bouts of rage, and I thought we had never had so many broken things in our house from chairs to dishes.

Coming home from school early one day to pick up a jacket I would need later, I saw him with a flat of eggs, chucking them at the back wall with all his might, his face contorted with anger. I was glad he wasn't beating up on a person, but I was embarrassed that the neighbors would see, and I was frightened that one day I would find him beating up on Mom. At other times, my father would sit in a corner of the living room all evening long, staring with glittering eyes at whoever entered and muttering to himself in low, unintelligible grunts.

He had snapped. I honestly thought my dad had snapped. I told no one except Will. He became my sole confidant, and he grew very protective of me. I spent more and more time with him although I felt so guilty leaving Mom by herself with Dad.

But I just couldn't handle being around Dad and the problems seething below and above the surface that I could scarcely understand. If only my sister was home and I could talk to her and try to make some sense of Dad's actions. But she was safely ensconced at college.

School was a refuge. It was our senior year, and I was tempted to get over-involved, but conscious of Will's comments the year before, I dropped out of student council and declined to run again for a student office. Honing my musical skills and spending time with Will became the two most important things in my life although I was elected as a princess of the homecoming court.

It was a special evening. Shivers ran up and down my spine as Will escorted me onto the field to stand in my designated place. The packed stadium erupted as we walked, and I knew that the cheers were as much for him as for me. He was still the undisputed best player in basketball, and was attracting the attention of many college scouts.

My mother and father were there, proud parents still keeping up the façade of perfect family and pillars of the community. As we reached our spot, Will looked down smiling, and I looked up, our eyes locked in a visual embrace, and I could tell he was enjoying the moment as much as I was.

Following the game, which our team did win, 24-17, we adjourned to the gym, decorated for the event in black, orange and gold for the dance. A dais had been erected at one end with places taped off for the queen and her court to stand.

It was right next to the band that had been hired for the evening, and the noise was so loud that we girls soon abandoned our posts and joined the swirling, gyrating crowd below. Even Pandy, our panther mascot, was moving wildly to the music and entertaining several girls. Quickly finding Will, we positioned ourselves for the Slide.

After a half-hour of energetic dancing, the band played the first slow song of the evening. I melted against Will, savoring the feel of his body, and I could feel his body responding to mine. He drew me closer still, wrapping his arms tightly around me, his head bent and breathing in the sensual scent of the perfume he had bought for me with some of the money he had earned at camp.

This was the closest together our bodies had been for a while, and mine responded with the sensation of an electrical current pulsing in the core of my gut and making me feel warm and weak all over. Thank goodness my parents had gone home.

From the shelter of Will's arms, I looked around the dim room with the kaleidoscope of muted colors flashing from the ball high above us. No one was paying attention to us. They were all locked in their own moment of time, so I surrendered to the sensations flooding through me. Will pulled me closer, and I was lost in the emotions his closeness stirred within me.

Will and I continued our habit of taking long walks through the woods behind his house. A golden October had melted into November, and as the Indian summer waned, the afternoon air gradually began to take on the tangy spice of autumn. I enjoyed these afternoons, usually three or four times a week, immensely.

Our relationship changed. We had built a solid friendship over the past few years, and now it deepened into a permanent commitment. Whether it was due to our isolation from others because of my father's deteriorating behavior or because we ourselves were maturing, we were drawn together in a more intimate relationship than we had ever had before. We now began to discuss college, of course, but also marriage.

Sitting on the deer stand, we discussed our college options.

"I'd love to do basketball, but really, it's more important that I get a degree in engineering. I want to get a good job so I can support you, Mary," said Will. "UC Berkeley's Engineering school looks great! They have all the classes I need, and their graduates usually get good-paying jobs."

"You'll just have to apply at another place around the San Francisco/Berkeley area," said Will. "If we attend colleges that are at least within fifty miles or so of each other, we'll be able to see each other more often."

And so we filled out our applications late in November and sent them off, hoping to be able to be near each other in the coming year.

Our physical intimacy increased as well. Often now, Will would draw me onto his lap and we would kiss with increasing abandon, our mouths roaming and tasting the sweetness of skin on the neck, chin, or jaw. Sometimes he'd hold me so tightly, he'd nearly crush my ribs. He explained that those were the times when he wanted so badly to go all the way with me, and the only way to keep from taking me was to hold on tightly until he could control his passions.

And then suddenly in December, the stability of our lives was destroyed.

It had been a relaxing and enjoyable Christmas. I made sure that my sister was included in most of my festivities especially with Will and his family. We had shopping to do together in crowded malls and in smaller stores sandwiched together along streets gaily decorated with Christmas lights and wreaths that hung from gracefully arched street lamps along the sidewalk.

On one of the shopping trips, Will, my sister, and I took his two younger brothers all over town. It was so much fun to experience the shopping trip through their eyes!

They were rather contemptuous of Santa Claus since they knew who really brought them gifts, but they were owl-eyed with wonder over the train set in Santa's Village. Each car was a foot high and wound through a snow-hilled town complete with figures skating on a pond—they really moved!—and miniature streetlights that really worked.

The next day was the program at church. My sister had been working on "O Holy Night" with her voice teacher at college. I was familiar with the music, so I accompanied her on the piano. It was achingly beautiful. As the last few notes faded away, I happened to glance at my mother. Her face shone with a heavenly beauty, and two beautiful teardrops slipped down her cheeks.

At that moment, I wanted to jump up, place my arms tenderly around my Mom, wipe the tears from her cheeks and hold her, promising her to protect her from my father and his abuse. She had always done her best for us girls, in spite of the obstacles placed in her way by my obsessive father.

But of course, I didn't jump up and do all those things. How could I protect my Mom? I realized that I had, up to this point, ignored the terrible things that were happening in my family. Was there any possible way I could change things, or at least help my Mom?

Sitting at the piano, I allowed the last liquid notes to fade and bowed my head, asking God to help me find a way to help my Mother.

Sunday's roast beef dinner was a more joyous affair than we usually had. Mom was expansive in praise of her "two talented daughters," and even Dad's face took on a gleam of possessive pride. My sister's reaction to Mom was tenderness, but I could tell that she resented Dad's obsequious praise of her talent.

As soon as we had finished washing the dishes for Mom, we made our escape to Will's house, once again leaving Mom with her antagonistic husband.

One glance at Will's face when we arrived sent my sister in search of his mother, and the two of us outside for a hike in the hills. We walked in silence halfway to Bald Eagle. Finally I could take Will's silence no longer.

"What's wrong?"

"I can't say."

"Will."

"I don't want to be ugly, and if I talk right now, I'll say some ugly things."

Throughout our relationship, I had never once heard Will say anything even mildly unkind or demeaning except about my father. It was an area of great strength in him, and I often wished I could keep control of my tongue the way he did. A frisson of fear whipped up my spine. It had to be something really bad for him to talk this way.

"I won't tell anyone, Will. You know that."

We were approaching the Knob. Will took time to make sure I was safely seated on the rocky surface, but he remained standing.

"It's my parents. My Dad really. He's being transferred back to Charleston, South Carolina. My Mom's ecstatic because now she'll be with her grandbabies," he said bitterly. "They've got my younger brothers excited about it, but what about me? What about us? I don't want to leave you, Mary. I won't leave you. But what am I going to do? Where can I stay?"

His first words hit me in the pit of my stomach. It was a good thing I was sitting down. "When?" I managed to whisper through dry lips.

"What?"

"When? When do they leave?"

"The end of January. I've talked to them about staying here. They're not very happy about it, but they understand, especially Mom. She's really concerned about you."

"She is?" That made me feel better, as if someone was on our side, and I was touched by her concern.

"Somehow, someway, Mary, I'm going to stay here with you." He ran his fingers through his blond hair in a gesture of frustration.

"I really want to finish my senior year here at Santa Rosa High. After graduation, I'll be going off to college, and I can live in the dorms. But I still have to find a place to stay February through August."

He shrugged his shoulders, but he was far from defeated. From my rocky seat he stood tall against the blue sky, and it is a picture that I will never forget. Sincerity and courage radiated from him as he stood defiant against the possibility of separation.

"We'll find a way, Will," I said with more conviction than I felt. I didn't possibly see how it would work, but his courage unlocked mine to face this new difficulty with more grace than I felt I possessed. Besides, I couldn't stand the wall of silence that had separated us at the beginning of our walk. We had learned how to communicate, and I wasn't about to let that go.

Will was restless, so we continued our walk around the hillside to the grove of pines with the tall scarred pine standing sentinel above the rest. The stream below, usually a quiet vernal pool during the spring, was once again a raging stream—not very deep, but still too wet to cross. Although the sun still shone warmly, a breeze whistled coldly down from the top of the mountain. We took shelter inside the copse of young pines.

Not only was it warmer inside the cathedral of young pines, it was dry. The deep border of pine needles at the base of the large pine was dried out from the rains of the previous week, and overhead the sunlight filtered down through the needled boughs, creating an intimate place of warmth and peace.

"Hold me, Mary," whispered Will. He turned to face me, and I gathered him in my arms, hugging him tightly. We rocked back and forth for several minutes while I willed with all my heart and mind for a peace to settle over us.

It did. Silence permeated the air around us, while a finger of sunlight reached down to play gently with Will's hair, burnishing it.

When I felt him relax, I pulled away and sat down carefully on the needles with my back against the sentinel pine. Then I spread my legs and motioned for Will to sit between them so I could hold him again. He sank down, and, once again, I gathered his much taller frame in embrace.

"This is no way to do it," Will said somberly but with a hint of humor. He flipped over and sat beside me, his arms around my shoulders pulling me closer and closer. His lips gently played with mine at first, tasting and teasing. But as I opened my mouth, he plunged his tongue deeper and deeper, voraciously drinking from a deep well of love. He pulled back his head and gazed into my eyes with concern.

"I'm not hurting you, am I?" he asked.

"N-no," I managed to stammer, shaken but pleased with his passion.

He lowered his head again, possessing my lips and engulfing me in a vortex of pleasure. Gently he pulled me to one side and lowered me to the bed of pine needles, the full length of his body half covering mine, left hand gently cupping my head. He nibbled on my lip, moved to kiss my nose and each eyelid, then ran his tongue along the ridge of my ear before nibbling on my ear lobe.

"Mary, Mary," he whispered brokenly. With his right hand, he began exploring my face, lowering his lips to kiss each spot that he touched.

He unzipped my jacket and moved his hand lower and lower until his hand cupped my breast through the thin layer of my pale blue turtleneck. I trembled with feelings I had never felt before, my whole body on fire, aching for his touch everywhere.

I reached up to unzip his jacket, and with one fluid movement, he flung it off, revealing his typical blue plaid flannel. Slowly I unbuttoned the top four buttons so I could reach inside and feel the taut muscles through his turtleneck. He pulled both shirts out of his pants and guided my hands underneath to explore his chest, finely etched with golden hair.

His hands felt so good on my body. I felt engulfed, swamped by myriad emotions, trapped in a maelstrom of aching need and pleasure, and I didn't want it to end.

I wondered why it had taken so long for us to get to this point. With that thought, some sanity returned to me, and I realized that two years of Will's careful restraint was about to go down the drain.

A brief vision of my mother made me realize that I was probably going too far. Could this be, as I had been taught, part of the relationship that should be saved for marriage?

My father's stern visage passed before my eyes, and I was surprised at the surge of anger that spurted through me. I realized that if I wasn't careful, this anger against my Dad would rule my life, imbuing it with a bitterness that would be difficult to overcome.

Will sensed my withdrawal and drew back, looking with concern at my expression. He had never lost control so much, and I could tell that he was worried. I smiled up at him and put my finger against his lips in a hushing sign.

"Don't say anything to spoil it. I've enjoyed every minute," I said, refusing to give in to the guilt.

Will threw himself back against the cushion of needles for a moment, and then propped himself on one elbow beside me. "You're so beautiful, Mary. I don't ever want to do anything to hurt you. If I get too rough or too passionate, just stop me. I won't be upset with you. I'll try to control myself, but gosh, it's getting hard."

He leaned over and gave me a quick hard kiss. "Let's go face the music."

Chapter Fourteen

The solution was surprisingly simple. Mom Merrill agreed to stay in California with her three sons until school was out while Dad Merrill moved back to Charleston. He flew back to California for Easter and for the final move.

It was a simple solution, yes, but I wondered, now that Will and I were talking about marriage, how Mom and Dad Merrill could stand being apart for so long. They had such a good relationship, especially compared to my parents. Their love seemed to be as alive and as strong and filled with passion as the relationship Will and I shared.

One day late in February, I asked Mom Merrill about it. She had received a card and gifts for Valentine's Day along with a very long phone call.

She grabbed my hands and pulled me forward in a quick embrace when I posed my question.

"Yes dear. It has been difficult, but I hope for the sake of my kids that I can remain cheerful. After all, when you've been married as long as we have, nearly thirty years, this really is a short separation." She sighed wistfully. "That doesn't make it easier, I suppose."

Then she looked at me intently. "You know, Will's Dad and I want you two to have the same kind of relationship. Do you mind if I'm frank?"

I nodded a no.

"You and Will have been dating a long time now, and I think of you and your sister as the daughters that God never gave me.

Your parents, bless their hearts, haven't provided you with such a good example of how to build a good relationship, but you and Will have done so in spite of that. You've learned to communicate and sometimes so well that there's no need for words."

It was true. Often now, I could just watch Will and know what he was thinking.

She continued. "I don't give two figs for the relationship of most young people these days, but you and Will are different. You've taken the time to build a relationship that's based on more than the physical, and you have a better than average chance of it growing into something permanent and lasting. So if Will should ask you to marry him, I want you to know that you two have our complete approval," she finished in a rush. "I know I'm speaking ahead of things, but I just feel as if time is limited."

I laughed and gave her a hug, unable to put into thoughts the tumble of words flowing through my mind.

"If Will doesn't ask you to marry him," she said darkly, "he's a fool. But he will." Her face cleared and cupping the sides of my face in her soft but careworn hands she said, "No matter what happens, I want you to know that you'll always be welcome in my home, both you and your sister."

She kissed me gently on the forehead, and I felt completely surrounded by love: her love, her son's love, and God's love for the first time in my life. After living with my father's unyielding disapproval, whether tacit or spoken, all my life, I felt the joyous freedom of basking in the love and approval of Will, of his mother, and through them, of God.

Will's basketball season did not end until the middle of February. The black panthers, on a roll, had made it to the state playoffs and had won the state championship. The final game had been held at the junior college, and the frenzied excitement had pulsed over the entire campus, sending wave after wave of thrill as each basket slowly added to the consummating victory.

Will had been at the top of his form that evening. When I look back, I try to remember him as "Will the Conqueror" as he had been dubbed that evening. He was cool and commanding, always in control of the game.

He quickly established a six-point lead early in the first quarter and maintained it throughout the remainder of the game. When the final bell sounded, the gym erupted in a cacophony of sounds and the court was flooded with screaming Santa Rosa Panther fans.

Will and I went out to Burger Heaven afterwards and sat in a back booth. He was ravenous after such an important game, and every time he looked into my eyes, it was as if an electric current was shooting into me, making every cell of my body tingle, and flooding me with an awareness of his masculinity. I hadn't seen him like this before, and it was both frightening and exciting at the same time.

His teammates began trickling in with their dates. We obligingly pulled a table up against the end of ours so all of the guys could sit together, glorying in their win.

Janet, who was currently dating Larry, sat across from me. We tried to carry on a conversation, but with Terrence on the other side of her, and Henry Taylor next to me, both trying to talk to Larry and Will, it was impossible. So we sat and listened proudly as the guys dissected the game, discussing it point by point.

Burger Heaven stayed open an extra twenty minutes for us. Todd, the cook, had graduated two years earlier, and Tina, our waitress, was sore that she'd had to work during the game. They gravitated to our table as the crowd dissipated, asking numerous questions. The guys were not loath to recapitulate each play again. But finally, at 12:20, they declared that they had to finish up, and we were locked out.

"You want to go for a drive?" asked Will. "I don't know if I can settle down yet," he added.

"You know I could stay up all night, especially if I'm with you," I teased.

"Let's do it," Will said impulsively.

"Do what?" I asked.

"Stay up all night."

"Will."

"What? Look, I'll call my Mom to let her know what we're doing. It won't be a problem with your parents will it?"

I shook my head mutely. It was true. Mom had complete faith and trust in Will, and Dad was locked into a secret world of his own. Most of the time, he seemed to care little about what anyone in his family did except for my sister. He followed her moves, her college life avidly. But he didn't usually bother Mom or me unless he wanted something.

As I saw it, my mother was nothing more than a slave, cooking his meals, cleaning his house, and going with him to church every Sunday to keep up appearances.

He ignored me unless he thought I had done something to step out of line, something that would make the neighbors think he was less than perfect. Thinking this through, I realized that if he found out about this, I would probably have to endure his rage.

His explosions didn't bother me much any more, but I felt sorry for my Mom. She made a pitiful picture, wringing her hands and wincing as vile language of hate and abuse poured from his mouth like an evil brew. Shaking off the mental image, I turned my attention to Will and what he was saying.

"We can drive over to the coast and watch the sun rise over the ocean." He went on, but I knew this would not work.

I stopped his flow of words. "No, Will."

He stopped mid-sentence, and stared, waiting for me to explain.

"There will be a terrible scene with my Dad if I'm not there when he gets up. Mom has been an angel covering for me, but I don't think she can do much about this one. She's so fragile these days, Will," I pleaded. "I don't want to put her through more with the monster." I tried to make him laugh over this appellation, but my shiver as I said it, made the joke fall flat and highlighted my concern.

"Maybe we could drive over to Bodega Bay and just walk on the beach for a bit and be home before sunrise," I suggested, not wanting to spoil his idea too much.

Will digested this information thoughtfully. Then he shrugged. "Sure. That'll work." He started the car, backed up, and swung forward out of the parking lot, heading for Highway 12.

I glanced at him out of the corner of my eye. This was one time that I could not interpret his silence; in fact, I had not been able to figure out what was going through his mind most of the evening. One thing was sure: before the sun rose, I would find out what was on his mind.

We rode in a comfortable silence while the miles flowed smoothly beneath our tires. Will's arms around my shoulders and the soft crooning of Elvis and Sinatra on the radio released all tension and I snuggled even closer into the curve of his side. Thank goodness he had showered and used his deodorant after the game!

Spring was on her way, but it was still cool outside, especially in the early morning hours. Will's arm kept me warm, and the scent of his deodorant and cologne awakened my senses, pulling on my desires and heightening my longing for him.

Will parked the car above the bay, and hand in hand, still in silence, we walked down the brief incline to stand on the gravel and sand of the beach. An outcropping of rock thirty yards down the shore beckoned, and as one, we turned and began walking toward it, gravel, wet and glistening in the moonlight, crunching beneath our shoes, waves, crashing and foaming, just daring to touch our shoes and then racing away again to the arms of the sea. A wind tugged at my hair, and now thoroughly awakened, I finally understood Will's mood.

As we reached the shelter of the rocks, Will gathered me in his arms, bringing his lips down on mine in fierce passion. Now his tongue probed, now his hands tugged at my hair as he moved his lips to my throat, now he buried his face in my hair, only to return once again to my mouth, igniting the passion in me that was only too ready to come to the surface these days.

All at once he stopped and wrapped his arms around me in a tight embrace, his body trembling with need and desire. When the trembling stopped he released me ever so gently and looked down into my face. I saw in his eyes his desire, but I also saw steadiness and deep purpose.

"Mary, I've loved you for so long now. I don't ever want to do anything to hurt you, but it's getting more and more difficult to keep from doing what my body wants to do. I want to ravish you, devour you, make passionate love to you until it hurts, then do it all over again." He rested his head against the side of mine for a moment. "Mary, will you marry me?"

I was stunned for a moment. So this is what had been on his mind all evening. But joy quickly enveloped me and I know that when I looked up into his beautiful eyes and whispered, "Yes," that my eyes contained more than the brilliance of stars because they contained all the love and longings of my heart.

Will pulled a small box out of his coat pocket. "I've had this for six months now; I bought it with the rest of the money I earned from camp last summer. This just seemed the right time to give it to you. At Christmas, I found out about my family moving, and Valentine's Day seems so, so expected. I wanted this to be a special time for just you and me."

While he was talking, I opened the box. Inside was a marquis diamond with two small chips on each side. I shyly held out the box to him.

"Will you put it on for me?"

He plucked out the ring carefully, and with serious intentness on his face, took my left hand in his and quoted, "With this ring, I thee wed to love and to cherish from this time forward; for better for worse, for richer and poorer, in sickness and in health, forsaking all others as long as we both shall live."

I was so moved that he knew the wedding vows. "I Mary, take thee, Will, to love and to cherish from this time forward; for better for worse, for richer for poorer, in sickness and in health, forsaking all others as long as we both shall live. You may now kiss the bride."

I raised my head to his expectantly, and in the solemnity of that moment, he gave me the tenderest of kisses, full of promise for a bright future.

On the drive home, I realized Will hadn't called his Mom. When I asked him about it, he laughed. "She already knew," he said.

Chapter Fifteen

My ring became the sensation of the school. Many girls became my "friend" so they could get all the details of Will's proposal, but I was shy of telling the intimate things that had been said, and only gave vague responses. That's when I realized how many girls had serious crushes on Will. We laughed together about it in private, and that's when I also realized how secure I had become in Will's love.

Will's mother was ecstatic, and his father sent his blessing via telephone, but the reaction in my family was quite different.

My father gave me an unnerving stare and said nothing. My mother said, "That's nice, dear," when I displayed my ring at the dinner table the following day. She glanced nervously at my father, but he went on eating. I caught him staring at me with what I could only describe as hatred mixed with a leer, but I brushed aside the uneasy feelings this gave me, and ignored him as much as possible.

Later, my mother came in my bedroom. She impulsively bent down to where I was sitting on my bed and gave me a hug. When she straightened, I saw tears on her cheeks.

"I'm so happy for you, Mary." Her face shone through her tears. "I know Will treats you with the respect you deserve. He'll never do anything to purposely hurt you like your Dad does to me."

This was the only criticism I had ever heard my mother utter about my Dad. She struggled to say what was on her heart.

"No matter what happens in the future, know that you have my blessing and one hundred percent of my support." She twisted her hands in her lap and played with the skirt of the blue gingham dress she wore.

"I may not be able to say much when your Dad is around. Oh, Mary, I do love you so much. You are very blessed though I don't think you know how much yet. I know I don't say much about spiritual things, but I pray for you every day, and God will be with you, no matter what happens. Well, I'd better go. Your Dad, you know…." She let her sentence trail away.

I jumped up off the bed and squeezed her tightly, but gently, she was so very frail. "I love you too, Mom. You're a very special Mom, and you've put up with a lot. I'm sorry if I've not been there for you when you needed it." I felt awkward, but I desperately wanted to say the right thing to such a sweet and long-suffering mother.

"No regrets, Mary, no regrets. Live your life with no regrets." She took my head between her hands and kissed me on the forehead. I watched her leave feeling blessed, but also feeling sad. Why did she put up with Dad? Why didn't she stand up for herself or even leave him?

Then it hit me in a blinding flash: she put up with him because she loved my sister and me so much. It was a truly sobering, humbling thought. I pushed my ring back and forth on my finger, absently watching it sparkle. Love was not all sparkle. Sometimes it was doing what you hated doing most. It was certainly unselfish.

We had not set a wedding date yet. Will wanted to get several years of college under his belt toward his engineering degree, and I had decided to major in music education at Berkeley if my performance major at the San Francisco Conservatory didn't work out.

At least, that's what we told everyone. We were trying to be practical, but deep down, we both wanted to get married right away and take our chances on how things would work out financially. I didn't want to take the chance of losing my scholarship at the Conservatory, and Will wanted to get his engineering degree.

We kept assuring each other that we would make it "for at least a year." That's the only way it seemed even slightly bearable that we would not be able to see each other on a daily basis come fall.

Prom that year was an unforgettable event. The setting was an evening of stars, and Janet's mom had a friend who made our dresses. I chose a midnight blue dress with a silver underskirt. The midnight blue fabric had a liberal dusting of tiny silver stars, and when Janet and I went shopping the Saturday before the big day, I found a headpiece, a spray of silver stars on a silver bobby pin to match the gown.

Janet chose a dress in mint green, one of her favorite colors. Her dress, a lacy confection that fitted her willowy figure, needed very little accessorizing. But she had her heart set on silver sandals, so we shopped at every large department store we could think of and then a few more before she found some that she liked.

"Hey, Janet," I called just as she headed for the cash register. "Look at this." It was a slim clutch purse in silver.

Janet knew without asking that her mother would never use money for something she considered unnecessary. We stood in the corner, and she counted the money she had left, but she was two dollars short.

Seeing the disappointment on my friend's face, I volunteered, "I've got two bucks."

"Thanks so much. I'll pay you back when I get my allowance," Janet whispered.

That could be days. Money was always tight in Janet's house, but this was a special night for us, our last prom together. If only a few dollars could buy what made us truly happy, I thought as I watched her make her purchases.

The evening of prom was especially poignant. The entire senior class voted for Will and me to be the King and Queen of Santa Rosa High. The gym where it was held was festooned with black, white, and silver garlands.

After we were crowned, Will led me out on the floor for the first dance, and as I looked around at all my dear friends, tears came unbidden to my eyes. This was one of the last times all of us would be together.

I looked at Janet, glowing on Larry's arm, and my throat constricted. I saw Sylvia, with Doug who had graduated last year, and I thought about all the times she had tried to cause trouble between Will and me. Yes, I would miss even Sylvia Strickland. At least there were no more world wars to tear these boys-turning-into-men away from us. Or so I wanted to believe.

Will's arm tightened around me, and I focused my attention on his face. Noticing my tears, he pulled me closer. "Tears, Mrs. Merrill?" he teased.

"Will, don't tease."

"I know. It's one of the last times this group, that includes all of our friends, will be together."

I was dumbfounded at the way he had just read my mind.

"But Mary, you'll always have me."

It was a promise, like an iridescent soap bubble so easily broken, but I put all pessimistic thoughts aside and enjoyed floating with him around the dance floor.

Janet and Larry, Terrence and Pam, Henry and Leah joined us, each of the girls' dresses creating a flower garden of color against the elegance of the boys' black tuxedos. More and more couples joined us, and now the music changed to a lively swing number.

When Janet and I retired to the lady's room several hours later, our feet were tired, but our enthusiasm unflagging.

"You and Will were so beautiful dancing the first dance of the evening together," said Janet. "I nearly cried. And you should have seen your diamond blazing when you put your hand on his back. I could hear all the girls around the room sighing, their hopes dashed for all times," she added melodramatically. "What did he say to you, anyway? You looked so sad for a minute, but then you laughed, and I knew you were all right."

My word! Did everyone want to hang on to every word of our romance? Ever since I had received a ring from Will, the rest of the student body had become obsessed with how Will and I spent our time together and what we said.

I felt like telling them all to go away. Our romance was really a friendship that had started several years ago in case they hadn't noticed.

"Oh, I was thinking how this was one of the last times we would all be together, and..." I really didn't want to give out all the details. "But Will called me Mrs. Merrill and made me laugh so I wouldn't get too weepy on him."

"He really called you that? You two haven't gone and gotten secretly married, have you?"

It was a thought that was beginning to cross my mind lately with all the hoopla going on about my ring, but I shook my head no.

When I recounted our conversation to Will on the way home, he threw his head back and laughed. "Well now everyone knows I called you Mrs. Merrill."

"Janet's my friend. She won't tell."

"Yes, she's your friend, but yes she will tell, just one person, mind you, but by tomorrow noon, everyone will know."

We had driven to our favorite spot to come to and talk whenever Will had a set of wheels, out Highway 12 above the city where we could see its lights and under a huge oak tree. Will turned toward me, his right arm still around my shoulder and his other hand toying with my fingers. "Do you mind being called Mrs. Merrill?" he asked tenderly.

"No," I said with my head down.

He lifted my chin so he could see my eyes.

"I can't wait 'til it's really true," he said before his lips found mine. Immediately my pulses began hammering, and the now-familiar sensation of longing for his body to possess mine began clamoring for satiation.

I pressed my body closer to his and returned kiss for kiss, first tasting the wine of his lips and then drinking deeply. His kissing slowed down, and he began the familiar rubbing of his jaw against mine while his hands, strong and sure began to massage the nape of my neck, my shoulders, and lower.

The moment his hands brushed against my breasts, I felt I was drowning in the pulsating sense of need and longing. I gasped with the pleasure of it, but he caught the gasp in his mouth and his tongue began an assault of its own, thrusting deeper and deeper into my mouth. I was on fire, shaking with frustrated desire.

My hands began their own play along the planes of his chest, unbuttoning his shirt as soon as possible, caressing and kissing as I moved down toward his waist. His hands slowed and his body stilled as he leaned back enjoying my touch.

I longed to go lower, but I dared not. We were getting into uncharted territory, and sanity was slowly seeping into my brain. Part of me wanted to recklessly go all the way with him, but the foundation of respect Will had created and the disappointment of his parents if they discovered our indiscretion helped to keep us in check.

Things were falling into place for us, and I didn't want to spoil things now. But occasionally lately, I had wondered if things were going too well. I felt like Juliet who had had her Romeo torn from her. If that ever happened to me, would I wish that we had done more so I could at least have a memory to keep me warm? A shiver ran down my spine. Will felt it and looked questioningly at me.

How could I explain? "You just have this effect on me, Mr. Merrill," I drawled in an exaggerated Southern accent. He laughed, a low gravelly sound, and started the car.

Chapter Sixteen

Graduation day dawned as bright and as clear as our futures. At least, that's the way I felt. I was ebullient, exuberant, and slightly nervous. The required white dress, purchased in early March, was lovingly placed over my shoulders by my mother. She patiently helped me find my shoes and style my hair. At last I was ready.

"Wait here in your bedroom for a few minutes," commanded my mother. She returned slightly breathless with a small white velvet box in her hands. I sat on the bed next to her as she opened it. Inside was a delicate gold chain with a small circlet hanging from it.

"This was your great-grandmother's, my grandmother's, wedding ring," she explained in a hushed tone. "Before my mother passed away, she gave it to me. You were a tiny girl then, and we already knew that your sister would have her ring.

But she wanted something special for you, too. She asked me to give it to you on your wedding day, but," she looked both confidently and wistfully into my eyes, "I feel very strongly that I should give it to you now." She hugged me and held me tightly for several long minutes.

"You look like a bride today in your beautiful white dress, Mary. I don't think I'll ever see you look more beautiful. You've made me so proud. Don't ever forget it," she said almost fiercely.

I was touched beyond words. The lump in my throat prevented me from saying anything, but this time, I reached for her and gave her a long hug.

Outside, the horn honked. The one down note on an otherwise beautiful day was that my sister was staying on at school for the summer to take some special classes.

When Dad had found out, he was furious. He ranted and raved the whole day, following Mom around the house while she meekly went about her chores. In the morning, he questioned my sister and her motives for staying at school, but toward the end of the day, his blame shifted to my Mom.

How he could twist things around to point the finger at someone. And in this case, it wasn't really a matter of blaming someone. It was just the way things were. When white appeared around my mother's lips, I knew she was emotionally exhausted by his verbal harangue. I was afraid she would just drop, so I invented an excuse to get him away for a while. By this time we were making dinner preparations.

"Dad, could you please take me to the store to buy some hairspray. I'm all out, and I forgot to get some last night."

He stared at me, but consented. While he was getting his keys and heading out the door, I gave Mom a quick hug and a peck on the cheek. "I'll handle him for a while," I whispered.

The grateful look in her eyes shamed me. How many times before this could I have stepped in and done something to give her a break? But I loathed being with my Dad and had always tried to stay away from him as much as possible.

But today was my day, my graduation day, and although I missed my sister being here for this important day in my life, I wasn't going to let anything spoil it for me. With one final look at my angel mother, and another last look around my room, I left for what would be the pinnacle before the depths.

Will met us at the junior college stadium where the graduation exercises took place. Already in his black graduation gown and tasseled hat, he looked so handsome.

Mom helped me on with my gown and hat while Will stood by carrying a small florist's box. Inside was a wrist corsage made up of one white carnation. Mom allowed him to help me on with it, and then went to join my dad in the seats allocated for parents.

The nearly five hundred seniors graduating were divided into two sections with an aisle between. Will was to my left and behind me, but if I sat catty-corner, I could watch him during the ceremony.

The traditional speeches were given by the valedictorian and salutatorian and the gift given to the school by the senior class was presented by the senior class president.

This year we donated a picture of a panther, ready to spring, to be hung in the main hall by the office. Some had wanted to get a picture of a gladiator to replace the picture lost in the fire of 1922, but most of the seniors agreed that such a picture would be too close to Montgomery's Viking mascot.

In spite of sweaty palms and trepidation, I managed to keep from tripping up the stairs, shook with the correct hand while receiving my diploma, and changed my tassel to the correct side without embarrassing myself. With that over, I relaxed and enjoyed watching Will.

He was so handsome. Our eyes met as he walked down, and I could barely contain my elation and joy. Instead, I sat and watched how the sunlight caused rainbow colored fires to dance in the diamond he had given me several months earlier. I caught Janet's eye in the row behind me, and she grinned, knowing all too well what I was doing.

Just before our graduating class was presented, the "Staffs," the male quartet from our school, stood and sang a farewell song. Most of us girls were getting teary-eyed, but when our class was announced as having completed our high school education, a tremendous cheer erupted.

I quickly found Will, and Janet and Larry joined us. Will's parents were the next to arrive at our little group. His father had flown in yesterday to see Will march and to help move the rest of the family back to South Carolina.

My parents stepped up while Mom Merrill was giving me an effusive hug and congratulating me. His Dad joined in with a firm handshake that he turned into a hug. It was the first time our parents had ever been together, and I was curious to see what my parents would do.

Mom gave Will her hand and then stood on her tiptoes to give him a kiss on the cheek. She next turned to me and gave me a hug. "Congratulations, honey, I'm so proud of you."

I returned the hug quickly, eager but dreading to see what Dad would do. He gave Will a handshake and said stiffly, "Congratulations." He turned to me, and I held my breath. Would he hug me? I fervently hoped not. Evidently that idea was foreign to him also. He shook my hand as well and said the same thing.

I looked at Mom and Dad Merrill. Mom Merrill, bless her heart, covered the awkward moment by crossing to my Mom who was beside me and talking cheerfully to her.

Will's Dad immediately demanded to see the "rock" his son had given me, and offered his congratulations on our engagement saying he couldn't have chosen a better daughter-in-law.

At least Larry and Janet had moved away to join some other friends before this exchange had taken place. I was embarrassed, but grateful to the Merrills for their gracious friendliness.

The Merrills arranged for me to go with them for a celebratory dinner. They invited my parents, and I could tell that Mom wanted to come, but Dad flatly refused. I was concerned for my mother as they left, but there was nothing I could do.

Dad Merrill took us to a restaurant for lunch. He said it was a double celebration both of our graduation and our engagement. He wanted to know if we had set a date yet. When we told him that we were going to wait, he looked rather grave like he wanted to say something, but he didn't. I got the impression that he would talk to Will about it later.

It made me terribly curious, but it was only a quick impression before Eric asked a question and the conversation flowed to other channels, and later events in the day drove it entirely from my mind for a while.

We all rode out to the Merrill's house. I looked lovingly at the white fence and the white frame house. I would sure miss the whole family when they moved, but in a few short months, Will and I would be going on as well to separate colleges. Just thinking about it brought a lump to my throat. It was the day for lumpy throats I thought whimsically.

Dad Merrill had picked up some boxes late the evening before, and now he put Eric and Caleb to work packing toys in their room. He made a game of it for them, packing books from a bookshelf at the end of their hallway and giving them funny and sometimes nonsensical answers to all their questions about their new house in South Carolina. Mom Merrill joined them after changing her clothes.

Will, always hungry, was foraging through the fridge for food, and I sat at the kitchen table, listening enviously to the cheerful banter from the other end of the house.

Will, catching my expression, pulled me up by the hand and surrounding me with his arms, held me close for a few minutes.

"It's hard to see them go, isn't it?"

I nodded.

"Actually, this is a new phase of our lives, Mary. We've had some wonderful times in high school, but we've got some more wonderful times ahead of us: college, getting married, having children."

I blushed, and Will laughed. He sat on one of the kitchen chairs and pulled me down on his lap. "You're going to have to get used to the idea of children. I want us to have several and to create for them a secure, happy home like the one my parents have created for me and my brothers."

Thinking of the cold austerity of my home, I agreed. Snuggling against him, I felt the circlet of the ring my great-grandmother had worn. Moving away from him slightly, I pulled the thin chain from beneath my dress, showing it to Will and explaining what my mother had said that morning.

"You really do have a special mother," Will said. He looked at his new watch, a graduation gift from his parents. "Let me change out of these dress clothes, and I'll take you home to change and check on your Mom, then maybe we can go for a hike up to Bald Eagle. I start work at my new job on Monday, so I don't know how many more times we'll get to go up there this summer."

Will had applied several different places for a job that would put him around engineers. Pacific Electric had called, had interviewed him last week, and had hired him. I could tell it made him feel like he was a real man now, part of the work force.

Before we could move, Mom Merrill entered the kitchen. Seeing me on Will's lap didn't even seem to bother her. She handed me a note.

"Here's something your sister sent for you. It was in a letter I received from her yesterday. If it's about what she wrote me about, I think you'll enjoy reading it," she said with a teasing laugh.

Will helped me off his lap and stood. "I'll go change while you read it," he said.

Alone in the kitchen, I read her note.

Dear Mary,

This has been a wonderful spring for me! As I write these words, I can hardly believe them myself: I'm in love! I've met the most wonderful man. His name is Marc, and he's from France. He came to the Conservatory on some kind of cultural exchange program in vocal studies.

He's witty and charming, which is, of course, what I'd expect of someone from Paris, but he's also very kind and understanding. We are starting to see each other by planning it and not just by accident. I'm thrilled to have been chosen to stay here for special study this summer; that way, I can get to know him more.

Now don't you dare tell Dad. Marc is special, and I don't want any interference this time. In fact, please leave this note at Will's house so there won't be even a chance that Dad sees it.

I'm sorry to miss your graduation, but I'm looking forward to showing my little sis around this fall.

Love,
Your Big Sis

Wow! She finally had a boyfriend that Dad couldn't chase away! I was really excited for my sister. I showed Will the note, and he dutifully took it back to his room. I chattered all the way to my house about how happy I was for my sister and how excited I was to be going to the same college. We talked about spending weekends together. Will was trying to find a map of the area so he could find out exactly how many miles we'd be apart.

When we pulled up into the driveway, I noticed that the car was gone. Good. At least I wouldn't have to face my Dad. If Mom was gone too, I'd leave a note for her. Entering the front door, I saw her sitting in a chair in the living room.

I started toward her, but my steps slowed as I realized how unnaturally calm, how pale she was. And then I saw the arm she was supporting held at an awkward angle, the white around her lips, and the single tear that slipped silently down her cheek.

"Mom! What's wrong?" I knelt beside the chair, a deep fear knotting inside my stomach. I wanted to hold her close, to tell her everything would be all right, but I was intensely aware of my awkward clumsiness around her porcelain fineness, and I didn't know what to do or how to do it.

"My arm is broken," she whispered. "I need you to take me to the hospital." It took so much effort to say those few words that she leaned her head back and closed her eyes.

I dashed to the kitchen for aspirin and a glass of water, spilling a bit as I anxiously returned and helped her take a sip with the pain reliever. How had it happened? But she was in too much pain to be questioned.

"I'm going to get Will. He'll help you to the car," I said softly, taking the hand of her good arm. She squeezed mine gently to let me know she had heard.

Once out of the room, I raced to the car. "My Mom. We need to take her to the hospital," I panted.

Will asked no questions. He gently helped my Mom into the car and sped to the emergency room. Mom would not let me in the examining room with her, and she insisted on coming right home as soon as she was given a sling. I could tell the young doctor was slightly troubled at letting her go, but my usually meek mother was surprisingly adamant.

Arriving home four hours later, my Dad was still not there. I helped Mom into a nightgown and into bed. Before I left her room, I gave her a kiss on her forehead. The additional painkillers from the hospital staff were beginning to work, and I knew she was tired. Drowsily she said goodnight and added, "I'm so glad you have Will, Mary. He'll be good to you."

Chapter Seventeen

Will's job kept him busy working twelve-hour days. With no point in sitting around moping, I applied for a job and began working at a small clothing store downtown. Our lives fell into a pattern of working apart during the week and spending time together on weekends.

I still did chores at home on Saturday mornings. In fact, with Mom's arm broken, I fixed breakfast and did most of the cleaning. Mom insisted on running the vacuum. She didn't need but one arm to push it she insisted.

I would not sit down at the table with Dad until Mom had sat down, nor would I sit a minute longer at the kitchen table with him after she finished her meal and rose to take her plate to the sink.

Although Mom told Will and me that she had broken her arm slipping on the floor and falling heavily against the doorjamb, the days following her accident she developed vivid, purple-blue, finger-sized bruises on both arms and a smaller one by her ear on the left side of her face.

I was certain Dad had caused the "accident," but how could I prove it? And did I really want to? I decided to leave well enough alone, but I was more careful of leaving her alone with Dad, especially if I could sense he was in a foul mood. We fell into the habit of taking her with us on

Saturday evenings to get a scoop of her favorite ice cream, orange sherbet.

It was during these times that Will and I began to see the fun-loving side of Mom along with a sense of dry humor that could keep us in stitches.

We'd sit down at the table in Burger Heaven, and Mom would make a gently sarcastic comment about the uniforms the waitresses had to wear or the song screeching from the jukebox in the corner. She was certain that the other patrons, usually teenagers, chose the jazziest tunes on Saturday night when they knew she was coming.

Two Saturday evenings a month during the summer, the owner of Burger Heaven, Mr. Glass, allowed us to push the tables into the back corner and dance to the tunes we selected on the jukebox. The mutual benefit from this was an increase in his business and a relief of summer boredom for us teens.

It was on these evenings that we discovered Mom's love of music and how well she danced. Once she figured out the moves, it wasn't unusual to see her moving around the dance floor with one of my high school friends. They came to love her, and I came to respect her even more as a person.

Sunday afternoons I could spend with Will without my conscience bothering me over Mom. My Dad fell asleep reading the paper, and Mom was free from him for a while. Will began coming to our house for Sunday dinner, and then we'd slip away to his house after the dishes were done.

It was a quiet, empty house with Will's family gone. At first it was almost unbearable, so we spent time walking in the woods, visiting our favorite places. Bald Eagle was too hot, so most of the time we'd climb the deer stand where we could enjoy the view and catch the breezes.

But as the summer wore on, it became a huge temptation to spend Sunday afternoons in the house where we would be alone without fear of interruption. The first Sunday in August was one such Sunday. The temperatures, always high during the summer, had soared to 108, and it was impossible to sit outside even in the cooler dimness of the forest's interior.

We sat on the floor at a small coffee table in the living room pretending to play a game of checkers with the set Caleb had inadvertently left behind. The air between us was charged with the frustration of denied longings.

I nibbled on my lip as I half-heartedly contemplated the next move to make with my red pieces. Will made a small sound in the back of his throat that caused me to look up to see his eyes riveted on my face with such a look of longing, that had I been the Witch of the East, I would have melted without any water.

The checker piece I had lifted clattered to the table as Will moved around the table, catching my hands in his and capturing my lips with his own mouth. Passion erupted inside of me, sending a quivering sensation in the center of my stomach and moving down, down.

His kiss was hard and insistent, and I matched it with my own hunger, my arms locked around his neck. The feel of his long taut body against mine as we moved to the floor sent shivers down my body, flowing into the center of burning need to be possessed by this man I loved so much.

Cradling my head with one hand, he reached under my shirt. Moving my hands from around his neck, I began unbuttoning the front of my shirt. Will's whole body stilled as he waited patiently for me to finish, but I wasn't done. Slowly, tantalizingly, I sat up slightly and unhooked the back of my bra.

When it fell forward to reveal my flesh, I heard him draw in his breath and saw his brown eyes darken with pleasure. Still cradling my head, he lay on top of me without moving, and I knew he was trying to control the passion he felt.

When he lowered his head to taste, sensation exploded in me, a thousand stars seemed to dance in my head, and I moaned with pleasure. I wanted to sob as intense, wild feelings ripped through my body, wave after wave of pleasure carrying me higher with the longing for more.

His shirt came off and we lay flesh to flesh from the waist up. The weight of his body on mine felt so good, but we both knew if we didn't slow down, we would finally complete what we longed to do.

Will buried his face in my neck as shudders rippled through his body. As the trembling slowed, he lay as a weight over me unable to move until I shifted slightly. He held his face up and gazed into mine.

"Your skin is as white and creamy as a magnolia blossom, Mary, and you smell so good," he whispered.

I shifted again.

"Am I too heavy for you?"

"No," I whispered back. "But I want you so much. It's so hard to wait, and it seems like school will take forever. Do you think we could get married next year? Maybe we could get secretly married."

Will chuckled. "If anyone found out, you'd lose your scholarship, Mary. Your parents would never forgive me." Again he whispered then lowered his face and rubbed it against mine with a sigh. Absently he ran his hands down the length of my body.

"Hey, don't do that unless you want to start something again," I protested.

He grinned, and the gleam in his eye told me he wouldn't mind. He began exploring my upper body, slowly this time, using both his hands and his lips. Again watching his face, I could see his fascination with the differences in our bodies, and could tell to the second as his eyes darkened and his breathing quickened when his need for me overcame his sanity.

Where it would have led we never discovered. What I thought was the blood pounding through my head was really the phone ringing. Will couldn't bear to stop and answer it, but he put his face between my breasts and led out a groan of pure male frustration.

The phone had stopped by now. "You realize that was probably my mother," he said, sitting up and running his fingers through his hair. "If I had answered right then she would have known what we were doing." He laughed ruefully. "We'd better stop. She will call back in ten minutes."

I sat up slowly, shyly, my innate modesty overcoming me. I'd had no inhibitions moments before, but now I had to will myself not to blush as I looked around for my clothes. Will clumsily handed me my bra and in spite of myself, I had to giggle at the expression of wonderment on his face.

"What are you laughing at?" he demanded.

"Your expression. It was so funny."

"Well, it's not every day I handle women's lingerie." He was still looking rather sheepish, and I couldn't help it, I laughed again.

I was saved from retaliation by the phone's insistent ringing yet again. Will answered. His mother must have asked him what I was laughing at. He told her that I was teasing him, and that seemed to satisfy her curiosity. When I talked to her a few minutes later, she asked what I had been teasing him about.

"Oh, a look he had on his face. You had to have been here to understand." Not for anything would I have had her anywhere close.

The following Sunday Mom wanted to go for a drive with us, and the Sunday after that we both had to pack for school, so our physical passion smoldered quietly underneath the surface ready to erupt at an opportune time.

Chapter Eighteen

My sister was on hand to greet us in front of the residence club on Sutter Street where she had a room. If I was a bundle of nerves, she was an overflowing container of excitement!

We were to share a room on the second floor complete with a tiny bathroom shared with the suite next door. Her roommate from the last three years, Lindsay, was next door with a second-year violin major from Japan, Suki.

Capably she grabbed two pieces of my luggage and the rest of us followed up the railed marble staircase, each with something in hand so that very soon, what I had brought for my first year in college lay in a heap on the floor beside the large closet that was mine.

She had her own closet on the other side of the room. Mom suggested that we at least hang up the dresses I had brought with me and store some of the smaller boxes at the bottom of the closet until I had time to unpack them.

"Here, let me help you," my sister volunteered. "We're going over to the music department to meet your piano teacher; he's a doll, I told him all about you, Mary, and then we're all going out to an early dinner at this restaurant that Lindsay and I just love. She and Suki and some other friends are going to meet us there. It's my treat, so don't say no," she implored turning first to Dad and then to Mom.

"Sounds fun," I said trying to help her out. It was obvious to me she had something up her sleeve, and I suspected it had something to do with the guy from Paris she had met. I was curious to meet him myself, but I could understand the delicacy of the situation with Dad around.

Mom quickly agreed with me, and Dad just shrugged, so that was that. He announced that he would wait for us all in the car downstairs.

When he had left, my sister visibly relaxed.

"So what's this really all about?" I asked crossing to my sister where she had sunk into a chair by the desk that was obviously hers. An empty desk with shelves above it on the other side of the room beside my closet would be mine.

"I wanted you to meet Marc without Dad knowing I've been dating him. Mom, you don't know about him because I wrote Mary about him, but mailed her letter in one I sent to Mom Merrill. I'm sorry, but I didn't want Dad to find out."

It was time for Mom to surprise my sister. "It's okay, I know about Marc." She kissed my sister gently on the forehead. "Mom Merrill called me before she left to invite me over for lunch. She showed me all the letters you've sent her that talk about Marc, so I've a pretty good idea that I'm going to like him, little girl."

She and my sister embraced and I could tell that my sister felt a great deal of relief.

"Well girls, let's go meet Mary's piano teacher, and then we can meet this wonderful man of yours," my mother said.

"Just be careful that Dad doesn't find out anything," my sister said. She continued, muttering "If he wasn't here, I could really enjoy myself."

"He won't find out from your sister or me," Mom said, placing a calming hand on my sister's arm. I shook my head in mute agreement.

The music wing was huge, with large classrooms holding fifty desks or more, smaller offices for the faculty, and even smaller, closet-like practice rooms. Never had I seen more pianos in one building in my life. Every single room except the bathrooms and janitor's closets had a piano.

I met Mr. Stevens, my piano teacher, and I could see right away why my sister spoke of him so affectionately. He was very short, only about five feet, with a large head full of graying hair, giving him a very distinguished look. And he was charming with an air of old-world gentility and grace.

"Good afternoon, Miss Mary," he said bowing over my hand after introductions were made. "And you must be the mother of these two very fine musicians," he said taking my mother's hand. "I am very pleased to meet you and your girls." He bowed and excused himself to go meet his wife for lunch. She taught English at the Conservatory.

We had our own lunch date, and I was very curious to meet Marc. Lindsay and Suki were already holding a table for us in the back of an Italian restaurant. Two men were seated with them. They stood as we approached the table, and since my sister was too nervous to make introductions, they introduced themselves.

Ron Brown was a senior conducting major, and Marc Montaigne was visiting from France as an exchange student in voice pedagogy. Ron was solidly built with large hands, hazel eyes and mahogany brown hair.

Marc was just as tall as Ron, but he was built thin and wiry with the warmest blue eyes I had ever seen and black hair. He had a very thin mustache on his upper lip.

I noticed that when he sat down, he was careful to sit between Suki and Lindsay. Ron, Lindsay's boyfriend, sat at her right. I sat across from Ron beside my sister, and Mom sat between her and Dad and across from Marc. Well, that had worked out nicely, I thought.

As the meal progressed, I could tell that my sister and her friends had planned the whole luncheon. Ron told amusing stories with contributions from Lindsay, Marc talked mostly to Mom about France, but was careful to include Suki with several stories of Japan, and when any talk became too personal for my sister's comfort, she coughed quietly into her napkin.

Afterward, in the privacy of our room, Lindsay, Suki, Mom, and I laughed with my sister until tears came. It was easily the most interesting dinner I'd ever been at, and a wonderful introduction to my new life at college.

Will called that evening, and I could tell that he was lonely. His father had purchased a used vehicle for him before the family had left for the south with the understanding that Will would work off the amount in the next few years.

With his drive, energy, and dependability, Pacific Electric had been glad to give him overtime, so the Buick was more than halfway paid off. After poring over a map, we had discovered that our schools were only about forty-five minutes apart. Will wanted to come over that evening, but I thought Sunday afternoon would be a better time. I was tired after this long day, and still unpacking everything that I had brought from home with me.

Sunday morning dawned bright and beautiful. A fresh breeze sweeping in from the Bay had cooled down the city. My sister and I feasted on a small breakfast of cereal and milk in our room before heading to a small church around the corner. Lindsay joined us later for the service along with Ron.

Will came after dinner. Joined by Marc and my sister, we walked around the neighborhood until we came to a park at the waterfront. It's hard to describe the peace I felt that afternoon. It felt so good to be on my own, to be seeing new things, to spend a sparkling, sunny afternoon with Will.

The sun was warm on my shoulders, but a small breeze off of the ocean kept us from being hot. We could hear the shrill cry of gulls as they seemed to perform an intricate reel dance above the glinting, glistening water.

I also watched Marc with my sister. They sat together on a park bench facing the ocean, the water nearly lapping at their feet, talking, sometimes quietly, sometimes animatedly, and occasionally with laughter.

She had taken French in high school, and now and then, he would lapse into his mother tongue and she would respond. She seemed to come alive when he was near in a way I had never seen before. It was obvious to me that she was deeply in love with him. Was he as much in love with her? Time would tell.

The following week was filled with frenetic activity. Registering for classes, learning where everything was, organizing my room so I could find things at a moment's notice, trying to carry on an intelligent conversation each evening with Will even though I was so weary, I could have fallen asleep fully clothed; it was easily one of the longest weeks of my life so far.

With the start of classes the following week, some sort of schedule emerged, bringing order out of chaos. I loved my classes and discovered new and exciting information about music every day.

I particularly enjoyed music theory. Most freshmen disliked the discipline of the course, but for me, it filled in the pieces of why and how music worked as it did, giving me concrete information to add to what I already knew intuitively.

Will and I continued to talk every evening. We were already strong in the area of communication, but our relationship grew to a new dimension.

Unable to see each other forced us to concentrate on nuances and tone of voice. If I detected a different timbre, I would quickly ask him to explain what he had just said. Not only did this heighten our understanding of each other, it also increased the ache of physical separation.

Most weekends we spent together. At first it was rather easy to race through homework, so that the rest of the weekend would be clear. But as each of us became more involved in our areas of study, it became increasingly difficult to find the time.

If I didn't have practices to attend, I had required recitals and performances to see. Will attended some of them with me. At least we could hold hands and cuddle in the dimly lit recital halls and auditoriums.

My sister and Marc spent as much time as they could with us, but as seniors, they had their own recitals and other group performances for which to prepare.

And Marc, on his way to becoming a tenor of some international acclaim, practiced often with the San Francisco Metropolitan Opera Company. They were performing *Aida* the week before Thanksgiving. My sister had auditioned for and received a small part as a member of the princess' court.

As the warmth of an Indian summer slowly slunk away before the onslaught of cooler weather, the leaves on the oak trees along some of the boulevards turned a beautiful gold and then russet color. I daily rejoiced over how my life was falling into place. I loved the school, I was passing my classes, and Will and I used moments stolen from busy schedules to be together. But I was homesick.

I missed the woods, and the long walks with Will, and the physical intimacy we had shared over the summer. I was also concerned about what was missing in letters from my mother.

It was difficult to place my finger of thought on exactly what was wrong, but at last I concluded that with both of her girls in college and an abusive man with whom she was living, her joy was being replaced by fear. She just didn't seem to be the same Mom with whom I had lived for the first eighteen years of life, or was it that I was just growing up?

Will and I made plans to attend one of the early performances of *Aida* and then take a quick trip home. His family's home had sold, but he was fairly certain that someone would let him have a bed for the three nights before we had to return.

My sister, with several performances during Thanksgiving week, was perfectly content to stay in San Francisco with Marc.

Chapter Nineteen

I breathed in deeply as Will's Buick headed down highway twelve. Finally I could relax from the whirlwind of activities in which I was involved at school. Gradually, dim, gray shapes grew more defined in the gathering light.

As the sun topped the crest of the mountain, it shot out a vibrant finger to curl lazily around the tendrils of grape vines, touched tentatively on a few fat orange pumpkins in a family vegetable garden, and then came to linger on Will's blond head.

The sun caressed his head much as I longed to do, but I enjoyed watching the strength in his hands as he handled the curves of the road and feeling the pull of physical longing.

Absence of physical closeness had brought an aching longing hard to deny, but at the same time it had created pleasure out of the merest of touches, poignancy from glances that caught, held, and heated.

Will, catching my look, chuckled joyously and tugged on my hand to pull me away from the door where I had propped my head against a pillow at the beginning of the trip to catch a few winks.

I snuggled in, savoring the warmth of his body and the spicy scent of his after-shave lotion. My normally hardworking boyfriend was carefree for a few days, and filled with a contagious exuberance, his chuckle turned into laughter.

My mind floated ahead to home and the surprise I would see on Mom's face when she saw us at the door. I planned to help her fix Thanksgiving dinner so I'd know how when Will and I were married. We had finally decided to get married the following Christmas.

Both of us loved the season, and after living several months in the Frisco area, we were confident that somehow we could find a place together. I might have to give up my scholarship and finish my music degree at UC Berkeley, but so be it. It was a step I was more than willing to take.

If I had to, I'd take a job and put Will through school, and when he had his degree, he could do the same for me. Confident of the future, I turned my mind to home. I wasn't much looking forward to seeing my father, but in the past, ignoring his presence had seemed to alleviate the necessity of acknowledging it.

We pulled into the driveway at 8:15 a.m. right after Dad usually left for work. I didn't know with Thanksgiving being the following day if he'd be at home or not.

Mom was seated at the kitchen table, a coffee cup on a saucer in front of her, staring out the window at the birds in the backyard. It was one of her favorite past times. When she heard my step and saw my face, the gray, tired look on her face was replaced with one of joy.

"Mary!" She stood to embrace me, and her arms felt warm and welcoming. "Mary!" she said again, resting her face against my shoulder, reveling in the joy of a daughter returned home.

"We decided to surprise you, Mom. I hope you don't mind," I said, motioning to Will who stood in the doorway to join me.

"Mind? Of course not. I was just sitting here wishing I could spend Thanksgiving with someone else beside your father, and then there you were! What a wonderful, wonderful surprise! Come, sit down you two and tell me all the news about school, and how you're getting on there."

She bustled around the kitchen, so very happy to serve us. I nearly rose to do it myself, but then I realized that it gave her joy to serve us, so I let her have her moment of joy.

Will and I told her everything we could think of though most of it had been written in letters or said over the phone. Somehow, coming from our lips in person seemed to satisfy a hungry place in her. We spent two hours talking, interrupting each other or letting Mom interrupt us with questions.

"Mom, we only have until Sunday after church, and Will and I have decided to get married next Christmas, so you have to teach me how to cook a Thanksgiving feast."

"Oh my. Well, the first thing we need to do is go shopping."

So we shopped. We arrived home in time to fix dinner. Dad seemed disappointed that no one else had come with us. He disappeared, surly and disgruntled, behind his newspaper. But Mom's blithe spirit kept us humming in the kitchen.

Will was at ease there. Since his mother had not given birth to any girls, she had made sure her boys knew how to make themselves useful. He chopped celery and onions, stirred the gravy, and even put on an oven mitt, lifting the meat from the oven so Mom wouldn't have to bend over the heat.

After dinner, Will and I went out for a drive. Dad, claiming to have a meeting, had left right after dinner. We assured Mom we wouldn't be gone long.

It was heavenly to sit under our favorite oak tree overlooking the town and kiss to our hearts' content. Both in playful moods, our lovemaking was playful too.

I tweaked Will's nose and he had to pin me down on the seat, pretending to bite my nose and then blow lightly in my ear. The steering wheel kept getting in the way, and Mom was expecting us back at a decent hour, so we reluctantly kept it short.

Will had made arrangements to spend the night with Larry Larson's family, but he promised to be at our house right after breakfast to help with the bird. Dad wasn't back yet, so I tiptoed into Mom's room to give her a hug goodnight. I knew she'd still be up.

"Good night, sweetheart. I'm so glad you and Will came."

I was glad too, and would be even more grateful that we had come in the months to come.

Thanksgiving Day was sunny and clear, warming up to sixty-five degrees by lunchtime. Will came shortly after I'd washed the breakfast dishes and again made himself useful in the kitchen. He kept one eye on the parades being broadcast over the TV in the living room, not wanting to miss any good floats.

We feasted at four on a meal made more wonderful by the fact that Will and I had helped cook it. Dad seemed to be in a better mood, so we spent the evening visiting a few friends who were in town.

On Friday, Mom insisted on going shopping. Will and I were longing to get away to go hiking to all our favorite places, but instead we spent the day with her.

That evening we even hit Burger Heaven where once again the tables and chairs were pushed together in the back to make space for dancing. Mom seemed to take on a new life whirling and gyrating to the music, but at last she was worn out.

"I'm pooped!" she exclaimed, dropping into one of the chairs at the table where I sat sipping on a cherry soda.

"Well, I'm not surprised. You've been shopping most of the day. I can't believe how much energy you have, Mom."

"It's you kids," Mom exclaimed. "I always seem to have more energy when you're around. I don't know why."

I could guess why. For some reason, Will and I made Mom remember her youthfulness. Did she ever wish that she could go back in time and marry someone else? It was a question that had burned often on my tongue in the last year, but I didn't want to make Mom feel bad about the choice she had made.

She answered my question without my asking. "If I had to do it all over again, but it meant not having you two girls, I wouldn't. But if it meant marrying someone else and still having you two, I probably would. I don't think I really knew your Dad. He was already in the military when I met him. I'm so glad you and Will have taken the time to build such a strong relationship. Don't let him go, Mary. He's one in a million."

Looking back, how I wished I had taken her advice. But even in black despair, God gives hope, and He gives us second chances, sometimes even when we no longer have faith to believe that He will.

Will and I found our time together on Saturday. We packed a lunch and headed out at ten. Another family lived in the white farmhouse that Will's family had vacated, so we had to hike around the long way to get to the deer stand. We hauled our lunch up with us and ate while watching the surrounding area like kings surveying their dominions.

Bald Eagle Knob was next. The air was warm, but had the wine of autumn in it, especially high up on the mountain. A few lazy clouds floated, titanium white against the cerulean sky. I breathed in the fresh, spicy scent of the mountain air, feeling invigorated and thankful to be alive.

The Cathedral was our next stop. Sitting at the base of the scarred sentinel pine with the smaller pines all around, we were secluded, set apart in our own little world without concern for time or others. Will stretched out on the soft bed of fallen pine needles, and I was only too glad to follow suit. The large lunch and winey air had made me sleepy.

Lost in my own thoughts, I was half-asleep when Will leaned over and tickled my nose with a pine needle. Perhaps he wanted to continue our play fight from several evenings earlier. But I was suddenly swamped with a longing for him.

Mutely I held up my arms. He willingly moved so I could wrap them around his neck, and began rubbing his lips against mine until I parted them, slowly, softly responding, first with little nibbles and then with nips and then with tongues tasting and drinking of a potent wine.

He began to move his body against mine, awakening it to the awareness of his straining against the boundaries and restraint of rules and clothes.

He shifted his weight so he could move his hands along my body, stroking and bringing alive with fire every part he touched. When his hand moved between my legs, I arched up and all the restraint I had been trying to hold onto left. My response fueled his, and kisses were no longer languid and exploring, but long and searing.

I let my hands do their own exploring, and when I unbuttoned and unzipped his pants, he groaned, murmuring my name in a ragged way that left me feeling heady with power over his poor man's body.

When he did the same, I no longer cared about who had power over whom, all I wanted was for him to possess me. His hands were everywhere, sending me higher and higher into longing until finally, finally he exploded in me, and we both shuddered again and again in the ecstasy of forbidden love.

He lay still on top of me for a while, and I held him to me, wonder flooding me at the beauty of what had happened. Will finally raised his head.

"I'm sorry, Mary," he said.

"No, Will."

"No, what?"

"Don't be sorry. That was beautiful."
"But I should have waited."

"We should have waited," I corrected him.

He was silent, and I could tell he was still troubled.

"Will, all my life my dad has been making me feel guilty. I'm so tired of it, and I refuse to feel guilty anymore for something that is so beautiful. Do you understand how I feel?"

"Yes, Mary, but sometimes guilt keeps us from losing our heads and acting foolishly. But I do understand about your Dad." He acted as if he wanted to say more, so I waited, respecting his need for time to formulate his thoughts.

"What if I got you pregnant?" he asked at last.

"We'll cross that bridge when we come to it," I said. "Besides, we can always get married. It's not as if no one knows we love each other. We're engaged, remember?" I said teasingly, trying to lift his somber mood.

He groaned and buried his face in my shoulder. I caressed his back, his head, his shoulders, using slow, loving strokes. When I stopped, he murmured, "Don't stop." I continued, and he began to stroke my body until we were both a quivering mass of passion once again.

This time we moved slowly, stroking and kissing, tantalizing each other until passion once again overwhelmed us. When we were finished, we dressed slowly, but lay down again holding each other close.

The waning sun warned us that dinner would be waiting. We walked slowly back to Bald Eagle Knob, past the deer stand and to Will's car.

I told myself defiantly that everything would be fine, that Will and I had waited long enough for this bit of heaven. By the time we arrived home, I had myself nearly convinced. Will's tenderness through the remainder of the evening made me feel even more special, and, unable to see the future, I vowed that nothing would interfere.

Chapter Twenty

My sister had glowing reports of the *Aida* performances and even more glowing reports of the handsome lead tenor.

Marc had evidently won the admiration of many fine musicians with his outstanding performances. She glowed and he was tender. I fully expected to hear of an engagement before too long.

I glowed too, but in a more subdued way. So many activities had been planned for December, and as a first year student, I think I felt even more pressure to do my best than more seasoned performers.

Exams loomed like thunderclouds ready to burst over our heads. When I was exhausted from the pressure and the sheer amount of activity that kept me moving from seven in the morning until well past midnight each day, I would pull out memories of Will's passionate lovemaking and tender concern.

The evening before we left to go home, my sister returned from a date with Marc with a ring on her finger. It was an emerald cut diamond with tiny chip diamonds all around it.

"Isn't it beautiful?" she exclaimed, holding it under the 40-watt lights, the highest illumination allowed, turning it at different angles to see which one caused the most sparkles. Even in the dim light, it sent rays of rainbows dancing around the room.

"So how did he propose?" This came from Lindsay. She and Suki had joined us for this impromptu celebration.

"Oh, you've got to hear this, it was so romantic and so typically Marc," she began. "After dinner, we stopped off at the theatre, something about a costume he wanted to see for the March performance of *La Boheme*. We stood for a minute on the stage, and I asked him what it felt like to sing for so many people."

Robyn stopped to catch her breathe, and then she continued. "He asked me to wait a minute. When he came back, he was holding a single red rose with a ribbon on it, and tied in the ribbon was my ring. But I didn't notice that at first because he sang this beautiful song to me about how life is all nothing without love. Then he showed me the ring and asked me to marry him."

We all sighed, it was so romantic.

"So when is wedding?" asked Suki.

In May, the Friday after school is out. I have so much to do, but, oh, I'm so excited!" She twirled around like a dancing butterfly. "And you all will be my bridesmaids, of course."

We all readily agreed.

"Is Marc coming home with us?" I asked, wondering if she had thought of Dad's reaction.

"He's coming the day after Christmas. That will give me time to make sure Dad understands that he had better behave. I won't have him throwing a temper tantrum and trying to manipulate me anymore. It's over, and the sooner he understands that, the better," she said with steel in her voice.

"What if he won't accept it?" I asked fearful for her and her newfound happiness.

"Marc and I have already made arrangements for him to pick me up and bring me back here if Dad won't behave himself."

I looked at my sister with admiration and awe. Something had freed her and given her purpose and hope. That something was love, and I began to understand how love can elevate us, change us, and even give us courage to face formidable fears.

Two days earlier, Will's parents had sent him a plane ticket, begging him to come home for the holidays. His Mom was especially excited because all of her children would be home at last. Will felt that he couldn't disappoint his Mom. I agreed although I knew I'd miss him terribly.

It would be the first time we had ever been apart for any length of time since we had started dating more than three years ago.

He told us that we could use his car since he wouldn't need it, as long as I picked him up from the airport; a classmate from Berkeley who had the same flight into Denver would take him.

My sister, still excited over her engagement, elected to drive. I tried to be cheerful for her sake, but I was tired and already missing Will.

Mom and Dad were waiting in the living room to welcome us home. Dad looked eager to greet us, his erect military posture just a little more stooped, and more iron in his hair. I saw him with new eyes now that I had been at college for a semester. If only he had always treated us with the eagerness and concern that he exhibited now.

Until he saw my sister's left hand. His body grew rigid with anger and his face contorted, changing to successively deeper shades of red. "What's this?" He threw the hand he was holding away in disgust.

My sister took a deep breath and said, "It's my engagement ring. Marc and I became engaged last night. Can't you just be happy for me, Daddy?" Once again, she was a little girl pleading for her father's approval and affection.

"You can't get engaged without my consent, and I won't give it," he roared.

"Dad, you listen to me," my sister said sternly. "I'm twenty-one and I don't need your consent any more. Marc is coming to visit the day after Christmas. If you won't behave yourself, he'll take me back to school, and we'll get married in San Francisco without you."

She took a deep breath and continued. It's your choice, Dad. The past is over, and I won't tolerate your outlandish, brutal behavior any longer. So make up your mind. I've made up mine." She turned disdainfully away from him and walked as regally as any princess to her bedroom.

Dad sank into his chair shaking. Mom flew to my sister's room, and I followed with our two suitcases.

"I'm so proud of you," she said, brushing my sister's hair back from her face. She turned to pull me into the hug she was giving my sister, glad to have us home again and the first crisis passed.

Miraculously, Dad behaved. Since Will wasn't there, I had plenty of time to spend with my mom and my sister. We went grocery shopping, and learned how to prepare some favorite dishes.

Christmas shopping was our next priority, and we spent a day buying beautiful ornaments to hang on the tree and stocking stuffers for every taste. It was such fun finding just the right gift for each person on our lists. We shopped, we laughed, we glowed as only two sisters who love each other and are in love can glow.

Will called every night, and we had long talks about what we had been doing and our future together. I felt that it had never been so promising, but I finally pulled out of Will an ominous sense of foreboding.

"Everything is fine here, Will. Dad is even coming around about Marc. Are you sure you're okay? Are you trying to come down with the flu or something?"

"No, it's nothing like that, just a feeling. I shouldn't have mentioned it." He tried to shrug it off.

I tried to comfort him as best I could, but I really couldn't understand. It was the first time, really, that we hadn't been able to discuss something and work an understanding of it out to our satisfaction.

Christmas Day dawned cold and clear. My sister, normally calm and sedate, chattered with excitement. It seemed she couldn't wait for Marc's arrival, she couldn't say his name often enough, she was driving us all crazy!

I got her out of the house by telling her I needed to go for a walk. We walked up to where Will's family had lived, but while calming my sister down, the walk just made me depressed, and I missed Will even more.

In addition to that, I was so tired, and I felt a little queasy. Falling asleep early, I even missed Will's call. I dreamed that Will wanted to tell me something, but when he opened his mouth, I couldn't hear any words. He kept pointing to something beside me.

When I tried to reach for his hand and pull him closer, he drew farther away until I couldn't see him at all. I looked down around my ankles to see what he had been pointing at and I saw a blanket with something moving inside. Pulling the blanket aside, I found a baby! And it was my baby.

Waking up, I sat up straight in bed, the terror in my heart and my head pounding at me until I wanted to cry out, but I dared not. Was that why I was so tired? Was that why I kept feeling off, like something I'd eaten hadn't agreed with me? Was I pregnant?

I lay back down, and then the nausea started to roll over me. I held myself rigid until my stomach calmed, but my mind whirled on. I needed to find out the truth. Wait a minute. Had I had my period this month? No. I hadn't. I moaned softly. Somehow, I would have to find out for sure.

Marc arrived. Dad watched him carefully, but Marc remained poised and charming. I could tell that Mom liked him immensely. Dad did not get angry and lose his temper, but he kept himself emotionally distant from the rest of us.

By the time Will called that evening, I had calmed down. He had been disappointed not to talk to me on Christmas. I told him about the walk we had taken and about how depressed it had made me, but I didn't dare tell him about my dream or what I suspected over the phone.

I dreaded nights now. I was afraid of having the dream again, and I always awoke with a feeling of dread. Then I'd remember my suspicions, and the waves of nausea would hit me.

To make matters worse, Mom caught a terrible cold four days after Marc's arrival and although she made sure we always had hot meals, she spent the rest of the day in her bedroom or sitting quietly in the living room.

I was almost relieved to be leaving the day following New Year's. I was worried about Mom, but I was more worried about myself, and I was wild to see Will. His plane would arrive the third of January, and I made plans to pick him up by myself at the airport so we'd have plenty of time to talk by ourselves.

My sister wanted to go with me, but I told her that I wanted to take Will out to eat after his flight came in and she would be *de trop*. What I really wanted to do was to stop at a drug store in a strange section of town and pick up one of the pregnancy testing kits that had just come out. They were expensive, but I had to know before I saw Will.

Chapter Twenty-One

The pregnancy test showed positive. I leaned wearily against the sheet-rocked wall in the tiny bathroom of a nondescript gas station. Will's plane would be arriving in two hours, but I had wanted to find out first.

So I had driven south of San Francisco, looking for an out-of-the-way drug store in an out-of-the-way town, and a gas station that was off the beaten path, somewhat busy so I would not be noticed, but not so busy that I would be disturbed.

On the way to meet Will's plane, I cast over and over in my mind how to tell him that he was going to be a father. He would accept it and be supportive I knew, but I also knew he would feel guilty as if somehow he had failed in protecting me from himself. I would have to remind him that it always takes two to tango.

Will's reaction was crucial, but not as critical as the reaction of my Dad. There was no telling what Dad would do about an illegitimate child. The steps Will and I took in the next several weeks could maybe make a difference in what my Dad would say.

What I really wanted was for Will to say we should be secretly married. But I didn't want to be the one to say it. I hoped fervently that Will would think of it. To me it seemed our only hope to reconcile my family to a baby.

"Mary, it's so good to see you!" Will hugged me close and buried his hands and face in my dark hair. "I've missed you so much." He stepped back to make a close inspection of my face. "You look tired. Are you alright?"

"I'm fine," I managed to lie. Fortunately, his luggage popped up at that moment, and he went to retrieve it. We wound our way through the maze of lobbies, corridors, and stairs until we were at the parking lot. Will took possession of the parking ticket, found his car, stowed his luggage, and we were off.

"Let's stop and get something to eat," Will suggested. Finding an A&W where we could be served outside in Will's Buick gave us the privacy we needed to talk.

I had never been so nervous about talking to Will, but I inquired about his family and his Christmas and told him about my sister's engagement, Marc's visit, and Dad's good behavior in more detail than when we had talked on the phone.

I had a difficult time eating my entire hamburger. I toyed with it trying to come up with something else to talk about. When I finally realized how quiet it was in the car, I glanced up to find Will studying me.

"What's wrong, Mary?" he asked gently.

I began to cry quietly. Taking a deep breath, I said, "I'm pregnant."

Will scooted over on the seat from behind the steering wheel and pulled me into his arms. He held me close without saying anything, letting me cry as he gently stroked my hair, nuzzling against it with his lips. When my crying was spent, he held me back away from him and wiped the tears from my cheeks with his thumbs, his hands still cradling my head.

"It's okay, Mary, we'll figure something out. When did you know?"

I told him about my dream and the results of the pregnancy test I had taken only that morning.

"Why didn't you tell me earlier?" he demanded. "It's not good to bottle things up inside you this way." He ran his hand through his hair in the gesture that was so characteristic of him. "I have to admit that I've thought about this all during vacation."

I looked at him in surprise, but let him continue.

"I kept wondering if you were pregnant and what we could do about it if you were. I think we should go ahead and get secretly married."

Throwing my arms around him, I felt relief pouring through me, so glad that he finally knew and so glad that he had put into words what I felt I should not.

"When?" I asked. "Where?" I was at a loss with how to proceed, but Will had evidently thought through most of this.

"There's a little chapel near UC Berkeley. I'll talk to the minister there and make arrangements, but how about if we do it Saturday? Is that enough time or maybe we should wait until the next Saturday."

He ran his hand through his hair again then grabbed my hands, and looking me directly in the eyes said, "Mary, I don't want us to just go somewhere and get married. I mean, I want us to write our vows and make it something special, something that we'll look back on and remember for a long time. So if this Saturday is too soon, just say so, and we'll make it later."

"No, I think we could do it this Saturday," I said slowly. "I have my white dress from graduation, oh, and look," I said, pulling the ring my mother had given me on graduation, "I have this ring from my great-grandmother."

Will reached into his pocket. "And I have this band that was my grandfather's. Is there anything else that we need?"

"What about flowers?" I asked shyly.

Will tried to do a bow from his seated position. "I'll handle that, Mrs. Merrill," he said. I giggled for the first time in nearly two weeks, and we hugged tightly.

"Oh, Will, I've been so nervous and confused. You always have this way of making everything right."

"Not everything, Mary. I'm sorry I didn't have enough control to keep us out of this predicament," he said soberly. "It's not the best way, but I want to make it up to you all the rest of our lives," he said, tenderness lacing the strength of his voice.

He kissed me lingeringly, and then he sat back against the upholstery. When he began to laugh, I looked inquiringly up at him.

"It seems funny to be planning our wedding at an A&W drive-in," he explained. I laughed too.

"Actually, it's rather nice not to have to go through all the fuss and bother of a big wedding. My sister was already planning hers with Mom before we left home. Well, I guess I'll miss it a little bit," I said thinking of my mother.

"It would be nice if my Mom and my sister could see it, but really it's better this way. Two weddings would probably do Mom in. She always seems so frail these days." I sighed.

Will leaned over and splayed his hand over my belly. "You seem a little frail these days, too. You've got to take care of yourself and our baby, too."

"I'll try, Will. The morning sickness hasn't been too bad. If I lie still when I first wake up, it goes away enough for me to finally get up and use the bathroom at least. It's going to be tough going to school and pretending nothing is happening."

"I'll do anything I can to help out," Will said, anxious to ease the burden but not really knowing how.

"Don't be silly, Will," I teased. "You can't smuggle into my room and hold me all night, and you can't bring me breakfast in bed every morning either."

"No, but we can spend all of our Saturdays and Sundays together," he retorted. "You can rest, and I'll, I'll . . .well maybe I can do your laundry or something." He ran his hand through his hair again.

Now I laughed outright at him. "You'll do no such thing, Mr. Merrill. But it is nice of you to think of it, Will."

I pulled his chin down and kissed him, my back pushing deeper into the cushions as he responded, his arms tightening around me.

Will stopped suddenly. "Am I squishing Junior too much?" he asked.

"No, Junior isn't big enough yet, Daddy," I said.

Will's face beamed. "It's going to be fun to be a daddy," he said. "I just hope the baby comes out all right and that you don't have any complications, Mary."

"I keep having a nightmare of my own," he said slowly. "I see you crying and crying, and your Dad is yelling at you, but I can't reach you to comfort you. I have a terrible headache, and then I see these big planes landing, and I have to go on them away from you."

He frowned. "I don't know why I feel so compelled to go on the plane, but I seem to have no choice. It terrifies me, Mary, to think of leaving you with your Dad. But I have to remember that it's only a dream." He turned then to look at me and see my reaction to his nightmare.

I was shaking inside, but I wouldn't let him see it. My Dad was my biggest fear, too.

Our wedding day dawned with clouds overcastting the sky in sullen gray. My sister left at eleven to meet Marc for lunch, and I quickly dialed Will to come pick me up. We had scheduled the event for two o'clock since I felt certain that the coast would be clear by then.

I dressed carefully in my lacy white graduation dress, fingers shaking with excitement as I put up my hair and dabbed on some special cologne. My face was too pale, my eyes hugely dark in the thinness Junior was causing.

I covered the dress with a large raincoat so no one would see the white peeking through. Grabbing the small handbag I had packed with a change of clothing and a few essentials, I glanced around the small room I shared with my sister.

When I returned I would officially be Mrs. Merrill. The thought caused the butterflies to begin their familiar dance in my stomach.

I walked slowly down the marble staircase of our residence club, savoring each moment and vowing to savor each coming moment as I said the words that would make me Will's and he mine forever. We had decided to say the vows we had said on the beach that long ago morning when he had proposed.

The chapel held six small pews, three on each side of a central aisle. Chandeliers hanging high overhead glowed dimly, several ornate pictures, obviously by masters decorated the walls, and candelabras at the front held already lit white candles, warming the picturesque scene and filling the hushed place with a waxy scent.

The minister met us in the back. His wife was already at a small organ playing softly. He explained in hushed tones that this was a War Memorial Chapel and that no kissing was allowed inside.

Waiting for our reply, he seemed to expect us to make a fuss, but it seemed fitting to me. Although we were getting married because we were expecting a baby, our relationship was based on so much more than physical passion.

The minister's wife slipped from behind the organ to greet us quietly. She gently asked if I had any favorite songs that I'd like her to play. When I requested classical music or hymns, she looked at me approvingly.

I had slipped off my coat and was holding the bouquet of flowers Will had picked up on the way. Will held my coat and a camera he had brought.

"You look like an old fashioned bride, Dearie," the minister's wife said. "Why don't you walk down the aisle just like a regular bride instead of standing at the front like they usually do. I'll play a real nice song, and," she looked at the camera Will was holding, "maybe I can call one of my friends to take pictures for you if you don't mind waiting ten minutes."

I murmured an assent in a small voice. Now that the moment was here, I was overwhelmed by emotion, but the minister turned and put a comforting hand on my shoulder.

"We can make sure everything is in order while Martha calls Mabel. Do you have rings?" he asked getting into the spirit his wife had created and willing to go the extra mile for us. He went over the vows and the small ceremony. It seemed beautifully quaint and simple to me.

Mabel, a white-haired, gray-eyed lady arrived. The twinkle in her eyes told me she was one of those people who, no matter what their age, remains eternally young in spirit. Will explained the camera to her and suggested several pictures, which we took before the ceremony as custom dictates.

Martha began to play the organ, Will and the minister stood at the end of the aisle, and I began a slow walk toward the man I loved, consciously savoring each detail: the slight rustle of the lace in my dress, the scent of the gardenias in my bouquet, the hushed, holy quietness of the chapel, the burnished gold of the picture frames that were echoed in the candelabras, restated in the chandeliers, and highlighted in Will's hair.

The ceremony, solemn and sweet, became a precious memory as well as a reality as the minister pronounced us husband and wife. As we walked to the back, I thought of how much I missed having my Mom and sister and Will's family present, but I fiercely banished the thought. I refused to shed any tears of regret on my wedding day.

We signed the documents, posed for a few more pictures, took one of the minister, Martha and Mabel, and made our way out the foyer door. The sun had come out, sending shafts of golden light to touch the day with beauty.

Driving south, we stopped at a quaint little restaurant for dinner. It was more expensive than we were wont to patronize, but Will had pulled some money from his savings account to make this a special day.

I was loath to return to my residence, and once again, Will surprised me. He took me to a small boarding house in a quiet neighborhood, and upstairs to a room facing east and overlooking a small garden.

"It's ours, Mary. I've rented it as a six-month lease, and I'll be moving in tomorrow. It's only a ten-minute drive to UC Berkeley. I thought we could come here when we wanted to be by ourselves," he added somewhat awkwardly running his hand through his hair.

I understood his awkwardness. We were married and allowed to enjoy each other physically. Yet why did I feel like a teenager sneaking behind her parents' backs? Eager to dispel his fears, I turned to him and hugged him tightly. "We'll be happy here, Will," I said.

And we were. Now as we made love on the double bed in the corner, we took the time to explore each other's bodies until the passion built, licking like a steadily increasing fire until we were totally consumed by it. I lay beside Will, still and satiated, running my fingers absently up and down his body and watching the sky outside fade from pale blue to the deep velvet of midnight blue. No matter what happened in the future, I would have blessed memories of this beautiful day.

Chapter Twenty-Two

With the growth of new life inside of me and the changes that it brought, the next few months at school were every bit as difficult as I had figured they would be.

I hadn't realized just how tired I would be, nor had I realized how difficult it would be to hide it all from my sister. I wanted to tell her all about it, but I knew how she would feel about hiding my condition to retain my scholarship.

The fear of losing my scholarship was not nearly as great as the fear of what Dad would say both about the loss of the scholarship and about the baby on the way. My sister had carried a scholarship all four years, and I knew Dad expected the same of me.

Will and I continued to spend Saturdays and Sundays together at his boarding room. He let me get the sleep I craved during the afternoons; my sister would have suspected something if I had done that at the residence.

Will did much of his studying while I slept, and I'd often wake to see him sitting at the little desk with his brow creased in concentration. I realized later that he studied then so he would be able to spend more time with me while I was awake.

One Saturday afternoon we received a frantic phone call from my sister.

"Mary, is that you?"

"Yes. Of course it's me. Who did you think it was?" I felt rather resentful over my interrupted nap.

"Never mind. We need to go home right away. Dad called this morning and Mom's been in the hospital with pneumonia for nearly two weeks. It's not getting better, and they told Dad to call us to come home. Is Will there?"

"Yes."

I held the phone mutely out to Will.

Her voice, high with anxiety was clearly discernible. She repeated the same story to him, asking if he could loan us his car. Will, instantly alert, asked if she could get some things together for me, and told her we'd be there in forty minutes ready to leave.

"And I'm driving. I just have to call one of my professors, and we'll be right there."

He suggested that she notify the dean of the Conservatory of our intended absence.

"I already have. I've been trying to locate you two for the past two hours." She sounded as if she were on the verge of tears. Will handed me the phone and suggested that I tell her what I wanted packed.

"Keep her busy," he told me voce sotto.

We left within the hour, and the trip, usually full of joyous anticipation at the thought of going home, seemed numbingly interminable. My sister sat white-faced in the back while I sat pale and sick up front. I clasped a pillow around me and tried to hold on to my stomach and its contents.

Will drove straight to the hospital, dropping us off at the front door while he parked the car.

"Room 212," the receptionist said when we inquired. She started to say something else, but we didn't wait to hear. We were on the elevator and on our way up in an instant.

As we entered the quiet room, I saw Dad, shrunken, pale, and unshaved sitting by the hospital bed. He seemed genuinely glad to see us. Slowly I swung my head scarcely daring to look at Mom.

She looked so small hooked up to the machines and monitors. Her face was white, and if I hadn't seen the numbers on the screen and heard the quiet whooshing of the machine, I wouldn't have known she was breathing. We stood on either side of her, each holding a hand.

"We're here, Mom," my sister said. "We came as soon as we found out."

Was I expected to say something? My mouth was dry and my heart seemed to hammer loudly in my chest cavity. I squeezed her hand and brushed her hair away from her forehead, avoiding the oxygen mask strapped to her face.

"I love you, Mom." My voice was barely above a whisper. I tried to will her to open her eyes, but they remained closed.

Feeling awkward and not knowing what to do, I was grateful when Will's tall figure loomed in the doorway. He stood for a few moments directly behind me, and I sagged against him in relief. Then he quietly pulled a chair over by the bedside so I could sit down. He did the same for my sister and sat in the remaining chair, his head bowed for a moment.

A nurse came bustling in, checked the chart, and made some adjustments to the machinery.

"How long has she been like this?" my sister asked.

"About a week now. She stayed home too long for us to give her the help she really needed. And her body has been worn down."

"Is she going to die?" asked my sister, bravely facing the question that was burning in all our minds.

"Now, Hon, you'd better ask the doctor. He'll know more about what to tell you. He's been in surgery all afternoon, but he should be here shortly." She made her escape quickly.

The doctor entered several minutes later. I moved to stand by Will, holding on to his hand tightly. The doctor looked at the monitors and at Mom's chart, listened quietly to her breathing through his stethoscope, then motioned for us to come out in the hall.

"There is no kindness in holding back the truth," he said after clearing his throat. "Your mother's body was already worn down when she caught this bug, and she let it go too long before getting medical attention." He cleared his throat again.

"I asked your Dad to send for you girls because I doubt that she'll make it through the night. The nurse has lessened the medication we've been doping her on, so she may come around before she goes. But I can't promise anything. Of course, she may just rally. At any rate, tonight is crucial."

He reached out for our hands, grasping them firmly. "I went to high school with your Mom, and I know she would want her girls here. If there's anything I can do, let me know."

We both shook our heads numbly, and he left us to begin our sorrowing.

Mom slipped away quietly that evening at eight o'clock. She didn't rally, and we girls were left in tears. At last Will suggested we go home; he said he'd get us something to eat. Touching my Dad lightly on the shoulder, he asked if he would like to ride home with us.

"No. I'm going to stay with her until they come for her," he said.

We left him there to make his peace in death with the wife he had mistreated in life.

The funeral was Tuesday. My sister had remembered somehow to pack the black dresses we wore for performances at school. Marc drove over Monday night; he and Will bunked in the living room. We had never needed the support of our men more.

It surprised me how many people my age came to Mom's funeral. But then I remembered those summer evenings at Burger Heaven, and the fun she'd had dancing with all of my schoolmates.

The memories brought on a fresh spate of tears, but they also brought relief at the thought that Will and I had protected her from Dad, had made her a part of our lives, and had re-awakened her joy in life. We had some precious memories that death could not rob.

Dad remained withdrawn and unemotional. He held aloof from our conversations around the dinner table. His coldness and quietness frightened me; I was much more accustomed to the Dad who ranted and raved, breaking dishes as well as the spirits of those around him.

We returned to school Wednesday evening. Was it presentiment that caused my sister and I to pack up most of the remaining things in our rooms as well as some keepsakes of Mom's?

It was certainly handy to have two cars in which to put our valuable childhood treasures. And it was certainly helpful to me not to have to hide my carsickness from my sister.

Two months after returning to school, we received the phone call. Dad had remarried. She was a woman twenty years his junior. I hoped he would be happy. I really did, but a leopard doesn't change his spots, and I really didn't think my Dad would change his actions.

Marjorie brought with her two sons in grade school. It surprised me that Dad could do this and retain his standing in the church. But then we learned that her husband had died nearly a year ago.

This news did nothing to quiet my sister's frame of mind. She was getting married in only a little over a month without the assistance of her own mother. Now she had a new stepmother about whom to think.

"What am I going to do?" she wailed. "I can't sleep in the same house with her. Besides, her two boys are probably occupying our bedrooms now. We are so lucky we moved our stuff out after Mom's funeral. But what am I going to do?"

"Well, we have a telephone. You know the numbers of everyone doing the flowers, cake, and catering. Why don't you just call them? We don't really have to be there until the day before the wedding do we? We can rent a motel room for one night."

I thought it was the perfect solution. It would certainly keep me out of the public eye. With my weight gain, someone would be sure to guess what was up. I was just surprised that my sister hadn't picked up on it. Fortunately, the dress I was wearing for the wedding was loose and flowing.

My sister interrupted my thoughts. "I can't arrive the day before the wedding and make sure everything is going to turn out alright." She looked at me as if I was crazy.

"Sure you can. Let's plan it all out, you know, what needs to be done when we get there."

She shook her head, but pulled out some paper. We discovered that we would need to get a motel for two nights. I could tell that she felt better after putting it all down on paper.

"Now go show it all to Marc. You know he might see some things that we've overlooked. And he might also help you find some shortcuts," I suggested.

She was due to meet him in fifteen minutes at the opera house. Her tears gone, she scooped up her bag, making sure that she had the paper we had just pored over. "Thanks, Sis," she exclaimed and ran out the door.

I sat back in the chair absently rubbing my belly. Boy was my sister a bundle of nerves. But she was my sister, the only real family I had left since Mom's death and Dad's remarriage.

Just then I felt a small flutter underneath my hand. My baby! My baby had moved! It was the first time I had ever felt the new life inside of me, and I wanted to shout for joy.

It was as if my baby was reminding me that I did have family, and overwhelmed with a fierce new love for this unborn child, I leaned my head on the edge of my desk and wept.

My sister walked in unannounced a few hours later to pick up some money she had left in a drawer of her desk. I had just taken a shower and was trying to decide what to wear for my little coffee shop date with Will. I was rubbing my naked belly, a glow still on my face.

"Mary!" She uttered the shocked exclamation and sank into the desk chair staring at me.

One glance at her shocked face told me that now was the time for truth. "Yes, I'm pregnant," I said.

"How long? I mean, how far along are you?"

"Nearly five months. I'm due in August."

"I can't believe this. Does Dad know? No I guess not." She answered her own question. How could you and Will...when did you and Will? Okay, Kid, start talking before I go insane or put my foot in my mouth or both. I just can't believe I didn't notice before this."

"It's not surprising, considering Mom's death and you getting ready to get married." I crossed and knelt in front of her, holding her hands in mine, a silent gesture, begging her to try to understand.

"It happened in November during Thanksgiving vacation. Something just snapped inside both of us, I think. Will has been so careful to not let our passion get the better of us, and he's been eaten up with guilt over this, I can tell."

It felt so good to finally talk to someone about all the questions going around and around in my head. "He never says anything, but I can tell it's just eating at him. I know we've both been raised to wait until marriage, but, well, it just happened. And it's not as if we didn't really love each other. I mean, we're engaged. Well, actually, we're married."

"Married?" my sister gasped.

"Yes, we got married in January after we found out."

"Wait a minute. You mean you've known about this since when, and you get married, and you don't even let me, your sister, know? I can't believe you." I could tell she was really getting upset now.

"I'm so sorry. I didn't mean to hurt your feelings. I guess I've not really been thinking about anything except not letting Dad find out."

She stared at me a moment and said soberly, "Dad will never let you keep this baby. What are you going to do, Mary?"

Replacing the towel I had scrambled for with my robe, I pulled the other chair by hers and sat down, wearily sinking my head in my hands.

"I don't know. I was hoping that when the time came, I would be able to talk to Mom, but now she's gone," I said bitterly, "and I don't know what to do. I've been so tired, and it's been so hard to keep up with my assignments."

"Oh my goodness, if the Conservatory finds out, you'll lose your scholarship." The thought was mind-boggling.

"I know. That's another reason why I haven't told anyone."

"I still can't believe this about you and Will."

I felt a sharp stab of resentment. "Look, if you're going to try to make me feel guilty, forget it. Dad's been trying to make us feel guilty about everything all of our lives, and I refuse to play his game. He's nothing but a hypocrite, pretending to be a good Christian, a pillar of the church when he hurt Mom over and over."

"I know."

It was only two words, but the look on my sister's face told me that she really did know. Some agony deep in her spirit was still being healed.

"Mary, you're getting God's moral law confused with Dad's moral law, and believe me, the two don't even compare. We both know that sex outside the bonds of marriage is wrong and only confuses the issues on which couples have to work. But I'm not going to preach at you."

Robyn took a deep breath. "What's done is done. And where Dad is concerned, I could write a whole book about the atrocities he's perpetrated, but this is not the time or place for any more revelations. Besides, I don't think I have the energy." She stood up and began pacing around the room.

Noticing the time on the clock, she exclaimed, "Oh no. Marc is still waiting for me downstairs. Look, I won't tell him, but I'm coming back early tonight. You and I have got to talk."

She hugged me, and, picking up her purse, left.

I cried again. It was such a relief that someone else knew. Maybe she could help me. The continual worry over where to have the baby, what to do next year about my scholarship, and how Will and I could make it through school with a child to care for had left me worn out and spiritless.

But the greatest fear still was how my Dad would react.

Chapter Twenty-Three

"You're going to have to come back here to San Francisco to have the baby. If you have it in Santa Rosa, Dad will have a fit. You know anything that would make him look bad, he'll not tolerate."

"Yes, I know."

"You and Will can stay at his place. That will keep people here at the conservatory from finding out although they'll probably find out eventually. Are you going to try to keep your scholarship here at the Conservatory?"

"I haven't figured that out yet. I'd really like to, but we'd have to have a babysitter, or Will would have to take night classes, or I'd just have to drop out. Besides, someone would be sure to find out, and I'd lose my scholarship in disgrace. I wouldn't mind giving it up as much as I would losing it."

"This is going to blow Dad away. You and Will need to talk and make sure you're both together when you talk to him. When are you going to tell him, by the way?"

"Well, I was thinking after the wedding. He'll probably be in a good mood then."

My sister looked at me strangely before she said slowly, "No, I don't think he will be in a good mood after the wedding, but it might be easier then. Not so much happening."

I didn't know what to say, and I was so tired. We had sat up until one o'clock, discussing the situation from various angles.

The wedding pictures that Mabel had taken helped my sister to realize that Will had taken time to plan things; it wasn't a ceremony that we had rushed into or taken lightly. We had laughed together and cried together, and we were both exhausted.

Before we fell asleep, my sister asked me if I'd felt the baby move yet.

"Yes, today, just after you left. I was hoping he'd move again, but he hasn't."

"He?"

"Well, I guess it could be a she. But I would really like to give Will a son."

"Oh, he'd be just as happy with a daughter. I can see her now wrapping him around her tiny little fingers!"

"You're right," I said, picturing it all too clearly.

"Mary, is Will a good lover? I mean, does he treat you right? He doesn't ever have you do things that are... degrading does he?"

I laughed in the darkness. "Are you kidding? Of course not. He's wonderful. He's gentle, but passionate too. You'll find out. Marc will treat you well, too."

"He already has. Not that we've made love or anything yet, but he's helped me so much with some problems I've had. Well, goodnight."

I wondered what had prompted her to ask, but I was so sleepy that I didn't question it at the time.

Final exams and juries came and went. At last it was graduation. I was so proud to see my sister graduating with honors. The fly in the ointment was Dad and his new family. Marjorie had insisted on coming to see us. She was a petite golden-haired woman, her calculation hidden by honeyed words and smiles.

I sensed her animosity immediately, but I couldn't fathom the reason for it until I realized she was afraid of losing his affection for herself and her two sons to us. I laughed inside with the irony of it.

We didn't have much affection for him, nor he for us. I hated to admit it, but I really hoped for her children's sake that he would show them some affection if he was capable of it.

They were all deserving of my pity. Two people trying to get affection from each other instead of giving affection to each other eventually starve. The two boys with the same golden hair as their mother and round, cherubic faces were to be pitied most.

We were all relieved when they left. My sister was grateful I had suggested phone calls and a motel for her wedding. I was grateful that the weather had turned chilly, and I had been able to hide my expanding girth under a raincoat.

My sister moved most of her things over to Marc's apartment. She would stay with him after their wedding. It was a busy week, and I was grateful for Will's tireless energy and calm presence.

The wedding day was sparkling and balmy, a perfect spring day. The church was decorated simply with white gardenias and bows on every other pew, two candelabras with ivy and gardenias climbing up to grace the base of each candle, and banks of ferns on either side of the altar with the unity candle and kneeling bench.

Lindsay, Suki and I were the bridesmaids (I was really the matron of honor, but of course no one else knew that), and my sister had opted to have us all wear white.

Our dresses, with an empire waist, flowed in a filmy, gauze down to our ankles. We carried bouquets of baby's breath and small white rosebuds with silver ribbons streaming down. Marc and the groomsmen wore white tuxes with black vests and silver cummerbunds.

The music for the occasion was exquisite. With their pick of top talent from the Conservatory and Marc's connections at the San Francisco Opera, strains from Mozart, Handel, and Mendelssohn spilled out of the open church windows from the mixed ensemble of strings and woodwinds.

When Marc's friend, Angelo, began singing in his rich baritone voice, I thought I would melt from the tender yet vibrant tones. His golden hair glinting in the lights made him look as angelic as his name.

Catching Will's tender glance as I came down the aisle, I wanted to hold the hands of time, to keep them from moving forward so this perfect moment would last. On this day of my beloved sister's wedding, I wanted to rejoice with her without any hindrances, but the cold hand of fear kept clutching at my heart when I thought of telling Dad about my pregnancy.

Marjorie and her boys sat where Mom should have sat. But my sister had decreed no tears on this day. Eliminating the flower girl had also removed the necessity for a ring bearer, so Marjorie and her two boys were mere observers on this special day.

Peeking through my lashes at Dad as my sister came down the aisle, I could see a nerve twitching in the side of his face, always an indicator of strong emotion. It did not bode well for the revelation to follow.

Will's warm brown eyes caught and held mine as the vows brought poignant memories back from our own ceremony. Mentally I repeated the words, and though some had been changed according to the couple's own preference, they steadied me.

With the power and peace of those words echoing in my mind, I wondered how anything or anyone could possibly separate us.

Just then, I happened to look at my Dad. His gaze was fastened on me with inscrutable intentness, and I wondered what was going on behind the cold visage. I would find out sooner than I wanted.

The receiving line took forever, and I felt the sly remarks about Will and I setting a wedding date keenly. It was over at last, and Will and I had just added my signature to the wedding certificate when Dad's corrosive and evil presence spilled from the doorway.

"Mary? I want to see you and Will at home immediately."

It was said with icy rage. My sister and Marc had already left for the reception hall next door. I glanced at Will with bewilderment, but he was looking at my dad with an alert and challenging expression.

"Yes, sir." Will's tone held respect mixed with iron composure.

"Mary, you're coming with me." My dad forcibly took my arm and pulled me toward his car. I couldn't cause a scene with all the people around, so I followed him, his hand still like a vise around my arm. Bruises would surely show tomorrow.

We were halfway home when he broke my nervous silence.

"You're pregnant, aren't you?"

I was too shocked to deny it.

"How could you come here displaying yourself in this ludicrous fashion at your own sister's wedding? I'm sure everyone knows by now. Well, I won't stand for it, you hear? You will not embarrass me by having an illegitimate child in this town."

"But, Dad...."

He cut me off. "What would your mother think now about this *fine* young man she allowed you to date? It's all her fault for letting you go to his house behind my back. This is what comes of disobeying your father's strict rules of conduct. Well, you've made your bed, and now you can lie in it by yourself."

By this time we were home and he was shouting, beside himself with rage. Will's car came to an abrupt stop beside my father's, and he flung himself out of it to race to my side, but my dad was already propelling me into the house where he flung me with loathing into Mom's chair. He turned to face Will who had followed us into the house.

"I want to see you in my room immediately."

"Yes, sir," Will replied, standing tall. He glanced at me as if to gain courage for the coming harangue, but all I could do was to look at him with pain and fear. I shivered in the chair, trying to pull a feeling of the warmth of my mother from this place where she had spent so much time.

But an alien spirit had entered the house. All around me I saw changes made by Marjorie. A new clock was on the mantel, and new drapes hung at the windows. The old, lumpy sofa was gone, and in its place was a smart new couch with a matching chair.

I could hear the low menacing sound of Dad's voice and occasionally the higher one of Will's. Discarding the idea of listening at the door, I sat in frozen numbness.

When Will finally came from the back room, his face was set, showing no emotion. Only his eyes blazed, a bright intense blue of cold heat. I'll never forget that particular color as long as I live.

He glanced at me once. I tried to read hope in his face, but could find none. There was nothing there, neither hope nor sorrow, only the pale mask and the bright burning eyes. Dad was right behind him. He watched from the window as Will left, and then turned to me.

"Now, Miss Mary," he snarled, "when is this bastard baby due?"

My voice stuck in my throat, and I tried to swallow to clear it enough to speak, but I felt a freezing fear that spread from my stomach to my neck, paralyzing me into numbness.

"Well?" he demanded.

"I'm due in August," I managed to whisper.

"You can't have your baby here. I'll not have anyone whispering about your loose morals in this town. I've got a wife and two sons to think about."

I was overcome with the injustice of it all. He cared for the wife he had now and her two children from a previous marriage, but he had mistreated the wife of his youth and cared little about his two natural children.

"You'll have to go back to San Francisco to have your baby," he continued. "In fact, I don't want to even see you until it's over. Pregnant women are ugly and disgusting."

Already drained of energy by the wedding and self conscious about my weight gain, this devastated me, and I began sobbing quietly.

"In fact, I want you gone before Marjorie and the boys get home. I'll call a cab."

He left the room at last. I was shaken and unable to think clearly, but I knew that to stay in this house any longer with my volatile dad would be very unwise, especially considering my suspicions of his abuse of my mother.

Where had Will gone, I wondered. Dad seemed to be very confident that he was gone for good. Maybe he would be waiting for me at the motel. I would go there.

He wasn't. The motel was already booked for the night I found out. My sister had left a note telling me she would be back the next day to get the rest of her things. I breathed a sigh of relief and sat down to wait for Will.

The emotional exhaustion took its toll, however, and the low drone of the TV put me to sleep. When I awoke it was morning, and Will still had not put in an appearance.

Marc and my sister came. She was glowing with happiness, but her radiance only served to remind me of my ungainliness, loss, and growing dread. The frozenness in the pit of my stomach was growing again, but this time, the hysteria was growing too.

If Will had not come by now, then something dreadful had happened. I had been crying for three hours, and one look at my red and swollen face brought my sister instantly to my side.

"Mary, what's wrong?"

"W-Will. Dad sent him away. I just know he's not coming back." The thought sent me reeling against the pillows with a fresh onslaught of tears.

"Hang on." My sister went to the bath area and brought a cool washcloth to place on my forehead.

"He called me ugly." More tears.

"Who called you ugly? Will?"

"N-no, Dad."

"Dad called you ugly? I can't believe it. Yes, I can. He's such a low-down, rotten snake." She turned to Marc.

"Do you mind if we make a detour in our plans and get her out of here? I don't trust him. He'll be plotting something in that sly, unbalanced brain of his. We can stop by Will's boarding place, and see if Mary can stay there."

Marc was instant solicitude, readily agreeing to the change in plans. And my sister's words gave me fresh hope. Maybe Will would be in San Francisco waiting for me. My sister and I packed up, Marc loaded the car, and we were off.

But Will was not at the boarding house. I noticed some things missing immediately. Spying a note propped up on the desk, my sister brought it to me to open. It read:

Dearest Mary,

Your Dad was as hard and unrelenting as you predicted. He has said some harsh things that I can't forget. I'm going to drive out to my parent's home in South Carolina and get their opinion on this whole thing, but I will be back before the baby is born.

I've paid the rent on this place through September, so please stay here and think on happier days. I wish I could leave you my car, but when I get back, I'll have it put in both our names. I hate to leave you, but I don't want your Dad hurting you or the baby in any way, and I desperately need to get the opinion of someone who is older and wiser than I am, but I can't imagine telling my parents about this over the phone. I need to talk to them in person. I hope you'll understand. I love you, Mary.

Your Will

He had gone! What had my Dad said to him? How could he have left without at least a goodbye kiss? I wanted him to hold me and tell me that everything would be all right, but he couldn't.

He was miles away by now, and anyway, how could he guarantee everything would be all right? He was a scared kid just like I was. Seeds of cynicism took root in my heart and refused to be dislodged.

Throwing myself across the bed, I finally faced the fear I had been trying to banish from my thoughts: Will was lost to me forever. He was not coming back.

My sister tried to reason with me, but I stared at her with a vacant look. Somehow my Dad had found a way to wrench my honorable husband away from me. I knew that Will would do what he felt was in my best interest. What had finally convinced him to leave, I would not know.

And I firmly believed that in spite of his best intentions to return, what Dad had begun, fate would complete, and I would not see Will again for a very long time, maybe never.

Chapter Twenty-Four

Somehow I survived the summer months, heavily pregnant, in San Francisco. My sister and Marc returned to San Francisco following their honeymoon, and deciding to rent a room down the hall from me, they became my support group. We did not hear from Dad, nor did we try to communicate with him.

My sister, bless her heart, tried to get me to face the future and make some decisions about my education, but I was focused on one thing only: having my baby, an outward manifestation of Will's love for me.

I still secretly hoped that he would show up, but June came and went, and July dragged its weary way to the thirty-first with no sign or word from him.

I examined every scrap of paper left by Will to see if he had left his parent's address or phone number, but I found nothing. I even begged the landlady for last month's phone bill, but when I tried to call the number, it had been disconnected.

My sister tried calling information, but no Merrills were listed in Charleston proper, and we did not know the names of all of the outlying towns and areas. We could only guess that they had moved again.

"Mary," my sister began one day at the beginning of August, "Marc and I have decided to go back to Paris in September. He needs to finalize his education there, and he wants me to meet his family."

I stared at her in stupefaction.

"We've talked it over, and you're welcome to come with us. Besides, to tell the truth, I'd feel a whole lot better about you and the baby if I knew you were safely out of Dad's reach. I don't think he's finished meddling with you yet; I just don't trust him with you and the baby. He'll try to mess things up somehow because if you ever came home, you'd be an embarrassment to him, and he won't stand for that."

I continued to stare at her, and she continued more hesitantly now but determined to finish her say.

"You don't seem interested in your education anymore, and if I leave, what will you do? You'll have to leave the baby with someone and get a job somewhere. How are you going to support yourself and your baby?"

I licked my lips, knowing the moment of truth had finally come. "I guess . . ." I faltered and then began again, my head bent. "I guess I've been hoping against hope that Will would show up and take care of everything. But I can't count on that, can I?"

Mutely my sister shook her head no.

"Okay." I sighed, suddenly drained of energy. "But he could show up at the last minute," I asserted.

"He could, but you can't count on that, Mary. It would be better if you plan as if he's not coming back. If he does, you can change your plans. But right now, you haven't made any plans for the future at all, and you just have to make some. I can't leave not knowing what's happening with you." She choked on the last word, and tears welled up in her eyes. "We're family, and we've got to stick together."

She was so right. Giving her a fierce hug, I returned to my seat by Will's window. The view was not that great, but the morning sun warmed me, and glints of golden sunlight sometimes reflected their way in once again during late afternoon.

I could sit and stare out of the window, whiling away the long hours with memories from the past and dreams for the future. It was the one way I could isolate myself from present and soon-to-be-present reality.

Lassitude and ennui enveloping me once again, I tried to escape into my dream world, but my sister's words had their desired effect, and I squirmed restlessly.

Not daring to venture out often lest I see someone from the Conservatory, nevertheless, my self-imposed prison was restricting, and I felt it stifling me like I hadn't felt it before.

I realized that I still had a keen desire to go to school. I was hoping against hope that somehow I'd be able to continue going to the Conservatory. When I told my sister, she expressed her doubts.

"You would have to tell them, Mary. You won't be able to hide the fact that you have a baby, and you'd also have to find someone to take care of the baby while you were in school. Look, maybe you should do what you told me to do about my wedding. Maybe you should write down your options on paper so you can decide which one would work best for you."

She was right. I lumbered to the small desk where I had so often seen Will working and pulled out a notebook and pen. We put Frisco at the top of one column and Paris at the top of the other column. Under Frisco we put the word Conservatory with a question mark.

"If you decide to stay here in San Francisco, I really think you should go talk to someone at the Conservatory and level with them about your condition. You might lose your scholarship, but you also might just find that they'll be understanding and helpful."

"What if I lose my scholarship?" I was certainly more cynical than my sister was.

"Couldn't you finish up at another school? There are a lot of schools in this area, and they're all good schools, too. You could even go to UC Berkeley. They have a good music program, and it would probably be cheaper than the Conservatory."

"I'd have to get a job."

"Yes you would."

"I wouldn't be able to spend much time with the baby if I had to go to school and work a job too," I protested.

"Maybe you could just go to school part time. It would take you longer to get your degree, but then you'd be able to spend more time with your baby."

"I should probably just drop out of school altogether for a year." It was so hard making these decisions. What if I made the wrong one? I could end up regretting it for the rest of my life. Looking back, I think that thought had held me in paralysis for most of the summer. I was so afraid of making an irreversible and damaging decision.

"Well, if you consider staying out of school altogether, what about coming to Paris with us? You could get a part time job, and I could watch the baby while you were working. Marc says I won't need to work. He'll make enough money for both of us."

"I don't want to go to Paris. I don't know the language like you do, so how could I get a decent job? And what if Will comes? He'd never think of looking for me in Paris. I'd hate it if I missed him."

"Maybe." She was obviously skeptical about Will's return. "You'd pick up the language, Mary, and we'd be together. It's bad enough losing Mom. I'd hate to lose you, too. And of course, Dad doesn't even count."

Her reasoning was so persuasive, but I wouldn't dare to miss Will's possible coming, and I needed to build some independence. I didn't know how to say it without hurting her feelings, so I let her think I was besotted with the idea of missing Will.

Actually I was, but learning to be independent was also important. Yes, I was scared to death of the terrifying decisions I was having to make, but she was right: writing it all down was helping me to see what I really wanted and needed to do.

My due date was August twenty-eighth, so Dr. Price wanted to start seeing me on a weekly basis. He said I was "progressing nicely," making me feel like a slab of meat hanging in a food processing plant. At least San Francisco was on the cool side during the summer with the nice Bay breezes coming in every evening.

My sister would be my coach and helper during delivery; I had a small crib and some clothes we had gotten at a garage sale; everything was ready. After depleting my savings account to pay the hospital and doctor bills, I really was down to nearly nothing. I would need to get a job about a month after delivery.

I was so glad that my sister was married and lived down the hall instead of in the same room with me because as my due date drew nearer, the longing to see Will intensified until I could have screamed with the longing.

I managed to cover my feelings during the day by conning the art of small talk and even counting backwards from ten when I felt most swamped by my feelings.

Where, oh where, was Will? I didn't have an address or phone number for his parents back somewhere near Charleston, and surely he would have called me by now. Nearly three thousand miles stretched between Frisco and Charleston; something must have happened to Will en route.

In spite of my sister's doubts, I was certain that Will would return to the baby and me as long as he was alive and in his right mind. Had he been in a car accident? Had someone drugged and kidnapped him? My vivid imagination worked overtime, often waking me in the dead of night with fearful images and dreadful visions.

During the day, a shroud of dread and depression hung around me threatening to engulf me, and even though I often resented my sister's married bliss and happiness, she and the baby kept me from going off the deep end. Dr. Price, concerned about my slow weight gain during the last month when the baby grows so rapidly, asked probing questions.

I let my sister answer most of them. She had a way of wording things tactfully, keeping me from embarrassing myself further than was necessary. I knew she was concerned for me. She had become the mother I had lost, and I was so very grateful for her support and care.

When my due date arrived, I was more than ready to have my baby. I was tired of feeling so heavy, tired of hiding in the small boarding room, and tired of not being able to get on with my life, whatever it turned out to be like.

The morass of gloom lifted somewhat, and I became curious about the new life about to be born. Would I have a boy or a girl? Would my baby look like me with dark brown hair and blue eyes or would my baby look like Will with his glistening blond hair and warm brown eyes?

More to the point, would my delivery be easy or would I be in so much pain that I would want to die? Dr. Price had insisted that I talk to a midwife these last few months.

Considered rather radical, midwifery was the latest craze in California. Dr. Price had taken the middle road by retaining a midwife on his staff, yet delivering all the babies himself. The midwife had answered many of the questions I needed to ask but felt stupid doing so.

Her name was Gretchen, and she compared the delivery of a baby to running a marathon. It was something you trained your body to do, it was physically taxing, and you didn't do it every day, but it was certainly manageable, especially for women who had more ability to endure physical pain than men did. When my due date came and went, I called Gretchen, tearfully wondering what was wrong.

"It's alright, Leubchen, the baby wants to take his time. He'll come when he's ready. You've been worried deeply about something, right? Baby hasn't gained all the weight he needs to survive because Mommy is troubled, so he's going to take a few extra days to get ready. Everything be all right. You just take a nice long nap like a cat, hm?"

Her common sense comforted me. Taking a long nap did help and I awoke refreshed, and filled with a desire to clean. I retrieved the cleaning supplies from the bathroom cabinet the next morning and spent two hours making everything sparkle. My sister arrived with boxes from the grocer around the corner and laughed at my energetic endeavors.

"That baby's bound to come soon. Your nesting instinct is coming out strong!" she teased. Then she sobered. "I had a scare coming home just now."

"What happened?" I asked, only mildly curious.

"I thought I saw Dad. He was driving a car around the corner, but he turned to stare at me, and I could swear it was he. What do you suppose he's up to now?"

I shook my head. I had no idea.

"You just be careful, Mary. He's going to do something about that baby of yours."

I shuddered, and tried to put the thought from me, but the idea marched forward in my brain and wouldn't retreat. "Just let him try," I said with a jolt of vicious anger. "Just let him try."

"Since you're in such a cleaning mood, how about coming down and helping me pack," my sister teased, changing our mood.

"You're on," I flashed back. We spent the next several hours in the front double room she and Marc were renting for the summer. They had plane tickets for September seventh. Anything they couldn't take with them on the plane had to be packed away in trunks to be shipped ahead of them to Paris.

We put a huge dent in organizing the nearly overwhelming files, stacks, and books full of music. There were also newspaper articles, bulletins, and brochures my sister had collected on Marc's international career to be put into scrapbooks when she had more time in Paris.

"After two or three months, I'm going to try to get a part time job so I can learn the language faster. But those first several months, I'll have time to find out just how I can best support Marc in his career and put all of these together."

My sister chattered away. She was obviously determined to be a great wife to her new husband no matter where his career took him.

The next four days I was filled with both lethargy and restlessness, and I took to prowling like a cat between my room and my sister's. Five days later after only six hours of labor, Davey made his debut.

He was a beautiful baby with the first signs of a full head of dark hair. As the nurse placed him in my arms for his first meal, I was able to examine him closely. I wanted to see if he shared any characteristics of Will's.

When he yawned hugely, putting his hands to his mouth, I saw the first thing. He had long fingers like his Daddy! But then he opened his eyes and I was once again looking into Will's beautiful warm brown eyes. I was flooded with an overwhelming love for my baby, and I fell in love with Will all over again.

How the events of the next few days fit together I played over and over in my mind, trying to figure out just how I lost my son. But four days after Davey was born, he was on a plane to Paris with my sister, and I was still in the hospital recuperating from an infection.

Chapter Twenty-Five

My first sign that something was wrong was when my Dad showed up in my hospital room.

Dispensing with the normal courtesies of asking how I was feeling, he cleared his throat and said, "I don't want you showing up in Santa Rosa with your kid and no husband. You also need to complete your education. If you'll sign this paper, I'll see that you retain your full scholarship at the Conservatory." He licked his lips nervously, and I grew more suspicious and wary.

The idea of staying on at the Conservatory was very tempting. If my dad would work things out, maybe I wouldn't have to get a job to support myself and Davey, and I would be able continue on at a school all at the same time.

Slowly I pulled toward me the sheet of paper and the pen he had put on top of the sheets. I was filled with dread, but also so very depressed and tired. An infection had me in its grip.

The nurses wouldn't let me feed my baby, so my sister came up every day to hold and cuddle him and give him his bottle of formula. How she found the time when she would be leaving for Paris in three days, I was too tired to question.

"What is this?" The top of the paper said "Legal Document." Wading through the legal verbiage, I managed to grasp the fact that I would be able to retain my scholarship only if I was willing to let my sister take Davey with her to France.

"NO!" The word exploded from my mouth, reverberating forcefully around the hospital room. At first, I couldn't believe he would ask such a thing of me, but then his words and actions began to make sense. He didn't want to be embarrassed if I took it into my head to visit Santa Rosa with a baby but no husband. If Davey went with my sister to France, my Dad would not have to face that possibility.

"You think about it. I'll come back later, and we'll talk about it more, but you won't get a better offer than the one I'm offering you now. If you don't sign, I'll make sure the Conservatory finds out about you and your precious baby, and don't think I'm going to support the two of you either. You'll have to get a job, and you won't have any time to spend with your kid anyway." With those salvos fired, he put the document in his briefcase and left.

Turning my face toward the wall, I wept. I was so tired, weak and sick that I couldn't think straight anymore. Let my baby go to France? Possibly never to see him again? How could I do this to the love child Will and I had produced?

On the other hand, to be in disgrace at the Conservatory, to be forced to live in San Francisco on my own, and to have to find a job and someone to look after Davey when I couldn't be there, and, on top of that, to try to finish up my education at another school? How could I possibly do it all?

If only Will would show up and take care of it all. I wept quietly, not wanting anyone to overhear and send the nurses running.

And then I thought of my Dad. What a scheming, selfish, scurrilous old bastard he was, unnatural toward his own children, and bent on causing grief for others in an effort to have things his own way.

No wonder my sister wanted to get as far away from him as possible. Then the thought struck me: would it be better for Davey if he were far away in Paris, too? Tears came afresh, as I faced the possibility that this might be for the best.

Hearing footsteps behind me, I willed myself to stop crying and breathe softly through my nose as if I were asleep.

"Surprise," I heard my sister call. I turned to see her come bustling in, her arms filled with several books, a small radio, two cassette tapes held in her right hand, and a bouquet of flowers in her left hand.

"You're probably feeling low still, but you'll be feeling better soon, so I brought . . . Mary, what's wrong?"

Hiccupping from holding back the tears, I felt the cloud of despair lift slightly. My sister would help me to see things in perspective.

"Dad was here," I began.

"And?" It was said quietly in a subdued voice.

"He wants. . . he wants you to take Davey with you to France." I began crying again, without any attempt this time to quiet the sobs.

My sister began to stroke my hair, but waited until I had calmed myself somewhat to speak. "He has talked to me, too," she said.

I jerked my head up and stared at her.

"At first I was appalled, but it could turn out for the best."

I was shocked into speechlessness.

She continued. "Davey would be safe from Dad, and you seem bent on going to the Conservatory. This way you could finish up there and then join us in France. I really wish you had tried to get a passport this past summer. Then you could just come with me, and I could take care of you until you got on your feet. But maybe this is the best way."

I was stunned at her opinion and anger rose in me, quick and strong. "How could this be the best thing for Davey? Do you think I'm not capable of taking care of my own son? How dare you?"

"Mary, listen. You don't understand what is really going on here. Dad is bent on killing your baby. When I came up here to feed Davey two days ago, Dad was standing in the nursery, with his hand on Davey's face. I'm sure Dad was trying to suffocate him. Davey had started to turn red, and when Dad saw me and moved his hand, Davey started crying."

I shook my head in disbelief, anger building and bitterness taking root. "Dad is a jerk, but murder? Come on. I can't believe this. It's too fantastical, even for you, Sis. You just want my baby because you're afraid I can't take care of him myself. I can, I know I can," I said stubbornly.

"It's not that at all. You've got to believe me, Mary. Your baby's not safe here in San Francisco, and since we don't know how to reach the Merrill's, it's best that I take him to France. Please, Mary. Promise me you'll think about this." She was nearly in tears, as if begging for her life.

But the bile built in me, and I refused to even consider that she might be telling the truth.

"Go away. I need to rest." I turned my back to her. Listening intently, I heard her draw in a deep breath and then walk to the door. She must have turned to look back at me, for her footsteps hesitated for a moment, then headed down the hall.

I cried again from sheer anger, from the frustration of not being able to hold my own baby, from weakness born of infection, and from self-pity. At last, exhausted, I fell asleep. My condition must have worsened, for when I awoke, a whole day had passed, and I felt weak but clear-headed.

The gall of bitterness forged my anger into a wall of iron-willed composure. Let the chips fall where they might, I decided to let my sister take my baby. I would graduate from the conservatory, and then I would fly to France and take him back. Let my sister get a taste of her own medicine when I came to claim what was rightfully mine.

When my father arrived, I was ready for him. Without taking time to read the print, I signed first one document and then another. In a cold voice, I informed my father that I wanted the amount of money needed for my tuition to be transferred to my account in one lump deposit.

He readily agreed.

I also told him that I never, ever wanted to see him again, and that if I discovered him anywhere in the vicinity of my living quarters, I would call the police and demand a restraining order be slapped on him.

His eyes flashed fire, but he readily acquiesced to my request.

My sister had been allowed to take Davey with her after leaving me the previous day. She was certainly greedy to get her hands on my child, I thought. She and Marc were to leave for Paris the next day.

Pressing the buzzer, I called for the head nurse and asked to be released. She soothingly told me that while I was on the mend, I'd had a relapse, so we needed to wait for the doctor to make his rounds.

"My baby is leaving for France tomorrow, and I want to see him before he leaves," I informed her in composed and clipped tones. "Please ask him to come this afternoon."

She gave me a strange look, and left the room. Several minutes later, another nurse came in, and again, in placating tones, she told me that the doctor had been called.

"Now why don't you take your medicine and a nice nap. Then you'll be ready for the doctor when he comes." Obediently I swallowed the medicine not realizing they had added a sedative to the antibiotics.

It was five o'clock a.m. when I awoke with a strange sense of foreboding. Oh no! I was still stuck in this hospital, and my son would be leaving for Paris in an hour with my sister. Quietly I lumbered out of bed, my stomach feeling hollow and my legs feeling like rubber.

I opened the blinds at the window and stared east toward faint ribbons of shell pink above the horizon that signaled the advent of the day, another day in which once again I would be robbed of what I loved most.

Cynically I thought that I would remember forever the date of my sister's wedding when I had lost Will and this date when I would lose my son.

At 6:05 I sent a prayer winging with the plane I couldn't see for a son I felt I'd never see again. If I'd been at the airport to see it, I would have seen a gray-haired man with military bearing watching a plane depart, his face hardened with selfish satisfaction.

Chapter Twenty-Six

A certified legal document from my dad arrived in the mail two weeks later. One of the nurses had been kind enough to drive me back to my boarding house. I was coolly thankful; after all, they had taken away from me a final visit with my son. A letter from my sister was propped up on the small desk.

Dear Mary,

I know you are very angry right now. I guess you have every right to be, but please try to understand. If I didn't feel that Davey was in danger of his life from Dad, I would never take him away from you. There are some things about Dad that you don't know. Now is not the time to tell you—you'll only think I'm lying again.

I'll take very good care of your little boy for you. I know you'd make a better mom than me, but I'll love him, and I'll tell him every day what a wonderful mother and father he has in the States.

We're hoping and praying that God will bring Will back to you. I know our family doesn't talk about God very much, but I truly believe He wants the best for all of us, and I'm praying that you will know this in your heart.

I love you so much, Mary. Please take care of your-self, and come to us soon in Paris.

Your loving sister,
Robyn Johnson Montaigne

Curling my lip, I threw the letter contemptuously on the bed. Of course she didn't mean it. She was just trying to play the innocent. But after a moment, I picked up the letter, smoothed it out, and put it in the desk drawer.

My stomach finally flattened, and I no longer felt as if someone had punched me in the gut. I missed the first week of school, and by the time I had registered and straightened out the financial arrangements, I felt as if I had been thrown into a flurry of activities with no time for anything else.

No time for anything else was precisely what I wanted. Only at night in the quiet of the small apartment which Will had rented and which I tenaciously hung onto, did I sometimes fall into the trap of missing my baby and his father. But not often.

I knew it would be emotional suicide to dwell for any length of time on the two people in the whole world who meant the most to me, so I crammed my days so full that I had little time for anything but to fall into bed at night. Most of my studying I did at the school library. Studying at the small desk where Will had studied would have dredged up memories too painful to consider. I also practiced my instrument at school, so I rarely spent time in the small apartment.

Surprisingly, I missed my sister, Robyn, more than I had expected. Each night my route to Will's apartment led me past the residence club where my sister and I had shared a room the previous year.

The lighted window, second story third from the end, put its warm fingers around my heart and delved into the memories stored there of long talks, shared secrets, and home-away-from-home comfort.

One rainy evening in late October, I hurried past the beckoning window, but the memories clutched at my cold, lonely heart. I passed another apartment, and saw a ground level window opened halfway. The wind caused the curtains to billow inward.

Someone must love fresh air, I thought wryly, pulling my coat closer around my thin body. From a small radio on the windowsill lilted the new tune from *Camelot* that everyone was singing: "If ever I would leave you, it wouldn't be in summer . . . ."

But he had left me. By the time I reached the tiny apartment, I was weeping, and when I reached its privacy, I threw myself across the bed and wept until I was hoarse and gasping for air.

With the dam of reserve I had built around my heart broken, each day, breathlessly busy, was followed by an evening of pensive thoughts and ragged tears. I grew thinner and thinner, and I could tell that my teachers were concerned, but I was determined to at least glean a stellar education out of the morass that my life had become.

Thanksgiving and Christmas were the worst. I spent Thanksgiving hoping for some news from Will. I was devastated when I received nothing and heard nothing.

By Christmas vacation, I had developed a severe sinus infection. I spent most of my time in bed, and in my feverish condition, had many vivid dreams of Will. These alternately elated and depressed me, and I finally counseled myself that something had happened to Will, and I was not to expect to see him ever again.

It was such a very difficult realization to achieve, but it gave me a certain measure of peace, and I was able to finish the school year in a calm if rather frozen frame of mind.

Summer did not catch me emotionally unprepared as I had been at Christmas and Thanksgiving. I used the three months to take additional classes. These counted toward my junior year requirements, and I decided to try to graduate early if possible.

I formed no new friendships. What I had been through had matured me, and I viewed life differently now than most of the students my age. Early my junior year I met Gilbert Livingston. He was dark-haired, quiet, intense, and passionately into his music. Something about him spoke of a deep sorrow.

I found, like Hester in *The Scarlet Letter*, that I could sense things in others because of what I had endured. I longed, sometimes desperately, for someone to talk to, but I had been hurt deeply, and I could sense that if Gilbert misinterpreted my interest for something stronger, he would be deeply hurt as I had been. It was not something I would knowingly inflict on anyone, so I held myself aloof, and he soon faded from notice.

Not willing to spend another Christmas like the last, buried in my room with too many thoughts for comfort, I took a job as extra Christmas help in a department store.

I lived very frugally, but I would not let my bank account get too low. I still had hopes of joining my son in Paris, and I would need to save quite a bit of money for the trip I planned to take. But life, again, had other plans.

My first indication of physical problems came when I fainted in Dr. Stevens' office. I had been sight-reading a new piece by Bartok when everything suddenly went black in front of me. I half-stood, but pitched over into my piano teacher's arms.

Coming to, I found myself lying on the sofa in his office, surrounded by a small handful of the faculty, and my head ached abominably. I insisted on going home; it was either that or let them call an ambulance. I couldn't let them call an ambulance. I was afraid they would somehow find out that I'd had a child.

A month went by without further difficulties. We were busy preparing for a production of *Tosca* with practices three and four evenings every week. I was weary in every sinew, but at least I didn't have to worry about dreaming of Will or Davey.

Then I suffered two more blackouts, fortunately on the weekend and in my own apartment. It scared me into going to see the doctor who had attended me for Davey's birth.

"Extreme fatigue and exhaustion. Young lady, you are on the verge of a nervous breakdown. You need an extended vacation." He placed an avuncular hand on my shoulder and looked down into my eyes with a look of concern in his own.

"I don't know all the difficulties you encountered in your family with the birth of your son, but I did hear of some of the circumstances." He looked very grave.

"My nurses reported some strange behavior on the part of your father that could have been cause for police involvement." He cleared his throat, obviously ill at ease and not quite knowing what to say.

"I would recommend a complete change of scenery if it could be arranged and time to deal with what you have been through. Your soul is disturbed, and your body is trying to tell you to do something about it." His slight German accent became more pronounced with this pronouncement. "I will write you a prescription, but your mind needs to give your body rest."

My mind whirled. I could not possibly get away, but a glimmer of an idea had taken root. His implication about my Dad sent a chill through me, but I determinedly put it away until I could spend more time mulling it over.

Three more fainting spells before the end of school had the teachers and administrators ready to take some course of action, but I had a suggestion of my own.

The week before school was out, I met with the dean of administration, the registrar, and the dean of women students. I had asked my piano teacher, Dr. Stevens, to accompany me for moral support.

I told them of seeing my doctor and his recommendation to take an extended leave of absence. I respectfully requested permission to leave the school for at least a year to recuperate, and upon my return, begged them to grant me my scholarship status in order to finish. Fifteen credits, a senior recital, and senior jury would complete my educational requirements. They granted my request.

Moving out of Will's apartment was the last tenuous link between us. If he looked for me now, he had very little chance of finding me. It was a bitter blow, but even I had the sense now to realize that I had pushed my body for far too long. The landlady was kind enough to keep my things until I returned for them.

"Don't you want to leave a forwarding address, Dearie?" she asked.

"I'm not sure yet where I'll land, but I'll let you know when I can."

"Well, I'm going to keep your room open for a while. I've got a little sum put by, so I don't really need the rent. If you need to come back, you just come. I'll find a space for you." She gave me a fierce embrace.

"Thank you so much, Mrs. Brady." Her kindness was unexpected and nearly overwhelmed my carefully kept composure.

"Is there any chance that your young man will come back? There, I didn't mean to pry, but he was so nice and thoughtful."

"No. I don't think so. I don't know where he is." I struggled to keep my voice clear though there was a lump in my throat nearly choking me.

"That's too bad, but you never know what will happen. You let me know where you are just in case, you hear?"

"Thank you, Mrs. Brady. I will." I had to get away before the tears surfaced. I gave her a quick hug, stepped into the car, and with a quick wave, left. The instant I turned the corner, the tears came, and they didn't stop until I was well on my way on the highway.

I had decided to try a long shot. Robyn and I had once talked about where we would go and what we would do if we ever truly needed help. A friend of our mother's had been a nun in a convent in the hills of California overlooking a lake. She had written a few letters to Mom telling of her work there.

The sisterhood was in the process of revamping their program to make them seem more accessible and in touch with the communities they served. Maybe, just maybe, they would allow me to convalesce there.

Tired and frightened, I was again overwhelmed when Mother Sebastiani calmly accepted my story and gave me a room and a job. For the first time in my life, I felt safe.

Chapter Twenty-Seven

Sorting through the memorabilia in the three boxes had consumed every spare minute and every spare thought. As I neared the end of my exploration, I instinctively knew that what I would discover would be the most important.

The last item in the bottom of the third box was a navy, cloth-bound journal. I lifted it out carefully, holding my breath as I opened the front cover. Robyn's name and Paris address were inscribed at the front. Flipping the page, I found the date of her departure written at the top of the first page. Sucking in my breath, I realized that each entry was addressed to me! What a surprise!

September 7th
Dear Mary,
I'm writing this journal to you so that someday you will be able to read about Davey's first few years of life. I know you hate me right now, and you think I'm stealing your baby. In a way I am.

Dad is a whole lot more dangerous than you know (someday you'll hear that story, too), and I'm determined that little Davey won't become one of his victims. No matter how you feel, I have to do what I think is best.

Look at it from my viewpoint, too, Sis: I'm entering a brand new marriage with a baby already. I wasn't planning on being a mother so soon. And Marc has been so very supportive. He knows about Dad, so he agrees with me that taking Davey is the best thing.

We wanted you to come with us to Paris. It would be so much easier for all of us. I'm just praying that God will reunite all of us soon. In Paris, we'll just tell the truth: that you needed help caring for your child because you've been sick. Some people, I'm sure, will still think it's our own child, but Marc says his family will believe him.

We are on the plane, and Davey is sleeping quietly in the seat beside me. He is so beautiful with your dark hair and Will's nose and beautifully tapered fingers. I think he has your mouth, Mary. It's smaller than Will's, but it shows the depth and warmth of your nature when you smile and laugh.

I'm so nervous about living in Paris. Will Marc's family accept me, will I adjust to this new life in a different country, will I be a good Mom to your son under these circumstances? I just have to do it. But I don't mind admitting that I'm a little scared. Well, I'm going to stop for now and get some sleep. I'll write more after we arrive.

September 10th
Dear Mary,
So many things to write about, but there has been so little time. We are living in the Latin Quarter in a little upstairs apartment or flat with two bedrooms a living room, kitchen and bathroom.

Marc says it is cheaper here because it is in the same area as the College de France and the Sorbonne; therefore, the demand for cheap student housing makes the rent lower.

And with the metro system, Marc can quite easily get to work in the Opera District.

Our trunks and barrels were already here when we arrived from the airport; one of Marc's sisters (Nadia, I think) came in and unpacked the bedding and made the beds for us, knowing, I suppose, that we would all be suffering from jet lag.

Because of the time change, we arrived on the eighth of September at about one o'clock in the afternoon. Marc's parents met us at the airport.

His mom is taller than I, about 5'8" with black hair and a svelte waistline. I felt like the gauche American schoolgirl until she gave me a warm and exuberant hug and began asking questions in her very French-sounding English. I love listening to the lilt of English on the French tongue!

Marc's Dad was more reserved, but he had a twinkle in his eye that revealed his sense of humor over human absurdities right away.

Anyway, I think I'm going to like them. They were smitten with Davey; I think they will spoil him terribly. (I hope this doesn't upset you, but since Davey will never have our parents spoiling him, I think God is giving him another set of grandparents; I hope you will look at it this way and not feel any more bitterness over it).

They drove us to our flat with instructions to come for dinner the next day. They stocked our refrigerator, so we could have a chance to relax after the long flight. I think Marc's parents are wise enough to understand that meeting the whole family—Marc has three sisters—will be rather intimidating.

Between tending to Davey and getting a supper together, I managed to unpack four boxes. Davey became pretty fussy while I was putting together some sandwiches for our dinner, but Marc fed him and rubbed his back; I think he had some gas.

Yesterday, I unpacked all of the big trunks and barrels. It's beginning to look like a home, I think, but we still need to get some necessities like shampoo, soap, toilet paper.

That's another thing to become accustomed to: they don't have rolls of toilet paper here. Instead, they have little squares that they put in a box, and we pull it out of a little opening at the bottom of the box!

I'll have to venture out soon to get these things, and it makes me rather nervous thinking about trying to communicate with sales clerks about what I need.

The dinner with Marc's family was very interesting. We left about four o'clock and went to the Metro station. The name of the station is Vavin. I'm trying to remember all of this so I can venture out on my own when Mark begins going to work on Monday.

He bought me a pass that lasts for a month. I put the little ticket in the slot, the gate opens, and I pick up the little ticket on the other side! It is so extraordinary! Marc laughed at me and said that they have a similar system in New York City, but I've never been to New York, so how would I know?

I feel rather bourgeois, but I suppose I'll become indifferent and blasé toward the novelty of it all soon enough. We left somewhat early, Marc said, to avoid the rush at five o'clock. The way he said it, I think it's a warning to avoid that time of day on the Metro with a small baby.

We changed lines several times and took a train (it's called the RER) into this little area near the Fontainebleau Forest called Avon. It's a beautiful area with miles of walking trails according to Marc. He told me that I should get his mother or one of his sisters to take me to the Fontainebleau Castle.

Marc's parents live in a six-bedroom house that backs up to the Seine River. His oldest sister, Natalie, is married to Paul. His second oldest sister is Margaretta. She is in her third year at Universite. And Nadia, the youngest, did make the beds for us in our flat.

Apparently the flat came furnished, (Marc sent some of the money he earned at the San Francisco Opera on ahead to his mother) but there was no crib for the baby, so they brought one borrowed from a friend to the flat and set it up for us.

The dinner went rather well, I thought. It is so difficult to follow the conversations in French, but they spoke in English most of the time so that I could join them. Actually, it made me feel as if I wasn't quite so stupid because several times they had to ask Marc and me how to say things in English.

Davey was wide-awake and alert during the trip out and dinner, but he became sleepy and fussy after dinner. Nadia asked to hold him, and she seems to love children. She fed him his bottle and rocked him to sleep. After dinner, we sat around the fireplace in the living room and talked.

Marc's family is really proud of him. Apparently his beautiful tenor voice caught the ear of his teachers at the Universite, but he chose to further his training in America.

On Monday, he begins working with a group at the Opera de Garnier, and everyone is confident that he will become well received and widely acclaimed in the operatic world. I have no doubts. He received rave reviews in San Francisco while he was there for two years.

Before we left, Marc's mother—she asked me to call her Gretta—pulled out some gifts for Davey. It seems everyone in the family had shopped for him. I don't think I'll have to shop for him for a while!

They bought some adorable outfits for him plus some blankets, bibs, a diaper pail, and a stroller which they call a *poissette*. Marc's Dad, Michel, took us home in the car. Davey slept the whole way home, and, I must confess, I was very tired too. I think I'm still suffering from jet lag.

September 11th

Dear Mary,

Yesterday I wrote while Davey was napping; today I'm doing the same. It seems to be a good time to sit down and collect my thoughts. Everything is unpacked, but I am making a list of things we need for the flat as well as groceries that we need. Marc will receive very little money until after the performance in three months, so we need to spend sparingly.

I have some money, still in American dollars, and Marc made quite a bit his last year with the San Francisco Opera Company, so we will have enough, I think. When Davey awakes, Marc is going to take me shopping.

September 12th

Dear Mary,

Shopping was a real eye-opener yesterday! The amount of francs needed to make purchases is so much higher than the number of dollars that would be needed.

I am so afraid of overspending that I forget I have more francs at my disposal than I would dollars. Marc gave me 200 francs and some change to spend on groceries and household goods.

He stood back and laughed at me as I made small purchases of bread and vegetables, but he was also very helpful when I needed to know how to ask things.

And I did have so much fun shopping at the little shops: first a vegetable stand, then a pastry shop for bread— he laughed when I drooled over the fine French pastries on display, then a boucherie or meat shop.

We finished up by stopping at a drugstore for soap, shampoo and the like. I think I'm going to adjust just fine shopping for things in Paris. We live close to the Jardin du Luxembourg, the Cimetierre du Montparnasse and a hospital, St. Vincent de Paul. It will be fun to go exploring; it is also comforting to know we are close to a hospital.

September 15th

Dear Mary,

Davey has been sick. He came down with a cold and has been having trouble breathing. Marc, of course, has had to begin work, and if it hadn't been for Gretta and Nadia, I don't know what I would have done.

Mary, I would be absolutely sick if anything happened to Davey. I've been so worried. Gretta has brought medicine and taught me how to help him, and Nadia has come every day after school in case I've needed help or needed to go somewhere.

He's not even two weeks old. I think he became sick because of all the traveling and being around so many new people.

We nearly decided to take him to the hospital, but he started getting better yesterday afternoon. I'm so relieved, but so tired. Since Nadia is here, I'm going to take a nap. I just hope and pray everything is all right with you, Mary. I sure wish you were here.

September 16th
Dear Mary,
Davey is definitely on the mend, and I'm so relieved. He is taking his afternoon nap, Nadia is at the kitchen table studying, and I'm sitting here in the rocking chair writing to you. I'm still tired, so Nadia has given me a time limit of ten minutes to write before she puts me down for a nap!

I never expected to feel so cared for here in France. Marc's family is wonderful. Maybe someday you will be able to know them, too. I miss you more than I thought I would. Every time I look at your son, I see both you and Will, and I think about what could have been. I'm having a difficult time accepting all of this even though I know I can't change it.

I also think of the things you are missing: smelling Davey's sweet scent after his bath, watching him drift off to sleep—babies are able to relax so completely when they sleep—watching for his smile.

He is just beginning to smile when one of us comes to pick him up from his crib. I hope reading this doesn't hurt too much, but I know you want to know everything about your son. Well, Nadia is marching toward me with a stern expression. I have already ignored her first two signals.

September 19th
Dear Mary,

This weekend was marvelous. We spent Saturday and Sunday with Marc's family. With so many babysitters, Marc and I were able to take a long walk along the Seine and catch up on us.

He had a really good first week at the Opera de Garnier. The director likes his work, and he can tell that the years he spent in America matured him and gave depth to his singing and experience. They are working toward a Novembre production of *La Boheme*. It really is exciting because he has one of the lead roles, that of Rodolfo, in the play.

Marc is thrilled that he landed such a big role for his first major production after returning from America. Apparently the publicists are going to bill him as "France's son returning from foreign climes," or some such nonsense.

He practices privately in the morning, has *dejeuner* (lunch) for two hours, and then practices with the rest of the cast in the afternoon/early evening. Dinner is usually around 8 p.m.

Such a late dinner hour is just an example of the many small things I am adjusting to here in Paris. He says that next week he can come home or we can meet in the Opera District for dejeuner. This week they've been fitting him for costumes, so he has been rather busy.

September 21st

Dear Mary,

Nadia is teaching me French! (We started this on Monday; that's why I am using French words and phrases in what I write). It is so much fun, and I know it will help me to get around Paris better.

Davey is smiling more each day now. He is so adorable! It's hard to believe that he'll be a month old next week. He does sleep a lot though.

September 23rd

Dear Mary,

Gretta came yesterday so I wouldn't get lost going down to the Opera District on the Metro to meet Marc for dejeuner. We met him at the back of the opera house. He was just coming out the door to wait for us—perfect timing!

The back doors are heavy wood, oak, I think, with black iron bars running the length of them, forming a grill and keeping out intruders, I suppose.

In the back of the Opera Garnier is a monument. It looks like it begins in marble (marble is very popular over here), but at the very top is a bust of someone in gold, and below the bust are some nude figures of men sitting with an arm raised up toward the bust. It is very picturesque and probably has something to do with the theatre. I'll have to ask Marc about it.

Four or five streets meet with the building acting as a hub, so it is a very busy intersection. We went down one of the little streets to the Brasserie Pub Opera, a quaint little café.

Marc was bubbling over about the aria he is learning. He was holding Davey, and Davey just stared up at him in fascination with Marc unaware of Davey's intense regard. It was so precious! Gretta noticed too. She says that Davey is going to be great with words; he is already so interested in the shape and sounds of them.

After we finished eating, Marc took us on a quick tour of the Opera House. He has a key for the back door. Going straight down the hall, he showed us a corridor to the left with dressing rooms on each side.

Huge trunks, double and triple the size of those we packed our belongings in, lined the corridor. Apparently, some of the singers/actors bring their own costumes for the shows.

We took the second corridor to the left. It runs right behind the stage. On the left hand side was a small room with a raked floor where Marc says the ballet dancers practice, the Danse Foyer.

It was ornately decorated, especially at the top. There, in gold frames, were pictures of former ballet stars. The mirrors were ornately outlined with gold, and the chandelier hanging from the ceiling was breathtakingly beautiful!

Of course, that reminded me of *The Phantom of the Opera*, and I wanted to see the house. So Marc took us along another corridor stage right, and we walked partway on stage. The house lights were dim, but I could still see the gold and red velvet everywhere. It is so lavish! And the chandelier was everything I had imagined. He pointed out box five where the phantom supposedly sat.

Marc had to return to work, but his mom took me in the foyer to show me the Grand Staircase. As I walked slowly down the stairs, I could hear the faint rustling of long skirts from many years back and imagine the intrigue and gossip that had swirled in the atmosphere.

I counted seven different colors of marble. It was all so different from anything I have ever seen before. Neither Santa Rosa nor San Francisco have such beautiful buildings on such a grand scale. Gretta grinned at me appreciatively. She was holding Davey who had fallen contentedly asleep in her arms.

"It is so refreshing to see my country through the eyes of a foreigner," she said in her accented English.

The day was warm, in the mid-eighties, so we took the Metro to my exit and walked to the Jardin (Garden) du Luxembourg. The air was lightly scented with perfume of many flowers.

I enjoyed talking to Gretta about Marc's childhood and how the family knew he was destined for great things. And now I know how to get to Marc's work as well as a new place to take Davey when I need to get out for a breath of fresh air.

*****

Reading Robyn's journal made me insanely jealous, and I found myself putting it down every ten pages or so to get a grip on my emotions, yet I couldn't bear to put it down for too long. I was so hungry to learn more about my son and how he had grown up in Paris. Picking up the book again, I voraciously began to read more.

Chapter Twenty-Eight

September 26th

Dear Mary,

Another lovely weekend in Avon. Marc's parents seem to want us there each weekend, so we go and enjoy his *maman's* fine French cuisine. This weekend she bought a large fish—it must have been about two feet long—and broiled it in the oven with some seasoned vegetables. It was delicious!

Now that I've been to Marc's workplace, I understand what he's talking about more readily.

I continue to learn more French. I am up to five words out of every twenty now. And I've started a little notebook of new words that I learn. Nadia is patient and never laughs at me for which I am grateful.

Davey is a contented little guy except when he wants his diaper changed or when he's hungry. He can't stand a messy diaper, and I really can't blame him, poor thing. He has begun to gurgle and coo just a bit now. It's as if he's found his voice and is practicing. I love to just sit and talk to him, watching him try to emulate the shape of my mouth and the sounds I make.

September 27th

Dear Mary,

This morning, I scrubbed our little flat until it shone after Davey went down for his morning nap. I'm used to cleaning on weekends, but if we spend every weekend with Marc's parents, I'll have to change that.

Mondays are difficult. We are adjusting to the flat again and picking up the pieces of city life, so I'm going to make Tuesdays cleaning day. I also need to get on some kind of schedule for laundry. Then I can spend the rest of my time exploring this wonderful city.

This afternoon Davey and I are going to go to the Cimetierre du Montparnasse. Apparently the Montparnasse area has been and still is home to many artists, writers, and even publishers.

I also found out from Michel that Voltaire used to hang out at the mill on the property there while he was a student at the Jesuit College de Clermont. It will be fun exploring some of these places. I can't believe I'm really here in Paris and away from my old life in the United States!

September 28th

Dear Mary,

Yesterday Nadia dragged Margaretta with her to come visit us; Margaretta is studying at the Universite Paris IV, not too far from us, but she is shy and concentrates on her studies.

Apparently, Nadia made her take a half-holiday so we could go sightseeing and window-shopping. We caught the Metro and went first to see the Notre Dame and then the Musee de Cluny.

The Notre Dame is so very beautiful! Inside the ceiling soars about four stories high, and people automatically lower their voices so as not to disturb the holy hush. I would love to sing in a cathedral like this: the acoustics must be marvelous! The circular stained-glass windows were beautiful, especially when they caught the sun.

Nadia assured me that the Sainte Chapelle is even more beautiful because upstairs, stained glass windows soar several stories above and all around, and when the sun shines, it is like being inside a kaleidoscope. But it is small and people are more talkative, she explained.

We strolled around looking at the altars dedicated to various saints located in nooks or niches along the walls. Sitting for a few moments in the quiet, I was filled with awe both that God has chosen to visit mankind and also that mankind could conceive building such a beautiful monument to God. When Bishop Maurice de Sully died, his vision continued several generations until the cathedral was built, another fact I also find amazing!

The Musee de Cluny is a museum of the ancient Roman baths and Medieval art, including tapestries, armor, and stained glass. It was mind-boggling to see such ancient tapestries preserved so well. In a way, the history in Europe goes back so much further than it does in the United States.

Davey became fussy, so we stopped at a little sidewalk café, and I let Nadia and Margaretta order some coffee for me. They also ordered some pastries, *brioches*, that were divine!

This is yet another language barrier I'll have to overcome: learning to order food at restaurants. We returned home after seven o'clock, and Nadia and Margaretta stayed and helped me prepare *diner* before Marc returned home.

September 29th

Dear Mary,

I am in a quandary. Though there is so much to see in this city, I get overwhelmed, so I am trying to learn things in small doses. However, if I don't go out and try new things, I'm afraid I'll get bored. So I've decided to work on my music.

After the flat is straightened, I'm going to practice my music for at least an hour every day. It did feel good to stretch my vocal chords this morning! I just hope I didn't disturb anyone in the building. Nadia can't come today, so I'm going to nap with Davey. Those girls tired me out yesterday.

October 3rd

Dear Mary,

Davey is one month old today! I wish I knew what has happened to you. I'm guessing that you are still at the Conservatory, and studying your music diligently.

Has Will returned? The more I think about it, the more I believe that if he hasn't come back yet, something has happened to prevent him from returning to you. Will is a very dependable person; you can bank on that.

Your little boy is so sweet. He takes a nap in the morning and in the afternoon, so I do have quite a bit of free time. He smiles a lot more and wants to see us in the room with him when he is awake. Sometimes I spread a blanket on the floor and let him lie on it just for a change from his crib and carryall.

Even though Marc is bone weary when he comes home in the evenings, he holds Davey and talks to him. It's really funny to listen to his conversation sometimes, but I learn about how his day has been by listening to him jabber. Davey loves watching Marc talk. I think Marc's deep voice fascinates him.

October 4th
Dear Mary,

After cleaning the flat this morning after Davey's nap, I ventured out with him to see the sights in the neighborhood. We walked around the corner and saw the *boucherie* shop where Marc took me to buy meat the first time I went shopping with him.

Several vegetable shops have open stalls right on the sidewalk. It was fun to browse, and I even bought some bananas and late grown peaches. And then there were the flower shops! The masses of jewel-like tones were as uplifting as prayer. I just had to buy some goldenrod colored mums to bring the sunshine inside.

We continued our walk until I saw this quaint bistro with several black iron tables and chairs outside. It was so pretty with bright pink and mauve potted flowers spilling out onto the sidewalk that I decided to sit and enjoy the sunshine, feeding Davey and sipping some coffee.

The waiter was very nice. I discovered that if I point to what I want and give the waiter more than what the posted price is, I can't go wrong.

The sidewalks were busier on the way home which was rather intimidating, but I decided to be brave and stop by the *boucherie* for some nice pork chops for diner. They were a hit with Marc when he came home, and he was impressed that I had actually bought them at the *boucherie* by myself!

October 5th

Dear Mary,

Today is overcast, but I have my sunshine inside--the mums I bought yesterday--and the memory of an idyllic afternoon. Davey is so sweet. I love to watch his little eyes drooping as he drops off to sleep.

His long, dark lashes delicately fan his cheeks, and his body totally relaxes until he is a precious heavyweight. His dark hair is starting to curl up slightly in the back and on top of his head. I think he might have naturally curly hair like Will. He often folds his tiny hands up by his face when he sleeps.

I am developing a repertoire of lullabies to sing to him including Brahm's famous tune, "Jesus Loves Me," "Sweet Child," "Les Berceaux," and more. Nadia has promised to teach me some French tunes as well, and I'm trying to get Marc to sing to him. Would you believe Marc is shy about it?! He thinks his voice will frighten Davey, but I disagree.

Marc can sing with dulcet tones, and who knows this better than I do? He won my heart first with his voice and then with his kindness. I know he is good for Davey. What I think he is really afraid of is succumbing to fatherhood. He is afraid of taking Will's place, just like I used to be afraid of taking your place, Mary. So even though he is a good papa, he tends to be reserved.

I'm going to talk to him about it because I think Davey needs Marc to totally be available for him. We can show Davey pictures of you and Will so he knows who you are, but right now, we are all he has. I hope this is alright with both of you.

And when you two return, I hope you won't wrench Davey away from us, but instead, plan to be here for a while. That way, we can become accustomed to life without Davey and he can become adjusted to a new set of parents. Actually, he should have four parents until we all become adjusted to the new situation.

I hope you don't mind my writing like this, but I have been thinking lately of those poor children who are just jerked around between parents, and if adults truly wanted the best for children, they would carefully consider the impact of their actions on children instead of thinking that children should just fall in with the plans of their parents.

The bottom line is that your little son has crawled into my heart, and I hope you will allow him to remain there. I know we could all live close to each other for a year when you return so that Davey has the best of both worlds.

Meanwhile, we are going to continue to let Davey crawl into our hearts and give him all the love we have.

Chapter Twenty-Nine

October 6th

Dear Mary,

The most incredible thing—I've made a new friend! My first friend outside of family here in France. Her name is Shannon, and she's a nanny from Ireland. She cares for a little boy two months older than Davey named Phillip.

We met at the Jardin du Luxembourg on Tuesday while watching some children sail boats in the pool there. I heard her say something in English, and my whole head flew around toward the sound.

I've heard very little English for a month now. When you think about that fact for a while, it seems strange. I just had to speak to her even if I might seem rather rude.

We jumped aboard the friendship train right away. Her accent is different, of course, from American English, and some of the words are different too, but we had a merry time laughing at the differences, and it is so wonderful to hear English again. I didn't realize I was missing it.

Shannon has five brothers, and two sisters back in Ireland, all of them older than she except for Donnell and Joseph, all of them noisy except for Jake, and all of them content to stay at home except for her. She has red hair that is very dark, more of an auburn than a red, with blue eyes and a few freckles on her small nose. I know you would enjoy her, Mary.

I had seen her before, but I thought Phillip was her son instead of her charge. He has dark hair and brown eyes like Davey, but he is shorter and more roly-poly. Davey is definitely going to be tall like Will. It will be fun for Davey to have a playmate. I almost hate to be going to Avon for the weekend, but we've made plans to meet several days next week.

October 10th
Dear Mary,
Marc and I had a fight Friday on the way to Avon, and I was so miserable. I felt like the typical, clingy wife. I hate it when I get that way, but he is gone so much, and he falls asleep so soon after he comes home at night and eats dinner.

And so I nagged which made me feel really stupid because him not spending time with me is not the real issue at all. Gretta helped me to see that.

She took me on a walk down to the Seine River with her, and she asked me what I would most enjoy doing if I knew I would be on my own for a month with no baby and no husband. I told her that I would find someone with whome to continue my vocal studies, and I would open a music studio. That conversation and opened a whole new world for me.

My real problem is that I feel as if my whole world revolves around Marc, and if he's tired or cross, I take it personally as a sign that he doesn't find me interesting anymore.

If I am pursuing my own interests, our times together will be more enjoyable because we both will be interdependent on each other instead of me being totally dependent on him for my link to an outside world.

The language barrier is also a problem, so she suggested that I take lessons. I might as well learn the language fast instead of slowly. Then I'll feel more independent and in charge of my life.

Saturday night we finally talked about it. I told him that my life and what I do every day, as a housewife, seems so boring compared to what he's doing.

He laughed at me and told me that I'll never be boring to him; he enjoys hearing about life in Paris from the perspective of someone who hasn't lived there long. It gives him a keener appreciation of those things he often takes for granted. He said that they can always use help at the opera house, but I like my idea of a studio better.

Making up was wonderful, but I'm sure you don't need me to tell you about all that!

October 14th
Dear Mary,
Shannon and I have had such a fun time the last few days getting to know each other. I couldn't have picked a better friend if I had looked all over Paris. We discovered our mutual passion for singing, and we've been yodeling ever since! She has very little formal training, but she knows many of the pieces I learned in high school and college.

I invited her to the flat along with Phillip on Wednesday and Thursday. After lunch, we put the babies on a blanket on the floor, and I pulled out my music. The babies just stared at us at first, and Phillip was a little fussy, but he soon quieted down.

They fell asleep as Nadia arrived. She rolled her eyes at us, raided the fridge, and began working on her homework. When we finally stopped, she taught us some music terms in French.

Your son is beginning to smile so much more now. When he woke up and saw Nadia, he beamed a sweet smile at her.

Margaretta is overcoming her shyness. When she came to collect Nadia, she told me about her classes. She is very quiet and soft-spoken, but her passion for medicine shows when she talks about it. She wants to be a doctor, but she has a great deal of training to acquire first.

November 2nd
Dear Mary,
Time has gotten away from me. It's nearly two months since Davey's birth and two months since we moved here, but my days seem to be so full. My French is improving so that I don't offend as many ears these days. I took Shannon with me to the Opera de Garnier yesterday so she could meet Marc and see what he does.

I could tell right away that she would love to be a part of it all. Maybe Marc can get her a small part in the next opera that he does.

The producers are talking about *Manon, Norma,* or *Andre Chenier*. They want to do something for the Storming of Bastille Day in July, and they are trying to decide which two to perform. Personally, I think *Norma* is too difficult—

the soprano part is absolutely grueling—but lucky me, I'm not a producer!

Davey is growing so fast. Gretta brought a scale over the other day. Davey is up to twelve pounds now. He has begun cooing when he wakes from his nap, he tries to hold his bottle, and he smiles at everyone. He's a charmer!

Novembre 20th
Dear Mary,
This is a rough time for all of us right now. Marc's performances begin this weekend. He is very nervous and stressed, but I know he'll do well. Davey is fretful, missing Marc's presence in the evenings when he comes in so late.

Marc seems to need to expel his nervousness with passionate lovemaking. Thank God for helpful counsel in this area or I would not know how to handle my intensely ardent husband. He still worries me, and it seems he is losing weight; I can feel his ribs, and his cheekbones seem more prominent.

November 28th
Dear Mary,
La Boheme is an astounding success as is the "incomparable son of France, Marc Montaigne." Isn't it wonderful?! The streets and all the papers are abuzz with approval and approbation.

Marc has five more performances left, but with all of Paris singing his praises (please pardon the pun!), he seems to have more fire and command in his performance. Word of the performances is spreading rapidly, meaning that our coffers will be full very soon, and we will have a wonderful Christmas.

Shannon is in alt. She is clipping all of the articles she can find for the scrapbook I'm creating for Marc. She has attended two shows and is learning the arias *Mi chiamano Mimi* and *Addio, senza rancor*.

Decembre 6th
Dear Mary,
Davey rolled over today! He's done it before but I didn't see it. Today I saw it, and he seems to want to practice it over and over. He holds his rattles now, waving them in the air, and when he wakes up in the morning, he often plays with his toes. It's as if he is talking to them! He is such a cutie pie!

It is too cold for Shannon and I to watch the little boys and girls sailing their boats in the pool at the Jardin du Luxembourg. She feels reticent about inviting Davey and me to the place where she is employed, so she comes to our place three or four times a week.

The directors at the Opera de Garnier were so impressed with Marc's performance that they have put him on a regular salary; this is in addition to his tremendous bonus from *La Boheme*. It is nice not to have to worry about money.

Decembre 19th
Dear Mary,
Nadia, Margaretta, Shannon, and I went Christmas shopping last Friday. We had so much fun! Even though I am learning French at a fairly good rate, I kept getting lost when talking to the cashiers and sales people. I'm very glad I wasn't alone.

Paris is so alive even in the winter. Despite the bitter cold, Paris pulls on her somewhat gaudy winter apparel and thumbs her nose at Jack Frost. I have been so used to the traditional red and green in the States, but Paris celebrates Christmas in all the vivid hues she can find.

Along the Champ Elysees, the trees are shrouded in some kind of see-through scrim to represent lollipops. After dusk, blue, orange and purple lights glow like giant bulbs hanging in the trees.

The Lafayette Galleries and Au Printemps, high-class department stores, use mechanical dolls in a variety of scenes to show off toys in their windows, and this year, orange mini lights crisscrossed over the sidewalk casting a glow over the droves of shoppers for blocks and blocks.

We went to the Place de la Madeleine in the Opera District first, a place to satisfy every gustatory desire. Nadia and Margaretta helped me choose gifts for their family. Gretta loves truffles, so I bought a pound of those for her. How she keeps her svelte figure, I'll never know, but every woman deserves chocolate.

Michel, or Papa Montaigne as I call him, is just as easy to please. He must have close to a hundred ties, but Nadia and Margaretta said that he wears every one of them at least once a year, and he likes getting new and unique ones. For clothing and more, we headed to the Galeries Lafayette and Au Printemps.

Natalie and Paul have had their eyes on some crystal stemware, so we all pitched in and bought not only the crystal, but also an ice bucket and a bottle of vintage wine.

While Nadia distracted Shannon, I bought her some wickedly sexy lingerie in an emerald green that compliments her coloring perfectly. Someday, she'll wear it for the man of her dreams, but she should also wear it just for herself, another thing every woman deserves whether single or married.

For Nadia I bought a skirt and blouse she had been drooling over, and for Margaretta, I found some small pearl earrings and a matching brooch that would work equally well for day or evening.

The others, filled with the energetic excitement of shopping, wanted to hit the Champ Elysees, but by that time the smell of crepes from a streetside vendor was tantalizing my taste buds.

I chose one with powdered sugar, and we all sat down at a small black iron table with the four matching chairs, the rest of Paris flowing around us. Nadia finished hers quickly and volunteered to feed Davey. Shannon had simply ordered a coffee and was already feeding Phillip.

Margaretta, looking at all of our packages and being practical, suggested that we save Champ Elysees for another day, so we invaded Lafayette and Printemps again, this time heading for the children's department.

It is so difficult to display discipline when buying toys and clothing for children, but a jack-in-the-box in the traditional Harlequin diamond outfit caught my eye, as well as a bright red ball, small enough for Davey to grasp, but large enough to prevent him from swallowing it.

I excused myself for a few minutes, leaving Davey in Nadia's care, and headed for the men's section where I found a leather attaché case for Marc's music. I also wanted to buy him some cologne, but Nadia and the others caught up with me and told me to wait—I could get a much better deal along the Champ Elysees or at Catherine's.

We wanted to make plans for dinner, but Shannon needed to take Phillip home, and Nadia and Margaretta needed to call their parents. The problem was solved when Margaretta called, for Gretta suggested meeting at a little Bistro around the corner for *diner* shortly after eight when Marc arrived home. Shannon could join us, and it would be their treat.

The atmosphere of the Bistro Charrone was small, intimate and convivial. Candlelight and laughter, the muted music of silver against china, the acceptance of a close-knit family made it a perfect ending to our day. Reluctant to leave, we all decided to make the Bistro Charrone an annual family tradition.

Decembre 26th
Dear Mary,
What a wonderful Christmas! Marc, Davey, and I joined his parents mid-morning of Christmas Eve. The most poignant time was the Christmas Eve service at the cathedral around the corner. It doesn't look like much from the outside, but when entering, people automatically lower their voices, and to me, it seems as if a holy quietude settles over the place.

The weather is bitterly cold, but the scent of a thousand or so lighted candles warms the lofty spaces, filling them with light. Then when the choir began to sing, the massive stone walls seemed to throb with such celestial sweetness that I'm sure the angels folded their wings and bent their heads to listen.

No wonder Marc has such a love of classical music. Paris has its share of other genres of music, but to hear classical music in a cathedral, where the notes can float like iridescent bubbles to tickle the very tops of the ceilings with wet kisses, is heaven.

When we exited following the service, a light mist was falling, turning the lights along the street into a magical fairyland. Marc put his arm around me, Davey looked up at us from his bundle of blankets, and I felt so happy and in love with life. When I was in high school, I never, in my wildest imaginings of the future, ever believed that I would be this happy.

With no children anxious to open presents, Christmas morning was lazy and relaxed. We ate a wonderful breakfast together before gathering around the tree. I received some wonderful gifts, but the thing that filled my heart with such wonder and contentment was experiencing the caring and love of Marc's family.

Our family was so dysfunctional. Marc's mother works as a private psychiatrist, and she has helped me to overcome many of the unhealthy behavior patterns that could sabotage my marriage and my new life here in Paris. I feel like I have so much freedom to bask in the comfort and concern this family gives.

*****

The full impact of the enormity of Robyn's sacrifice was now striking me full force. How dramatically her life had changed from that of a student with a fiancée to that of a wife and also a mother living in a foreign country all within the space of three months. Yet everything she had done, she had done with grace and elan.

Her death was a tremendous blow to me. Reading her journal, I was getting back my sister and the close relationship we had shared. Reading her journal, I was also losing her again, and the raw emotions of grief and guilt punched a devastating blow to my hard-earned composure.

Chapter Thirty

January 4th
Dear Mary,

What a wonderful time we've had! Parisians really know how to celebrate New Year's! Gretta and Michel elected to stay home, but the rest of us went to the Champ Elysees to watch the lights on the Eiffel Tower being lit and to see the marvelous fireworks along the Seine.

I have never seen anything like it in my sheltered experience! Hordes of people everywhere overwhelmed me somewhat, but to actually see in person something so breathtaking was awe-inspiring.

Davey was as good as gold. As long as someone is holding him, he is fine. He fell asleep, and every time a boom occurred, we covered his ears. Margaretta finally popped into a store and bought a little hat for him, and we put extra padding over his ears.

Natalie and Paul wanted to hold Davey much more than usual. I wonder if they will have any news for us soon!

Shannon came over yesterday with Phillip. She had a wonderful time with her family in Ireland. She laughingly scolded me for making her wait to open her gift. Unsuspecting, she opened it in front of her family, and did her brothers ever tease her about the lacy, green negligee I bought for her!

Marc returned to work yesterday for just a few hours. Not everyone is back yet because of Twelfth Night celebrations coming up on the sixth, but I can tell he needed some time on his own to practice the music for the upcoming *Manon*.

He is playing the part of Chevalier des Grieux, and because this opera is so popular all over France, all over the world, actually, he is determined to do a fantastic job.

January 5th
Dear Mary,
I am in a very reminiscent mood today. I suppose it is because of the New Year. New years always make me pensive about the coming year and what it will bring. Davey will grow, taking his first steps and saying his first words, and you will miss it. Part of me longs to write to you, but Marc thinks it is a bad idea.

It would look odd if you are not at the conservatory to receive a letter from a sister who should know where you are. And we both know how nosy the secretaries at the school are.

Suki's friend, Anna, told her once that the secretaries sometimes open the mail, especially if it is from or to one of the eligible men on campus. So many girls were green with jealously when I married Marc. I'm afraid a letter might get into the wrong hands and ruin things for you, so I will wait and try to be patient.

January 25th

Dear Mary,

Davey is sitting up by himself now. When Shannon brings Phillip over, they play together more, and are their personalities showing! Phillip is the busy little boy who is always looking for something to do or something to play with. Davey is much calmer and content with whatever toys are around him.

When Shannon and I start singing, we have to be careful to keep a close watch on those two. Phillip will scoot around on his belly and take toys away from Davey. This usually doesn't bother Davey, but yesterday while we were singing a duet, we heard an awful howl.

Phillip had accidentally scratched Davey with his long fingernails. Shannon and I decided to trim their nails so that won't happen again soon.

They are so close to learning to crawl. They get up on all fours and rock back and forth. It is so funny to watch! They are like two bulls getting ready to charge each other!

Marc had some interesting news when he came home from work yesterday. An Italian director, Zefirelli, is directing *Manon*. Some people are complaining that he is too picky about the details of the setting and costume, but Marc says he likes directors who are exacting about details. The performances usually go well when the director knows precisely what he wants.

He says that Zeffirelli and M. Pretre, the music director, deal well together because they are both master craftsmen. It does make for long practices, however.

February 1st

Dear Mary,

Davey was unusually fussy during our weekend visit to Avon. He wanted to be held and bounced or rocked all weekend long. And now we know why! He has two bottom front teeth coming! One is already peeping through the gum, and the other one is nearly there.

Gretta told me to wet a washcloth and rub it gently over the gums, but with pressure. It will create more room for the tooth to grow and relieve some of the pressure he's been feeling. That idea worked. She also suggested letting him gnaw on an ice-cold carrot to numb it some. That works, too, but I have to be careful that he doesn't choke on any pieces.

Shannon talked to her employers. They are going to let her have some evenings free each week so she can audition for some small walk-on parts for the opera. She is absolutely glowing about it! Me, I don't really mind staying out of the limelight, but Shannon seems to crave it, enjoy it, and have the personality for it. I'm thrilled for her.

It has been too cold to be outdoors much, but every now and then, we'll bundle up and take the babies for a walk. I love this little neighborhood where we live, but I will enjoy exploring Paris more in the spring.

February 15th

Dear Mary,

Davey finally did it! He's crawling! And it was so fun to watch! Shannon came over yesterday, and we put the babies on a quilt on the floor. We were sitting on the sofa looking through some music when Shannon said in her "look-but-don't-look" voice (usually reserved for when she sees a cute guy), "Look at what the boys are doing, Robyn."

I turned my head slowly, and there they were side by side on all fours, mimicking each other and actually moving forward. They finally realized they had moved across the room, and the expressions on their faces were so adorable: wonder and then glee at this achievement. After that, there was no stopping them, but they were sure tuckered out by naptime.

February 23rd
Dear Mary,
Shannon's part in *Manon* is that of Pousette, an actress. We practice her music often, and her voice is improving. Marc says that the directors have their eyes on her for more important roles in the future. In addition, they want me to work part time down at the Opera House helping out with the vocal training. I'm thinking of doing it as long as it remains on a part time basis.

March 2nd
Dear Mary,
I'm so sorry that I'm not keeping up with this journal as I'd like. My goal was to write a little each day so you could have a very clear picture of Davey's first several years, but somehow I've become so much busier than I expected.

Three days a week now, I join Marc for *dejeuner* in the Opera District. We are really enjoying working together again like we did at the Conservatory in Frisco (it seems so long ago). I feel so much more connected to him; the dynamics in our relationship have changed and we are so much closer. It shows in our sex life too!

Following *dejeuner*, I work with various female cast members on their music. I've been told by M. Pretre to concentrate on vocal quality, especially with the actresses.

M. Petre explained to me that with a Chevalier des Grieux of Marc's abilities and a Manon sung by someone as virtuostically flawless as Sutherland, our support cast must, indeed, support these wonderful artists. Apparently they are also interested in the perpetuation of quality musicianship, very admirable.

We have blocked off and child-proofed a room for Davey, and for Phillip too, when he comes. Although Shannon's employers have few objections to her evening rehearsals, they do have qualms about their son being "brought into contact with opera sort of people." Their double standards are amusing, and mostly we just laugh at them.

March 23rd
Dear Mary,
Two more weeks until production. Everyone is working their hardest to pull the sets, costumes, music, and all the rest of the details together. One of the set crew brought in a crib so Davey can sleep in it.

I'm afraid I've overbooked myself again. It is so easy to do when working on a production. I've been helping to finalize details on the costumes, such as gold braid on Lescaut's soldier costume and those white pearlized sequins on Manon's white dress in the final scene when she dies. The sequins sparkle prettily in the light without looking too flashy for a young girl.

I miss relaxing times with Shannon, and I definitely want to explore more of Paris, but on the other hand, my relationship with Marc is so much closer than we've had in a while. He is so passionate before a production. Guaranteed to knock socks off and curl toes!

April 17th
Dear Mary,

The production was a major success, and Russia has put a man in space! Of the two, *Manon* is of much more importance to me although I understand that with the competition between Russia and America, the news of Russia beating the United States in putting a man in space is extremely irksome to many Americans.

Marc was very nervous about singing with Sutherland, she is such a fine musician, but Marc did a wonderful job, and between the two, they brought Paris into the artistic spotlight.

Marc even received a letter from de Gaulle congratulating him on his success, both for himself and for his country, France. I think it gave the media something new to write about instead of the problems de Gaulle is facing in granting Algeria its independence. Tensions seem to be running high over that issue these days.

And there is more news about your wonderful boy! He is eating baby food now, causing him to sleep so much better. He enjoys baby cereal, applesauce, and pureed carrots, among other things.

We also let him eat oat rounds (in the States they're called Cheerios!). He loves to pick them up with his thumb and first finger. And did I mention peek-a-boo? Nadia keeps him laughing with that game, and it was fun seeing the stage crew and cast unbend to play it with him, too!

April 19th

Dear Mary,

Davey called Marc "Pa-Pa" today! It is hard to write this to you because I know you are probably thinking that Will is his Daddy. You are right, and when Davey is old enough to understand, we'll tell him the whole story. Marc just glowed though I could tell he has the same thoughts I do.

In fact, we talked about it for a long time tonight, and we decided to make a picture book for Davey with pictures of you, Will, the Merrills, Marc and I, and his Grandma and Grandpa Montaigne. Davey is showing interest in picture books, so I think this will help to put you two in his mind and hopefully in his heart as well.

May 4th

Dear Mary,

Spring is here, and Shannon and I have time now that the opera is over to go exploring! Tuesday we went to the Sacre-Coeur in the Montmarte district. Montmarte, as you probably already know, is where part of *Louise* takes place, and I wanted to see it for myself since that is the next opera the directors are discussing for fall production.

The Sacre-Coeur is every bit as beautiful as the Notre Dame but somehow has a different ambience. The mosaic of Christ with outstretched arms, the smell of waxy candles, and the statues of saints, such as the Virgin Mary and Joan of Arc, all are so uplifting to ponder.

How can people see something like the beautiful mosaic of Christ and not realize that religion can indeed be a very personal relationship with God? I was also struck with the symbolism of having a cathedral called the Sacred Heart of Christ that sits on a hill overlooking the entire city of Paris.

Thankfully, Shannon listens to my passionate outbursts, and I even think she tends to agree with me.

We walked around the Montmarte district, enjoying the sights, sounds, and smells of Paris in the spring. Montmarte is an exquisite gem in the setting of Paris, with a quaint, old-world atmosphere all its own. The artsy people like to spend their time in the square here that is surrounded on all four sides by whimsical shops and cafes. One café had hand-painted vines and grapes twining around the windows and door.

We could smell a delightful mix of coffee, meats, and pastries all around us, so who could resist stopping for tea? We sat at an outside table watching the artists trying to con tourists into having their pictures painted—they are really quite good, too—and enjoying small white clouds scudding by in the blue sky ahead of a sun-warmed breeze.

The trees around the square were in bloom with tiny white and yellow flowers and large stone urns overflowed with a riot of purple, pink, white, blue, red and yellow blossoms.

May 17th
Dear Mary,
My exploring with Shannon was short-lived. She auditioned for a part in *Andrea Chenier* and made it. She is to be the Countess de Coigny. So now we spend our mornings practicing her music, and if I'm lucky, I get to drag her to the Jardins in the afternoon.

Marc is playing the part of Andrea Chenier, of course, so when I am not listening to her practicing, I listen to Marc. He is working on the *Improvisso*, the beautiful aria from Act I right now. I get chills up and down my spine listening to him, and when I begin to ponder the political nuances of this play, I get even more chills.

I've been studying French history lately, and this country has spilt more blood, not just in the pursuit of freedom, but in the pursuit of what is perceived to be freedom when it is not, than many other countries.

And blood is still being spilt. We live so close to the Universite de Paris and the Sorbonne that I overhear certain things being discussed by the inquiring minds of students. One of the hottest topics right now is Algeria's determination to gain independence. I hope this doesn't result in more bloodshed.

Even bigger news than this is that the Kennedys are to visit Paris at the end of this month, and the entire city is readying itself with an almost giddy anticipation. The biggest questions are "What will Jacqueline Kennedy be like?" and more importantly, "What will Jacqueline Kennedy be wearing?"

What a unique city! Fashion and freedom being discussed with equal passion!

Chapter Thirty-One

May 25th

Dear Mary,

Marc surprised me by taking me for a three-day, two-night trip to the French Riviera for our one-year anniversary! We stayed in a little town called Menton since neither of us is into exotic hedonism.

The town does have its touristy side which we tried to avoid. It reminded me somewhat of San Francisco with its hills and beaches. We enjoyed several walks on the beach, exquisite sunrises and sunsets over the Mediterranean, luscious meals, and passionate love-making. Davey stayed with Gretta and Michel, and I missed him, but I wouldn't trade the wonderful time with Marc for anything.

June 5th

Dear Mary,

Davey took his first steps this past weekend while we were at Marc's parent's house! It was the third, exactly nine months from his birth date. It was so exciting! I bought a camera recently, so I took pictures of his debut.

It occurred right after *diner*. We were all seated in the living room, enjoying our coffee. He had pulled himself up to a standing position beside the coffee table, looking at us with these huge expectant eyes. Balancing himself, he took three steps and then collapsed against the sofa, holding on for dear life so he wouldn't fall.

He had everyone's complete attention! We all clapped for him. Gretta told Marc that he wasn't the only performer in the family!

We watched the broadcast of the Kennedy's visit. Jacqueline is very beautiful and very chic. All of Paris is in love with her. It made me feel proud of America.

June 13th
Dear Mary,
I've been asked to help out at the Opera House again. Do I have the energy for this? Davey will be more of a handful to watch now that he's walking. And I do value the quiet times I get to spend keeping my home and exploring Paris. On the other hand, sometimes it becomes too quiet when Shannon can't come over, and when Marc is so busy.

Feeling closer to Marc because I understand his work better and because we can spend more time together is another bonus, an important one for me. Some days I feel as if I'm the luckiest woman on earth to be married to such a wonderful man.

He is so good-looking with his dark hair and eyes, but more important to me is his kind, but passionate spirit. I never in all my dreams imagined that I would have so much to be thankful for when I had so much going against me in experiencing such a great love.

My childhood was so much different than yours was. I've always said the right things to you because you are my little sister, and I felt responsible for you. But my soul was so dark with hatred and anger and bitterness; despair, too. And yet, look at what I've been given. Life is amazing! Someday I'll tell you more about it.

June 20th

Dear Mary,

Paris is abuzz with the news: Nureyev, the great ballet dancer, has defected from Russia! It happened last Friday at the Le Bourget Airport. As they were getting ready to board the plane, he broke away from the people he was with, ran toward the police, and cried, "Protect me!" Very dramatic.

Madame Tousselaire and the other ballet dancers who work at the Opera de Garnier are ecstatic. He is a marvelous dancer, and now that he has been granted asylum by France, he will be performing with some of them. There is talk of including him in *Sleeping Beauty*, the ballet they are readying for performance.

Meanwhile, *Andrea Chenier* opens in slightly over two weeks, the weekend before Bastille Day. Most of the actors are familiar with this play since it is based on France's history, so things are progressing rather smoothly. It should be a grand production.

July 25th

Dear Mary,

Another astounding success at the Opera de Garnier! Marc brought the house down with his performance! "Never has the part of Andrea been performed with such fire and passion," said the newspaper. I am so lucky to be part of such a charmed circle.

Shannon was wonderful, too. She has a natural acting ability, and her voice is ripening into a full woman's voice.

She has a husky lower range that she's cleaning up, but her upper range, now that she is using her diaphragm and all of her head passages, is becoming more and more clear and round.

The directors have asked her to sign a contract with them for a year. She will probably say yes as it has been a dream she never thought was attainable. Her employers will probably release her condescendingly, feeling that they have saved little Phillip from a life of immoral associations!

Wouldn't it be great if she and Marc sang opposite each other? She has kept her family in the dark until now; I expect they'll come to as many performances as possible once they hear the news.

Davey's vocabulary is growing. He now calls me "Maman," and when he sees your picture, he calls you "Mommy" and Will he calls "Daddy" although with a French accent. He is going to be one well-connected kid when he grows older and is finally able to meet and know you and Will.

August 3rd
Dear Mary,
One more month and your dear boy will be a year old. I can't believe how fast time has gone by, nor can I believe how Europeanized I've become. Another European would laugh at me, I suppose, but I feel as if I've grown so much in the eleven months I've been here.

My French has improved, my worldview has changed, and I feel so much more confident. I think I have matured from a scared, little girl into a young, capable woman.

Davey is very affectionate but only when others are not around. Yesterday he had been playing quietly with his wooden building blocks while Shannon was sharing her good news—she is to be released by her current employers at the end of this month and will begin working with the opera in September! I am thrilled for her!

While we were standing at the open door saying final good-byes, Davey stood watching with a block in his hand. As soon as the door closed, he ran to me, hugging me around the knees. Then he went quietly back to playing with his blocks! It was so cute!

Most of Paris is on vacation this month. Marc is talking about two weeks on the coast or in the mountains of Germany. I think I'd rather go to Germany. Too many vacationers on the beach, and we went south to the Riviera in May for our anniversary.

August 22nd

Dear Mary,

Just returned from two wonderful weeks in Germany! Very restful and relaxing. We have both learned to take things slower with a little child around. Davey enjoyed walking between us, holding our hands or being carried in a little knapsack contraption on Marc's back. You and Will would really enjoy all the hiking trails. I didn't realize how much people enjoy that sort of thing over here.

Before we left, the Montaignes threw a huge combination birthday party for Marc and me with all of our friends from the opera as well as many family friends. They waited until *Andrea Chenier* was over since we were crazily busy before the show.

I don't think I've ever been to such a large party before this one. It was intoxicatingly fun! They have a largish patio area in the back with slabs of black stone on the ground, wrought-iron patio tables, benches and chairs, and huge trees as well as smaller bushes and flowers. Both Gretta and Michel enjoy gardening, and it can be seen in this beautiful garden setting. They strung little lights up for the party and hired an eight-piece string ensemble for the evening.

I met some more of the family friends, including Gretta's colleagues at the teaching hospital where she works, two members of the police force, several medical doctors, and a number of the professors from the Universite where Michel teaches French Literature.

He also delves into philosophy quite often, and I noticed that a passionate discussion was occurring as Marc and I went outside to dance. I told Marc how fascinating it would be to curl up in a corner and just listen to them. He told me he had heard it all his life, but I was welcome to listen whenever I pleased; just leave him out!

At the end of the evening, Paul and Natalie made their announcement about being *en famile*! Their baby is due in February. Gretta and Michel are thrilled that they will be grandparents, and Nadia is, of course, in raptures that she will have another baby to care for whenever they will allow her. I see her as a kindergarten teacher, but time will tell.

September 6th
Dear Mary,
Davey's first birthday party was enjoyable! Gretta, always outgoing, wanted to throw it, so I let her. And with Nadia to help, very little was left for me to do. We played several childhood games, ate little cakes (petit fours), drank

quantities of punch and opened gifts. Gretta had a gift for each child to open.

Gretta also had something up her sleeve. She invited Philip's parents, as well as Shannon. It seems that Gretta has some clout in this city, and a social invitation to her grandson's birthday party is not to be dismissed.

So they came, expecting the worst, I'm sure, but Gretta's charm and Nadia's sweetness dispelled their fears, for now they profess themselves to be avid opera fans and can't wait "to see dear Shannon perform."

I very nearly burst out laughing, but Gretta accepted it as a matter of course, praised Shannon's vocal abilities, and insinuated an invitation to a soiree she will give following the last performance of *Louise*, so they are now dedicated patrons of the arts!

Speaking of *Louise*, Marc is hard at work on the part of Julien, and Shannon will play the principal part of Louise, opposite Marc.

Shannon is both tremendously excited and understandably nervous, but she has plenty of time to work on her arias, much more time than Mary Garden who, as an understudy, stepped into the role one evening when the leading soprano took ill, winning instant success. That happened in April 1900.

I am helping Shannon three days each week down at the Garnier. She also has the added pressure of wanting to sing well for her family who are all very proud of her and will be, for the first time, attending an opera in which she performs.

Decembre 11th

Dear Mary,

Louise has been a great success. It was billed as a "poignant picture of Paris" with "impressionistic music and a passionate pair of lovers." The alliteration is NOT mine! The publicists must have spent hours dreaming up all those "p's! Shannon was absolutely priceless—oh no! They've got me going, too! She brought down the house with her breathtaking rendition of *Depuis le jour*.

Shannon's family joined us at Gretta and Michel's following the final production. Her family is incredible— filled with joie de vivre and so close together in spirit.

Emil and Jake are the two oldest of Shannon's brothers. Emil has blond hair, Jake's is very dark; Emil is talkative, Jake is very quiet. Both are married, and both have two children each, left back in Ireland. Taking time out from the construction business they own was difficult, and they are returning tomorrow. But the rest of the family will be staying until early Wednesday morning.

Jenny and Janice come next. I expect I'll get to know them better when we all do some early Christmas shopping together tomorrow before they leave.

Shannon's mother arranged for someone to take care of their kids so they could have some time off. Between them, they have five children, "good, Catholic boys and girls, everyone," according to Mother McKinnon. Rather short and rather plump, but with a gleam in her eye and a ready smile, she exuded a vivacious friendliness and grace.

After Jenny and Janice were born, Denton came along, then Shannon. Donnell and Joey are her two younger brothers. Denton is engaged to a wonderful girl named Alice who came with him (Jenny and Janice kept teasing him about being his chaperones; I think Alice became tired of it, but she smiled and changed the subject. Dennie told them to "bugger off," so they finally ceased their teasing.)

Donnell and Joey are "still looking" according to Mother McKinnon. They are of medium build, sharing that same rich, mahogany hair that Shannon has. Donnell has an air of deep purposefulness about him; I found out that he is in some kind of intelligence unit in Ireland. Joey seems restless, as if he hasn't quite found his niche in life.

Gretta left the small lights up out on the patio, so early in the evening Father McKinnon danced with "his girls" and even his boys. He is an energetic, gregarious man, full of good humor and jokes.

Later in the evening following a delicious buffet dinner, we discovered how musical this family is. Marc and Shannon had schemed to bring some instrumental tapes of Irish music.

When they began playing, first one and then another of them would burst into song, and soon they were all singing wild, gay melodies or throbbingly tender tunes. A few of them danced as they sang, and I soon began to realize where Shannon's love for music had originated.

They pulled us into the dancing and singing with some well-known opera tunes as well as into their lives with their friendly teasing and loving jokes. I know Gretta and Michel, Natalie and Paul, Margaretta and Nadia enjoyed them as much as Marc and I did.

And I now have a deeper understanding of and appreciation for my dear friend, Shannon.

Chapter Thirty-Two

Decembre 14th
Dear Mary,

We had our girls' Christmas shopping day Tuesday. Shopping with Janice and Jenny, Shannon's older sisters, was a blast! Evidently they had been saving up their "mad money" as they called it for this excursion.

Nadia, Natalie, Margaretta and I were agog watching these two pranksters in action. They had a list between them with the name of every member of their family and suggested gag gifts as well as serious gifts for each.

We headed first to the Place de la Madeleine. Gretta has been experimenting with mustard in her cooking, so I bought a set of twelve different types of mustard for her to try. I also bought her a box of chocolates with a generous portion of truffles, her favorite.

Over in the corner of the store, Jenny began to giggle. Janice hurried over to her, and Jenny held up some eggs. They looked real, but she suddenly threw one at Janice. The panicked look on Janice's face was comical once we realized that the egg was rubber.

"Ooh. This will be perfect, love, for Mum. Maybe we can try them out on Donnie and Joey first," Janice said in her lovely Irish accent. "You know. Bachelors. And they won't tell Mum if we get to them first."

"Okay. Let's buy a dozen. And let's get this apron for Da that says "Kiss the Cook." He and Mum ought to have loads of fun with that one," replied Jenny.

"C'mon you two," said Shannon. "We have a lot more shopping to do. You see what I have to put up with when I go home?" she said to me. "They were really impressed with your trick last Christmas."

"That wasn't a trick, Shannon. I honestly didn't suspect that you'd open it in front of everyone."

"I know," she said giving me a quick hug. "But you've left them with the impression that you have impeccable taste and a wonderful sense of humor to boot."

We continued our shopping expedition with much laughter, hilarity, and fun. Davey was wide-eyed at the window displays at Au Printemps and Galeries Lafayette. He especially enjoyed the Christmas elves in one window doing all kinds of mechanical movements making toys for girls and boys all over the world.

I must say, I was fascinated by the display, too. In every single corner the elves were doing something different whether it was nailing a toy boat together or dropping a completed toy train into Santa's bag.

Gretta joined us at a little bistro called Bistro Le Sancerre. We started out with *soupe a l'oignon* (onion soup) and moved to *canard with legumes* (duck with vegetables). Absolutely delicious.

Following our relaxing meal, we decided to shop the Champ Elysee. With so many stores to shop, we decided to section off each four to six shops, meeting out in front every twenty to thirty minutes or so. That way, each person could shop the stores they wanted, yet we could still stay together.

I found a pair of boots that Shannon was ogling, making sure first that Janice and Jenny wouldn't purchase them for her. Giggling, they added two pairs of net stockings to go with the sexily heeled black boots. The store also had some beautiful leather coats. Gretta helped me choose a beautiful black coat for Marc, and I added some soft, black, kid-skin gloves, too.

At another store, we found some beautiful linens-- towels, sheets, and pillowcases--for Paul and Natalie. Gretta was in alt over the silky, soft smoothness of them, so I knew Natalie would enjoy them. We just had to add some linens in a pale yellow for the coming baby as well.

Nadia is always easy to buy for: her eyes lit up over clothes in every store. I found a cute sweater and skirt set for her, even adding some stockings, shoes, and earrings.

Margaretta had requested a watch, and Marc and I had been elected to do the honors. Finding one that was not just beautiful but had a second hand for all those pulses she would be taking was a challenge, but with Gretta's help, we both settled on one that was perfect.

Jenny and Janice came giggling out of the next set of stores. They had found a box of rubber nails for Emil and Jake in a theatrical supply store, and a police "mike" that repeated "Hands up or I'll shoot" for Donnie.

They had also somewhere along the way discovered a huge fake diamond ring for Denton and Alice. I hoped Alice and Dennie would take it in the fun it was intended.

Shannon let me in on her secret. She had persuaded both Janice and Jenny to buy huge brassieres for each other as gag gifts. She knew they had bought something outlandish for her, so she had plans to get them back with some lacy underwear and some teddy bears—don't ask; they have a thing about teddy bears!

I had already found my gift for Michel in a quaint little used bookstore in the St. Germain area. It was a set of two rare edition books by one of his most admired American authors, Hemingway. I know Michel will be thrilled.

By then it was half past four and time to head back to Gretta and Michel's home to avoid the metro rush hour. We had agreed to meet the men there to freshen up and prepare for diner, including Shannon's wonderful family in our annual holiday celebration dinner at the Bistro Charrone.

The evening was magical with the murmur of contented voices, the muted sound of silver against crystal, the intoxicating aromas of excellent food, and above all the feeling of absolute bliss in belonging and being a part of these two special families. I have a feeling that the McKinnons and the Montaignes will continue as family friends for a very long time.

Decembre 15th
Dear Mary,
The apartment is all decorated, the gifts are all wrapped, and we are ready for Christmas. Marc has been going in half days since *Louise*, to begin work on *Rigoletto*.

He teasingly says he doesn't want the costumers to be without work so close to Christmas.

He also said he doesn't want me to feel let down with the departure of Shannon and her McKinnon clan, so we are going to a ballet tonight. I'm so excited! I've not seen much ballet. It has mainly been opera for me. Marc's friend in the ticket booth finagled the tickets for us, box seats up on stage left of the house.

But he wasn't finished surprising me. He took me shopping this morning for a dress, a gorgeous midnight blue with shoes to match. We enjoyed a leisurely dejeuner at a little restaurant close to the pont Neuf and the Samaritaine with Marc treating me like a prized and delicate piece of crystal. The intense look in his eyes made me feel deliciously quivery inside.

When we came home, he brought out a large box for me to open, and I found a beautiful dark fur coat inside. Obviously, he's had a very successful season, and he's going to spoil me rotten, but I have to admit, I love it!

He had to slowly spin me to the bed wrapped in the soft, silky furs, and after a wonderful kiss, I asked him why he was regarding me so intensely. He said that it had occurred to him that if he studied me like he studied his opera scores, doing his best to make me happy, we'd have a terrific relationship.

"If every man studied his woman, devoting himself to making her happy, the divorce rate would decline rapidly," I said as I snuggled closer in his embrace. "Women, well, most women," I amended, "would treat their men like kings if they were treated like queens, just like I'm going to treat you now!"

Decembre 19th

Dear Mary,

We've had so much more time to relax now that the opera season is off. Marc and I are enjoying Davey so much.

He is picking up new words daily. He calls me "Maman" and Marc "Papa." He calls Nadia "Nadi." He asks for his "ba" or bottle, his "ba ba" or blanket, and his "ball." He is learning "no" but really, Mary, he is so eager to please that I don't have to use that word too often.

It's really cute to watch Marc get down on the floor and build towers with Davey's blocks or make "vroom, vroom" noises playing with the cars and trucks Davey has. His favorite game is rolling his red ball back and forth.

He is also learning to point to parts of his body like his nose, his eyes, his mouth, his toes. It is his favorite game with Gretta because she'll end up tickling him, sending him into peals of laughter!

It was a good thing Marc and I had box seats last Friday evening. Once people recognized him, we were the object of every set of opera glasses and every set of eyes. I am so glad I had a new dress. Visitors kept coming to the box before the performance and at intermission. At least they had the courtesy of not coming during the performance.

Marc and I had to leave early or we would have been swamped. It was like losing a tail. When we were sure we had lost anyone who recognized him, we collapsed in laughter in the car we had borrowed from Michel for the evening.

We spent the weekend at their house. Gretta had already picked up Davey, and Marc had packed a few things for us, so we drove straight there after losing any paparazzi at the ballet.

Gretta wasn't quite finished decorating for Christmas, so we spent a quiet weekend decorating, wrapping gifts, and enjoying some real French cuisine.

January 10th
Dear Mary,
It's a brand new year! I always wonder what a new year will bring. When I was younger, I viewed new years with skepticism, but now I am cautiously optimistic.

Ironically, I still have a difficult time believing all this happiness and joy I've been given can really be mine, and I can't help feeling that some awful being—I won't say God because I believe God gives us good things and only allows bad things to promote our growth—will snatch it all away from me, and I'll be lost in sadness and misery forever.

So I think my goal for this year is to truly enjoy my blessings without feeling guilty, without feeling selfish, and without feeling as if a huge iron ball will crash down on me any minute sweeping it all away.

January 16th
Dear Mary,
Marc received a tremendous offer in the mail today: he has been invited to sing at Covent Gardens in London! His hard work is paying off! He is so thrilled! We telephoned his

parents immediately and then met to celebrate over diner at the Bistro Charrone.

The ticklish part is to approach the directors correctly. Marc's exclusive contract with them will be up in August; this invitation is for November. He wants to continue to work here in Paris, but he also wants the freedom to perform in other "operatically important cities" as he puts it, as well.

Michel, the philosopher, is sure things will work out fine as they always have, but Gretta really has a keen business head. She and Marc wrangled over finer points until they nearly got into an argument.

She patted his hand and said, "I just want you to be prepared for any obstacles you encounter, dear. I'm sure you'll be able to come to a workable agreement."

I will be on nails for the next week or so, I'm sure.

January 26th
Dear Mary,
What an explosive week and a half. Marc's request, simple enough, caused a furor with the directors. They called three emergency meetings before finally agreeing to release Marc to work with other opera houses.

This shouldn't have come as such a surprise to them. He is their biggest star and greatest asset, though Shannon should become a huge moneymaker for them as well.

And that is where the rub comes, I suppose. They are loathe to lose the financial gain that Marc inevitably brings. He is promised for *Rigoletto* this spring and *Carmen* late summer, but is released to do *Aida* again in the fall in London.

Incredibly, another offer has come in for Marc to perform *Tosca* in Rome in February of next year. Of course, he will accept. It is a dream come true!

Gretta and Michel are, of course, thrilled for their son, and Gretta is scouting around for an agent. She thinks that sooner or later Marc will need one. Shannon declares that she will use the agent Gretta engages, as well.

Meantime, Marc has buried himself in preparing for his part as the Duke of Mantua in *Rigoletto*. Shannon has the part of Rigoletto's daughter, Gilda. We are working on her aria, *Caro Nome*, in the mornings as well as her part in the quartet.

She also has some duet work with Marc. Although he works better rehearsing by himself at the Opera House with his instructor, he has agreed to work a few mornings each week with Shannon here at home when they've both learned the music separately.

Davey is his precious self. His vocabulary is growing to include numbers. He is so proud of himself when he recognizes numbers while we are walking or riding about, and he will sit still longer now to look at books. He also loves to color pictures in his coloring book.

February 10th
Dear Mary,
Emily Anne was born yesterday afternoon at 3:10 p.m. Mother and daughter are doing great, but Paul is still weak-kneed and in disbelief of how tiny yet perfectly formed his daughter is.

Natalie looked like a picture of the Madonna as she bent to kiss Emily on the forehead. It reminded me so much of you when Davey was born. It's incredible to even think about missing out on the wonderful life I have here in Paris, but honestly Mary, I'd give up at least some of it to know where you are and what you are doing.

Have you gone to the safe place we talked about as girls, or are you lost, alone, and miserable? I feel it is the latter because if you had found your way out of your ice castle of frozen misery to Will, you'd be over here in a heartbeat to complete your family with Davey.

You always were more independent and stubbornly proud than I was, and it will prevent you from searching for Will. You will expect him to come and find you. There is a point when pride must give way, or you will miss out on some of the most precious years of your life.

But who am I to preach? It took me long enough to break away. Each person dealing with emotional dysfunction is on a different time schedule of overcoming their past. I just hope it doesn't take you too long.

And Mother Sebastiani at our safe place (you will know the place I'm talking about) will know where you are. She told me to stay focused on creating my new life here in Paris, and I've done that. I think it's time to make sure you are all right.

******

Wait a minute, I thought! Robyn was writing as if she had been in contact with Mother Sebastiani during her first year in France. How could that be? I had to know more. Almost feverishly I kept reading.

Chapter Thirty-Three

February 12th

Dear Mary,

Some terrible things have been happening in Paris these days. Marc has invested in a car, and he has forbidden me to use the metro for a while.

On January thirty-first someone planted a bomb at the Foreign Ministry, killing a mailroom worker and injuring quite a few others. Then on February eighth, another bomb exploded at the home of the Cultural Affairs Minister, Andre Malraux, and protestors stormed the Metro crushing eight people to death.

It is all over Algeria's bid for independence from France. Some people will stop at nothing to prevent Algeria from gaining their independence. I don't know much about French politics, but I do value our lives, and I honor Marc's care for our little family.

He and his parents have even talked about us closing down our flat for a little while and staying at their home along with Paul and Natalie and the new baby. They have even welcomed Shannon so she won't have to travel the Metro by herself. We can work on the music at their house, and when she needs to go in to the Opera House, she and Marc can travel together.

It is a generous offer, and though I will miss our little flat, I think they are right. Marc is especially concerned because we live so close to several Universities, and students tend to get very riled up and passionate about causes. This seems to be an even more serious issue than usual.

I just hope Natalie will be all right with it. Sometimes when you have a new baby, you need time for just you and your baby without people hovering. Gretta is usually very intuitive about these sensitive kinds of things, so we should be able to settle on a workable solution.

Well, onward with the packing.

February 16th
Dear Mary,
We are all ensconsed here at the Montaigne home. They have six bedrooms plus a little three-room cottage in the back with a bedroom, sitting/kitchen area, and bathroom. Michel uses it for an office, but they let us use it since there are three of us and no baby.

Natalie didn't seem to mind. And now Shannon, Marc, and I can yodel to our hearts' content without feeling as if we are bothering the others, especially the baby. We have established a routine of sorts that seems to work well for everyone.

Michel, Gretta, Margaretta, and Paul rise first and breakfast. Margaretta travels with Michel into the city where he drops Paul off and then Margaretta, later picking her up directly at her building and then doing the same with Paul. Gretta goes in with them on the days she needs to be there. She is fortunate to be able to set her own schedule much of the time.

Natalie quit her job a few weeks before her due date. She works on a pair of needlepoint pillows when she is not caring for Emily Anne, or she reads.

Shannon is a slug-a-bed, so I knock on her door, and we usually enjoy morning coffee together. About an hour later, we congregate in the sitting room of our cottage. By then Marc is up and about with Davey. He has decided to stay here several mornings each week and work with us so there is a man about, at least this first week. I'm sure he'll get too bored eventually.

We are accomplishing a great deal actually. When Marc needs to work separately, he goes up to the main house while Shannon and I work on her pieces here. Natalie comes sometimes to listen with her cross-stitching.

In the afternoons, Shannon and I take walks down toward the Seine with Davey. She has confessed that she does miss Phillip though she wouldn't go back to being a nanny after gaining such an entry into the opera world.

I tell her she needs to find a man, but she just laughs and says she hasn't found anyone worth dating although there are a few young men at the opera who have caught her eye.

March 20th
Dear Mary,
We are back in our flat! I enjoyed staying at the Montaignes, watching Emily grow—she is already turning over onto her back and lifting her upper body with her arms—and seeing everyone in the family on a daily basis, but I'm glad to be back, too.

A truce has been signed, ending the war between the Algerians and the French. Maybe we can all get on with our lives now.

Less than a week until opening night and everyone is frantic as usual. Shannon is learning to keep her poise. She is ready with her music and so is Marc. The problem is with the gunnysack scene.

Shannon simply can't stand having that gunnysack over her head. When they first put it over her, it was so dusty and smelly that she nearly died of dust inhalation. It had to be sent down to the costumers to be washed. It is difficult for her to sing her final farewell with a tickle in her throat from the smell of the gunnysack.

Davey has discovered climbing now. While we were at the Montaignes, I found him one morning trying to climb up on top of the piano. Marc was in the bathroom shaving.

When I'm at the Opera House, and they call me frequently to help, I have to have someone watch him constantly now. We caught him trying to climb up one of the ladders that leads up to the catwalk for the lights. The costumers are the ones who usually help, and they don't mind taking a break from the work they are doing to watch him for thirty minutes at a time.

Davey has two teddy bears that he received at Christmas from Gretta and Nadia, and yesterday, one of the costumers, Elena, called for me to come quick. He had propped them up on either side of him on the piano bench in the ballet practice room. He would play the piano a little, but when one of the teddy bears slid down, he stopped, shook his finger at it and said, "No, no!" He propped it up, played a little more, then stopped and said "Sing!" It was so cute!

He is still unsteady on his feet, so if there is no one to help him, he will push his laundry basket of toys around to balance himself. He is nearly potty trained by now. He will come running and tell us if he needs to use the bathroom.

April 3rd

Dear Mary,

Rigoletto was another smash hit! The directors are beside themselves with joy, and it was a fun opera to do, but we are all rather glad it is finished.

I think though, that both Marc and Shannon were so well prepared with their music this time that they were able to concentrate more on the acting and putting the scenes across to the audience. It was certainly very well received and highly acclaimed by the critics.

Word has leaked out that Marc will be performing in London later this year and then in Rome. It has given him more notoriety, so the performances were even better attended than usual. He is nearly as popular as a movie star now, a situation with both an up and a down side.

The up side is the same as the down side: popularity. It is nice to receive notice for a well-done job, but too much notice interferes with our lives sometimes. Now that he has a small car, Marc is thinking of purchasing a house out toward Avon near his parents. It will be more of a commute, but should provide a quieter lifestyle for us.

Maybe then the teenaged girls will stop following him, begging for his autograph and giggling. Marc can't stand the giggling. I must say though that he is nice about it. He says that although they giggle much of the time, they still bring in ticket sales, and he must never forget that they do.

April 10th

Dear Mary,

Spring has arrived in Paris, Marc and I have more time to spend together, and I'm so happy that I just have to write about it! We have been house hunting together for several days now, and the countryside is just gorgeous! It is refreshing to get away from the hordes in the city.

One house in particular we keep returning to see. It looks Bavarian in style on the outside. Inside, it has four bedrooms, a studio, a kitchen, separate dining room, living room and two baths. Trees surround it because it is built on a hillside overlooking the town of Avon. I can see just a tiny part of the Fontainebleau castle from the kitchen window.

If we want to go for a walk, we can loiter down the road, or we can hike into the Fontainebleau forest via our backyard. It is a little pricey, I think, but Marc says we can afford it, and it is only fifteen minutes from his parent's house.

April 17th

Dear Mary,

We bought the house! The transaction transpired quickly because the house has been vacant for four months and the owner relocated to London. Hopefully we will be moved in by the end of this month. Marc has already begun work on *Carmen*, and I need to work with Shannon on her pieces.

Shannon is getting top billing now, and people are beginning to recognize her in the streets as well. Actually, it isn't difficult with the beautiful red hair she has. Gretta has found an agent for both of them, and Shannon hopes she will soon get some international offers like Marc has.

Davey is priceless. He likes to line up all of his toys, especially his bears. The other day he pretended to feed them. Somehow he had found a spoon, and he offered each one some pretend food, saying, "Num, num!"

May 8th
Dear Mary,
Our little house has received an Irish blessing and a French housewarming. Gretta threw a surprise dinner and party for us last week after Marc, Shannon, and I had been at the theatre most of the day. It began with just the family for dinner with friends of the family and from the theatre dropping in after dinner.

Of course, with Gretta, things flow smoothly, but they develop, and before the evening was over, pockets of people were discussing philosophy, politics, opera, and books while others were dancing or refilling their plates with the heavy hors d'oeuvres Gretta likes to serve.

Marc and Shannon have begun work on *Carmen*. Marc sang some of these pieces during his pre-San Francisco days, and Shannon has often belted out these numbers at the top of her lungs in the McKinnon living room at home in Ireland. Actually, of the two parts, I think Shannon's part as Carmen is much more demanding than Marc's part of Don Jose.

The director, M. Rouleau, wants Shannon to concentrate on the drama, the acting skills necessary for this opera, so the music must be like her second skin: so well-known, she can sing it without any thought. Her personality is much more flamboyant than mine, perfect for this work by Bizet.

I usually help with the costuming, but M. Rouleau wants my input coordinating the acting and music for Shannon's pieces. It is an honor to be allowed to help out with this aspect of the production although I did train extensively in this area at the Conservatory.

The costuming is going to be outstanding. With Shannon's fair coloring and rich, deep-red hair, the costumers are going with emerald green and a shimmering deep purple color contrasted with red for her gypsy costume.

May 15th
Dear Mary,
There is so much energy these days at the Opera House. We have a little over a month until production, but everyone from the set construction crew to the music director and the orchestra to the cast, has a feeling about this production. This is the big one, the one that is going to revitalize the entire theatre scene.

The press that Marc, and now Shannon, has received began the upward trend of interest in the opera. It was a bold gamble, to bill Marc as the returning son of France, but it sparked the press's interest, and put a stop to the decline.

The electricity of *Carmen*, however, is going to bring the interest to a very definite crescendo. The public following has been building, and though work hours are long, we are all eager to make this the best performance France has ever seen.

Davey spends so much time with us at the O (we've adopted Shakespeare's name for the theatre), that it's like his second home. Most of the time, we are at the Opera de Garnier like we are for *Carmen*, but there is talk of using the Garnier exclusively for ballet and moving operas to the Theatre du Chatelet or the Opera-Comique.

Anyway, Elena, one of the costumers, has become our favorite caretaker for Davey here at the opera. She has been so helpful that Marc and I are going to give her a bonus check at the end of production. We also have a new babysitter if by any chance Gretta, Michel or Nadia can't do it.

June 18th

Dear Mary,

A little over a week away from production and the atmosphere at the O simply crackles with excitement. When the cast and crew are this keyed up, the danger of the production stumbling and falling flat is even greater. Perhaps two days off before production will help.

The other problem is more international in scope. Tensions have escalated again in Algeria. Many "panicked Europeans" are leaving the violence there. The bottom line for us is to, as always, go on with the show.

July 10th

Dear Mary,

The show was a phenomenal success! The press is ranting about the ravishing performances, the rousing music, the rare and refreshing acting.

For the first time, Shannon received more raves than Marc did. And she was truly remarkable. She scorned, she flirted, she seduced, she scintillated with colors and with passion. After the first night, all succeeding performances were sold out.

The directors' plan to stick to well-known operas has worked. When they discovered that Marc is doing *Aida* in

London in September, they asked, no begged, him to consider performing it two weeks later the first of October here in Paris. Marc is seriously considering it. With the huge success and rise in opera attendance, he feels he has a vested interest in ensuring its continued success.

Gretta made sure the McKinnons knew of the expected success of this performance. Jenny and Janice couldn't both come, so Jenny agreed to stay home with the children. Emil and Jake were both able to come. They brought their wives, Maggie and Jillian, respectively, for a small vacation.

Denton and Alice came. They have invited us to their wedding on the twenty-sixth of this month. Denton said he had to drag Alice along; she has been so overwhelmed by wedding preparations, she needed a break. Joey came, but Donnie is working on a top-secret case. They weren't even able to contact him to tell him about their plans.

We all slept late after Saturday evening's final performance. Around two p.m. Sunday afternoon, we loaded Davey in the auto and headed to Gretta and Michel's house. The McKinnons arrived at the same time we did. And then did the fun begin!

Emil and Jake seemed to be serious businessmen last time they were here, but with their wives present, they were relaxed and full of jokes. They teased Shannon incessantly, but their pride in her was very evident.

As the eating slowed, the music began. What a sight and sound to hear the whole McKinnon and Montaigne clans singing the "Toreador Song" from the opera. A few fiddles appeared, and then the dancing began. When Emil and Jake tired of playing the fiddles, Father McKinnon and Dennie took over.

When the tunes slowed to dreamy and tender, Joey and Shannon took their turn so their parents could dance, Gretta and Michel joined them, and it was precious to watch Emil and Jake with their wives. Dennie swept Alice into his arms and then it was my turn with Marc. His ardent glances and tender touches promised a wonderful postlude to the evening.

Chapter Thirty-Four

July 23rd
Dear Mary,

We have arrived in Killarney, Ireland for Alice and Denton's wedding. Killarney is located in the southwestern tip of the island in County Kerry at the base of a beautiful mountain range. Even in the summer, the mists rise in the morning, imbuing each day with spirits of the past and blessings on the future.

We are to stay in one of the three cottages on their old farmstead. It belonged to Mother McKinnon's family, but since Father McKinnon does not have a knack for farming, Mother McKinnon established the McKinnon Cottages as a bed and breakfast/boarding house enterprise.

The cottages are small, but quaint and extremely cozy. The towels are large and fluffy, the soaps are scented, and each kitchenette has the basics of tea, coffee, sugar, and real cream directly from surrounding farms. I have never seen cream quite like this. It is not poured; it is spooned into the coffee!

Shannon met us at the airport in Cork. She says that Alice has everything under control. They want us to relax and enjoy ourselves, and, of course, we do want to do a lot of sightseeing. Shannon laughed when I said that, saying, "I'll send Da right over to you. He'll want to do the honors."

An hour after lunch spent in the main house with Shannon, Joey, and their parents, Father McKinnon had his jaunting car, a trap pulled by a pony, ready for us. He is a *jarvey* or tour guide during the high season. In the off-season, he told us he writes travel pieces for various magazines and lectures at the Killarney School of English. He has also had a book of Irish history published.

I am amazed! How did I miss all this? I am sure Gretta and Michel know about this literary side to Shannon's family. Why didn't I?

July 25th
Dear Mary,
It seems I am to learn many more things about Shannon's wonderful family. Last night we went to a pub called The Laurels where they had some traditional Irish singers. Some people called it a ceili.

We heard Julia Clifford sing, Seamus Ennis and Willie Clancy, both fantastic uilleann pipers, and Padraig O'Keefe on the fiddle. Later in the evening, Margaret Barry arrived. She sang, accompanying herself on a five-string banjo.

Some of the music was lively, encouraging the dancing of jigs and reels, while other music was sad and mournful over a lost love. Some of the words were difficult to understand, but I particularly enjoyed the music describing the history of the area.

Opera music is different, totally different. Irish music is like raw silk: unrefined emotions, but extremely pleasurable to the senses. Marc finds it restful that he can listen unrecognized.

July 28th

Dear Mary,

The wedding was absolutely beautiful with the McKinnon and O'Leary girls all in a rainbow of pastel colors. Denton was surrounded by his brothers and Alice's twin brothers, Danny and Davey O'Leary.

Following the ceremony, we were treated to some more Irish music and dancing, not to mention the wonderful home-cooked food. Mrs. O'Leary and Mother McKinnon must have spent several days preparing the Irish stew, roasted duck, and racks of venison. We also gorged on mussels, baked cod and salmon, and potato cakes as well as fresh homemade brown bread.

Alice and Dennie were radiant, but tired by the end of the evening. I can understand now why they chose a Thursday on which to be married instead of a Friday. It reminded me of my wedding somehow, except that they were surrounded by so many of their family members.

But I won't be filled with nostalgia or sadness. Instead, I remind myself fiercely of the wonderful family I have acquired since moving to France. If you and Will were here, I would have all the family I need.

Today we toured the Ross Castle, and then we drove over to Blarney Castle, touring the grounds and the castle. I didn't kiss the blarney stone. Someone has said that doing so is just an excuse to lie for the next seven years! I think they may be right.

Davey has charmed his shy but rambunctious way into the hearts of Shannon's extended family. Janice and Jennie both have volunteered to baby sit for us; one more won't bother either of them.

Their children have heard of his history, especially the older ones. They think his story is highly romantic and treat him like a young prince. He is very close to becoming spoiled. His sweet nature, I hope, will prevent this.

July 31st
Dear Mary,
We have regretfully put Ireland behind us though we take many fond memories of the scenery, the music, and, most of all, the people.

Now we are in London. Marc wanted to get a feel for the theatre and audience at the Royal Opera House. His new agent, Andre Mulligan, was able to obtain a flat for us in a neighboring area. He said the immediate area is rather shabby. When we went to view the theatre, it was easy to see his reasoning. Shabbiness is one thing, but the seediness of the people there was appalling.

The theatre itself is very old and very beautiful. Marc introduced himself to the costumers; they went ahead and took his measurements though I'm sure Andre has such things on file. He introduced me as important to the opera scene in Paris. After talking shop for nearly an hour, I could tell that they respected him. Not all opera singers are as nice to the costumers as Marc is.

August 31st

Dear Mary,

It is so good to be back home again! When Davey awoke yesterday morning, he walked around making delighted noises as he touched things familiar to him! It was so cute! He is very contented to play with familiar things.

Being tourists on the London scene was fun. We saw most of the sights for which London is famous: Buckingham Palace and the Changing of the Guard, Westminster Abbey, the Houses of Parliament, the Tower of London, and various museums.

We also enjoyed listening to some wonderful concerts all the way from informal jazz at some pubs in the evening to concerts in the parks and cathedrals.

Of course, Marc has a difficult time staying away from work, so he went several times to the Opera House to meet with the director of *Aida* and work on his music. I didn't mind. It gave Davey and me several idyllic mornings to ourselves.

Now we have one more month before Marc flies to London for the final weeks before his big debut there.

September 11th

Dear Mary,

What a busy month this is turning out to be! Gretta, Michel, and the whole family are delighted that we are back. Gretta threw a small party for Davey's second birthday with Phillip and Emily in attendance, as well as a few other children of family friends. The theme was outer space in celebration of the space age we are entering. The decorations of planets, spacecraft, and astronauts was too cute!

On the eighth, she turned right around and hosted a welcome back party for family and opera friends to celebrate our birthdays. Shannon's two younger brothers were visiting her. Joey may stay on as a technician at the opera, and Donnie at first said he was on vacation from his job, but later, while dancing with him, he admitted to being in Paris on official business.

Mum's the word with me. I just hope he isn't involved in anything dangerous. He assured me that he was basically here on a fact-finding mission; otherwise, he wouldn't stay anywhere near Shannon or us, putting us in any danger. "I wouldn't be telling you any of this either, if it were top secret!" he added wryly.

It was the longest conversation I've ever had with Donnie, and I felt afterward as if he is stable, strong, and stalwart, a person to trust when in dire circumstances.

October 8th

Dear Mary,

Marc left for London Friday evening, and I miss him so much already. Our relationship has deepened tremendously this year.

Of course, I have come down with some sort of bug. I have felt so nauseous lately. I must get more rest. Gretta, Michel, and I plan to fly to London for his performances. Nadia and Margaretta will stay at our house with Davey for the week we are gone, and I'm sure Gretta will want to do some strenuous shopping.

Davey did the cutest thing last week! Natalie brought Emily over with her for the afternoon. After her nap, Natalie gave Emily her bottle, but while Natalie was rinsing something at the sink, Emily began choking. Davey, all concerned, trotted over to her high chair and tried to pat her on the back. She gagged again and Davey patted her shoulder again. She caught her breath, and then they started giggling at each other. Children are precious!

October 15th
Dear Mary,

Sit down and take a deep calming breath: I'm pregnant! No wonder I have felt so nauseous in the mornings. I'm so excited! Wait until Marc hears! I can't tell him until after his last performance, but he'll probably guess with the beaming face I display.

We decided in May to start trying to have a baby, knowing that for most couples, it takes a year. We didn't expect this to happen so soon, but I'm so glad that it has. Marc was so wonderfully relaxed all summer long. We enjoyed such passion in Ireland and England, but apparently when we returned home, it happened.

Gretta is in alt, and Natalie is thrilled for me. Nadia is excited to have another niece or nephew to babysit, and Margaretta, who is a dear but rather reserved, just squeezed my hand when she heard the news. Shannon is relieved. She was very concerned about my "sickness," especially since she knows I want to see Marc's performances in London.

Fortunately, we leave on the plane in the late afternoon. With some ginger ale and crackers, I should make the trip easily enough.

November 25th

Dear Mary,

Morning sickness, bah, humbug. It's afternoon sickness and evening sickness as well, and it has had me gripped at the throat for nearly two months now. I have learned to carry a bowl with me wherever I go.

Davey has been a dear. "Maman sick?" he asks. Then he pats my head and holds my hand. He is old enough now to do simple tasks for me such as bringing me crackers or tissue. He has learned, out of necessity, to dress himself. Instead of the usual morning ritual of "What should we wear today?" I have learned to lay his clothes out in the evening when I seem to have more energy.

We still try to go out in the afternoons for a short walk. On one of our walks several weeks ago, we discovered a rock that soaks up the sunshine. It is about my height, but it must seem enormous to Davey. We sit on top of it and play a game called "How many things can we see?" It teaches Davey about things out in nature, and gives me a chance to rest.

Sometimes we bring along some cheese, crackers, and juice for a "picnic." I have become quite fond of cheese and other dairy products lately. At least my cravings don't include sardines with ice cream!

Marc was a tremendous success as the Egyptian soldier, Radames, who falls in love with Aida, the slave of the Egyptian princess, Amneris, who also loves Radames. Joan Sutherland sang the part of Aida, and in the final scene of the tomb where he is condemned to die, and where she has been awaiting him three days, their duet was so tender, it brought tears to my eyes.

Now Marc is singing it here in Paris, bringing in raves and filling the coffers. Shannon is singing the part of Aida, and again I am moved to tears. Is this part of pregnancy? Gretta assures me it is.

Gretta has given me some very helpful advice. She told me to do a load of laundry every day so that no matter how I felt, I could at least feel as if I had accomplished something. Actually, I try to do three things each day: a load of laundry, something with Davey, and a simple supper. Marc has been washing up the dishes whenever he is home. I am so thankful for his supportiveness.

Gretta and Natalie assure me that morning sickness doesn't last forever. I am two months along now, so maybe around Christmas, I'll feel better. I fervently hope so.

January 16th
Dear Mary,
Send up praises; I'm feeling much better! Marc did Christmas this year. He put up decorations, brought in a tree and decorated it, and bought gifts for his family. We spent quite a few cozy evenings snuggled together in front of the fireplace discussing what gifts to get each one. Then he shopped, brought them home for my approval, and we spent some more lovely evenings wrapping gifts together. The only gifts I had to buy were for Marc and Shannon.

Shannon, Gretta, Natalie, Nadia, Margaretta and I did our annual shopping. They pampered me, allowing me to sit often. Actually, I didn't mind a bit. It was enjoyable to sit watching people and admiring the decorations.

The Christmas story was very poignant for me this year. How did God ever allow His Son to come as a baby to this earth? Already my maternal instinct is so very strong.

Mary, how did you do it? How did you allow me to take your precious son all the way to the other side of the earth? Somewhere in your subconscious I think you must have realized the jeopardy in which your infant son was. Dad was determined to kill him.

I have not received word from Mother Sebastiani yet about you. I trust her implicitly, so I know that when she has news, she will send it along.

Marc is preparing for *Tosca*. He has the part of Cavaradossi, the painter who is killed for harboring a political fugitive. He will leave for Rome in several weeks, and we are both dreading the separation. He would love to back out of his contract for my sake, but I wouldn't dream of allowing him to sacrifice an international career for me. Davey, baby, and I will do fine, especially with all of the support from his family.

Chapter Thirty-Five

February 3rd

Dear Mary,

Marc left for Rome this morning and already I miss him. Thankfully, I am feeling much better. Saturday evening I felt the baby move for the first time! What a thrill! I am so glad Marc was there to share the moment.

I think so much of you and your pregnancy with each day I go through mine. I am so glad that Will was there for you at least through the first six months. You were so strong even at the end when he was gone. How did you do it, Mary? You are a marvel.

Shannon is working on *Lucia de Lammermoor*. It is an opera she has wanted to do, and now she gets the chance. Her natural flair for drama will enhance the "mad scene" in Act III. We are also working diligently on the beautiful aria and duet in the "fountain scene" when she and Edgardo profess their undying love before he leaves.

The directors have engaged Pierre Prilliou to sing the part of Edgardo. I will go into Paris to the O at the beginning of March to work with both of them on the duet. Performances begin March twentieth.

Meantime, Andre called to report that Marc has received offers from the Metropolitan Opera in New York and the San Francisco Opera. I invited Andre to dinner on the twenty-fifth so we can all sit down and discuss Marc's upcoming engagements.

I am due at the end of May, so we must work around the birth of our son or daughter. Nadia assures me that I am "cute as a crumb," but I just feel incredibly ponderous and heavy.

April 17th
Dear Mary,
Diner last evening with Andre was a lighthearted affair. Gretta insisted on providing the food. She and Michel came along with Nadia, who happily agreed to care for Davey during our "business discussion" as she called it, and Shannon, who has had several offers as well as Marc and wants our more experienced input.

I know I am becoming a greedy little piggy, but truly, the meal was delicious! Tender, rosy roast lamb redolent with aromatic herbs, served with baby carrots and small peas, salad greens with a special herbed mustard oil dressing, delicate cheese and yogurt (she usually includes a creamy yogurt following every meal, claiming that the active cultures aid digestion), and *pot de crème* for dessert.

Marc has been asked to play the part of Wilhelm in *Mignon* in July. Shannon has been asked to play the part of the actress Philene. She wanted the Mignon role, but they gave it to someone else. She has done such superb acting in gutsy, seductive, gypsy-type roles that they are beginning to type cast her into these roles automatically.

Andre, always calm and supremely efficient and confident, told her to make the most of these roles while she waits for an opportunity to prove that she can play the wilting, lovelorn, feminine heroine.

He encouraged both Marc and Shannon to accept these roles, stating that it is always good to stay on good terms with the company that gave you entree into the opera world. In the fall, Marc has a contract with the New York Met to do Rodolfo in *La Boheme*; three weeks later, he is to perform *Rigoletto* in San Francisco. It is a grueling schedule, but Andre and Marc are both confident that Marc can handle it.

Meantime, Shannon is to perform as Rosina in *The Barber of Seville*, in London in the fall. It is a role she has dreamt of playing, and she is thrilled. She has also been asked to perform her most memorable role, Carmen again, in Texas.

Apparently, some of the wealthy oil ranchers and their wives are determined to put their larger-than-life state on the map operatically, proving their culture and refined taste. I told her to watch out or she would lose her heart in Texas. They are known for their largesse. But she stuck her nose in the air, and pretended not to hear me.

One more month and baby will be here. Will it be a boy or a girl? Will it look like Marc or more like me? I am tired, but also restless, very restless.

May 28th
Dear Mary,
It's a girl; a beautiful six pound, four ounce girl, born on Sunday, May twenty-fifth. We named her Elyssa Mary

after you and Marc's grandmother. She has dark hair like both of us and beautiful blue eyes.

I am totally spoiled and so very much in love all over again, both with my husband and with this tiny girl. She looks so fragile and sweet, but she does have a mighty pair of lungs when her diaper is wet or when she is hungry.

And Marc. He is enthralled, enraptured with his daughter. She already has him totally wrapped up in her fingers, but doesn't know it—yet! He says he doesn't mind her crying because she will follow in his footsteps and become a famous singer.

I smile and indulge him. After all, this is his first, though we have Davey. Don't worry. We include Davey in all we do. When Elyssa receives gifts, we make sure Davey gets a little present as well.

Actually, he is just as enthralled with her as Marc is. He is so very careful around her and tends to be very protective. Whenever she cries, he is at the side of her bassinet instantly, patting her awkwardly and shushing her. It has been love at first sight for him as well.

June 23rd
Dear Mary,
My how motherhood keeps a person busy! Many women report having postpartum depression, but I have avoided that problem, I think. Between Elyssa's diapers and Davey's perpetual motion now, I rarely have time to even think about feeling depressed.

Marc is also busy with *Mignon*. They had some difficulty with the fire in the castle, but sheets of plastic loosely fitted over battens blown slightly by small fans and lighted by red and yellow gobo lights did the trick.

Shannon and I are working on her aria, *Je suis Titania*. She is determined to play her role to perfection. But she is also working on her pieces from *The Barber of Seville*. It is a joy to work with someone who demands such attention to detail.

August 6th

August 6th
Dear Mary,
The strangest events have landed our little family in a foreign, though not unfamiliar, country. Marc and Shannon did wonderful jobs in their respective roles in *Mignon*. Gretta and Michel, as usual held a large celebration for everyone following the last performance.

The next day, Marc went to the O to pick up the remainder of his personal belongings since his next engagements take him to America. As he was leaving the back of the theatre, he overheard some men in a heated conversation. He didn't pay much attention until he realized they were making plans to assassinate Charles de Gaulle.

He tried to leave quietly without attracting attention, but they spotted him, chasing him through the Metro. Crouching down in one of the cars, he managed to write a letter to me in case he didn't make it back home. It read

Mon Cherie,
I have uncovered a plot to kill the President. Two men with dark hair are chasing me through the Metro. I keep doubling back in the cars and changing trains, and I think I have lost them, but just in case I don't make it back, I want you to know the truth.

One man is tall and walks with a slight limp to his left leg; the other has a handlebar mustache and an old-fashioned watch on a chain.

I love you more than words can say.
Your Marc

Knowing he shouldn't go home and expose us to danger, he finally made his way to a police station and told his story. Under unobtrusive but heavy guard he was escorted home. We had to pack and leave the next day. Gretta came to help, and most of our belongings are now stored in the upper rooms of Michel's study.

Apparently, the men Marc overheard are part of an international terrorist organization and killing Charles de Gaulle is only one part of their plot to wreak havoc.

Our protectors took no chances. Marc traveled separately from Davey, Elyssa, and me. The children and I were helped by a secret service agent named Elaine--she was wonderful with the children—and took a more direct route through Spain to, of all places, Ireland. Marc's route, more circuitous, landed him here with us two days later.

I was so afraid he wouldn't make it here safely, but the agents traveling with him were also wonderful. We are now staying under the protection of Shannon's family in the smallest of the McKinnon Cottages, the one farthest off the road. Donnie has been assigned to watch over us.

Am I living in a time warp? It seems so strange to be here again, but we are treating it as another vacation. We do try to keep a low profile since the town is swarming with tourists.

August 13th

Dear Mary,

So many questions to be answered. Late last evening, Donnie came to talk to us. They haven't caught the terrorists yet, but Marc's quick actions prevented an attack on the President. Since *Mignon* was over, our absence has not been commented about. Everyone thinks we are taking our normal vacation.

Assuming that the terrorists are not caught soon, Marc will still meet his obligations since by now it should be obvious to these evil people that the police have been notified. What would be the point in killing him except for revenge? He will have security detailed to him when he travels.

Not only are we being protected, but Marc's family is being cared for as well. Donnie says that he is not the only one assigned to us, but he will be the only person who will talk to us about this situation because they want us to live our lives as normally as possible.

His superiors wanted us to go to a place where we had no previous connections, but they were persuaded by Donnie that we would be kept safely here, and they are also confident that the terrorists will be caught soon.

Meantime, I am enjoying my new baby girl. She is nearly three months old and loves to "talk" to Davey. He will tell her all about his day playing with his new "cousins" (Janice and Jenny's children), and she will coo right back at him, smiling and gurgling. She loves her big brother!

Marc is restless. He is not allowed to sing. I finally suggested that he either find a new hobby or find a way to help the McKinnons with their responsibilities. He left in a huff, but I later heard him whistling as he loaded kindling and peat in a wagon to be carried to the main house for Mother McKinnon.

Because the day was warmish, he took his shirt off. He sure looked fine without a shirt! Maybe I'll have to seduce him tonight! (Don't mind me; Janice and Jenny are rubbing off on me!)

September 9th

Dear Mary,

Our cottage is clean, Elyssa is down for a nap, and Davey is playing with his "cousins" up at the main house. Jenny went to do a spot of shopping, and then she will stop by for a cuppa. I am becoming more and more European, I suppose; I enjoy stopping for tea in the afternoon.

We are becoming anxious about Elyssa. She is full of smiles and joy, but she is so tiny. Jenny and Janice think I should take her to see a doctor. When I ask what exactly they think is wrong, they shrug and can't seem to come up with anything specific.

I try to remember what Davey was like at her age. He was certainly more energetic, always trying to push up with his legs. Elyssa seems content to lie still and smile at everyone.

On a less sober note, Davey's third birthday party was simple, but fun. We had an old-fashioned party with all his new friends, playing "Pin the Tail on the Donkey" and eating cake and ice cream outside at some tables. The children chased one another among the trees while the adults caught up on local gossip.

It is hard to believe your son is three already. I am so thankful you allowed us to have him for this brief time. He is no longer a baby but a small boy, serious and mannerly, but with a twinkle in his eyes that ignites when fun is about.

September 16th

Dear Mary,

Jenny took Elyssa and me to their family doctor last Wednesday. He examined her, taking especially long with his stethoscope. He told me, as kindly as he could, that he thinks her heart is having difficulties keeping pace with her growth. His receptionist called a friend of his in Cork and set an appointment for us on Friday.

It was devastating news for Marc. He questioned Jenny and I over and over again about what the doctor did and his exact words. The entire McKinnon family joined us for dinner at the main house Thursday evening with the exception of Shannon. They have become our family, sharing birthday celebrations, cups of tea, and now our anxiety.

Of course, no one can stay down for long with their good cheer and, as always, music. I will never forget the song Donnie sang with his father's violin for accompaniment. It was about friends remaining friends through many long years, and though I haven't known the McKinnons long, they seem like very close friends.

Friday morning early, Donnie, as our friend and bodyguard, drove us into Cork. Dr. Kilpatrick, prepared by the phone calls of his friend, Dr. Connelly, put Elyssa through a battery of tests. We will not find out the full results until our appointment this coming Friday, but Dr. Kilpatrick concurs with Dr. Connelly and told us to brace ourselves for the worst.

September 22nd

Dear Mary,

The news is not good. Elyssa has a hole in her heart that will grow larger as she grows. She also has a problem with one of the valves. She desperately needs surgery, but she is too small. So we play a waiting game: we wait for her to grow even though growth means an increased chance of her death.

Gretta is nearly mad with worry for us. She wants to come on an extended visit, but I told her that her husband and her girls need her too. She calls us twice a week now on a "clean" phone, one that is definitely debugged and can't be traced.

If this had to happen, at least we are with the McKinnons. It would be awful to go through this trouble in a strange place with no one to lean upon.

Meantime, Donnie brought a letter to me from Mother Sebastiani. I nearly forgot that I had written to her. I read it with tears in my eyes and in my heart. You have been ill but are recuperating there at the convent.

How wonderful that you are there where she can watch over you. And how sad I am that you choose not to find Will. A mystery is there. He would never leave for this long unless there was a reason. I hope for your sake that nothing has happened to him.

When I was very little, life was good and sweet. Then, a great evil entered my life and I felt that life would never be good again. Marc entered my life, and life became very sweet and good again. Now I am entering another stormy time, and I am convinced that we must learn not to only accept the sorrow along with the joy, but to embrace it as the very thing that will bring about greater joy.

October 6th

Dear Mary,

Marc left Friday afternoon from Cork for New York via a private plane. It was previously engaged to take a few operatives to New York, so the expense is not great. He was reluctant to leave, but now is the best time for him to go. Elyssa has gained two pounds. She must gain ten pounds total to be considered for surgery. Loathe as I was for him to leave, I know I'll need him more later.

Meantime, Elyssa smiles and laughs at Davey's antics to entertain her, and he seems to be thriving in his new surroundings. I think it is because he has more children with whom to play and interact. We have chosen not to say much about Elyssa to Davey. He is too young to realize that anything is wrong. As long as she smiles for him, his world is secure.

Marc called to say that his flight was uneventful. He and his operative, Cecil, saw nothing suspicious. He has promised me that he will wear a bulletproof vest during his performances. He will be gone until the eleventh of November.

Chapter Thirty-Six

October 23rd

Dear Mary,

Fall has come to Ireland, and it is so beautiful. In back of our cottage the MacGillicuddy's Reeks Mountain Range flirts with the clouds that come to play. Up past the main house and across the road is the lake. I am learning the many moods of the water.

As evenings turn a mite cooler, we gather around the crackling fire fueled by the peat that is so abundant here on the Emerald Isle. It is very relaxing to brood over a cup of tea, contemplating the lake or the woods or the mountains.

Now that I have learned her ways, I do my best to help Mother McKinnon. My laundry is done on days she is not busy with laundry for her family or the guests. I keep our cottage cleaned and even help clean the other cottages or rooms when guests leave. Since tourism has slowed some, I am learning how to prepare traditional Irish dishes so I can help in the kitchen as well.

I miss Marc dreadfully, but I am trying to stay busy.

November 25th

Dear Mary,

Marc, the love of my life, has returned, and our precious daughter has made it to six months! Great reasons to celebrate. Elyssa has gained a total of eight pounds, but as she gains weight, her heart strains to keep up, and now she has a definite bluish tinge to her skin.

Two terrorists were captured as they tried to enter Marc's final performance. Donnie says they have about eight more to capture including the two top ringleaders.

Some other wonderful things have happened, as well. Shannon's performances of *The Barber of Seville* received raves, and she is home. It is so good to see her again. She has brought an aura of vitality with her as well as more music, if that is possible.

Gretta, Michel, Margaretta, and Nadia have booked one of the other cottages for three weeks around the Christmas holidays. Donnie's boss is not pleased, but Gretta can be very persuasive! They have arranged for private transportation from London, so no records will alert the wrong people of their comings and goings.

So in spite of the cloud hanging over us with Elyssa's health problems and the terrorists still at large, we have much rejoicing to do at the special season approaching.

January 3rd

Dear Mary,

What a wonderfully relaxing time we are having! Gretta, Michel, Margaretta, and Nadia have several more days here. Most of the gifts I bought here in Killarney, but Gretta also did some shopping for me.

Supporting the wool industry in Ireland, we went in for sweaters as gifts this year. For Michel we chose a lovely wool sweater in gray with a gorgeous deep blue pattern as accent. Margaretta's was in a deep green, and Nadia's was in a rosy red. Gretta received some of the famous Waterford crystal. We are sending sweaters back with Gretta for Paul, Natalie, and even little Emilie.

The McKinnon's were more difficult to buy for, and we went overboard, but as our gifts are also a heartfelt thank you for their hospitality and friendship, Marc's family approved.

We chose an electric clothes dryer for Mother McKinnon. They have just come out and better models will be produced, but with the amount of laundry and cleaning she does, we thought it would help her workload.

For Father McKinnon we bought a new typewriter. He types his books and essays on an ancient model that only he knows how to coax along.

Marc and I decided to leave the pranks up to the McKinnon family this year. While he was in San Francisco, he found some Indian jewelry, delicate silver and turquoise bracelets for Jenny, Janice, Maggie, Emil's wife, Julia, Jake's wife, and Shannon and me, too!

For Emil and Jake, we gave them each gift certificates to a hardware store in Cork that supplies many of the latest tools and equipment on the market. They also stock home supplies, so that gives Emil and Jake the choice of buying something for their business or their homes or both. It seemed like a good gift, so we also purchased gift certificates for Johnny, Janice's husband and Ralph, Jenny's husband, too.

Alice and Dennie have been wanting to modernize the kitchen in their new home, so we made arrangements with Emil and Jake for the work to begin.

Joey, the party-goer, likes clothes, so we gave him a gift certificate to a nice men's clothing store.

Donnie we saved for last. Marc and Donnie have become as close as brothers. Donnie's personality is quieter than Marc's, but they both have a similar intensity in their attitude toward life. We racked our brains for something special for him. Since he often travels and at a moment's notice, Marc found some travel gear for him: an entire wardrobe change with all the travel accessories and accoutrements in a compact, briefcase-sized travel case.

Shannon went in big for perfume and colognes from Paris this year. She had perfumes made especially suited to Janice and Jenny's personalities. When they put them on they smelled awful! Janice and Jenny began threatening Shannon, but started gagging. They had to run to the bathroom and scrub to remove the offensive odors.

When they returned, they ganged up on Shannon with pillows, until laughing, she pulled out the good stuff. Of course, all the men suspected the colognes, but Shannon assured them her tricks were only for Janice and Jenny.

We decided to include Davey in choosing gifts for his "cousins" this year. Children are always easy to buy for, and Davey was very proud to have a part in it.

With the additional support from Gretta and Michel and Shannon, I felt calmer than I have since Elyssa's first trip to the doctor.

Gretta and I had a long talk about death since Elyssa's chances are only fifty-fifty. She and Michel lost a child before Marc was born. Those were very difficult days for her. She was not prepared for it, and it nearly destroyed her. She wants me to be prepared either way. Normally, I would resent this as a major intrusion, but coming from Gretta, I felt oddly reassured.

Shannon was there, too, in the small kitchen of our cottage as we talked over the inevitable pot of tea. Communicating with her has been absolutely forbidden as it would give the wrong people clues to our whereabouts. I felt comforted and embraced with the love and concern from both her family and Marc's.

We look forward to a very tough year, but leaning on the support of others will get us through. Gretta said that forming deep friendships like this is the last step in my recovery from the terrible trauma I went through in junior high and high school.

Shannon stirred more sugar in her cup, then licked the spoon delicately. "Having a husband is highly overrated although I do plan to snag one eventually."

Gretta and I laughed at this.

Shannon grasped first my hand and then Gretta's firmly. "Having close girlfriends, no matter what their age," she said with a nod to Gretta, "is just as important. We will be there for you, Robyn, in spirit and thought if not in actual presence."

Gretta grasped my other hand, and we formed a circle of complete love, trust, and friendship. It was a special moment.

February 26th

Dear Mary,

I am in the blackest of holes and can't find my way out. On Monday evening the sixteenth of February, Elyssa went into cardiac arrest while we were eating dinner at the main house. Everyone reacted quickly and efficiently. Donnie had the car at the door in less than two minutes, Marc grabbed a diaper bag, and I ran with Elyssa to the front seat.

The drive to the doctor's house was accomplished in five minutes, but it was too late. When we arrived he placed her carefully on the floor and did CPR, all to no avail.

I will never forget the terrified look in her eyes, her body growing limp, and then the warmth slowly fading to a stone cold. Oh, my beautiful, Elyssa. I miss you so much. Did I do everything I could? She was so close to the operation. She was to go in that Wednesday morning. I keep telling myself that even the operation might not have saved her, but I continue to question myself.

Marc is absolutely torn apart. I am so glad that he has Donnie. I feel unable to support his grief as well as my own.

The funeral was last Friday. We have become part of a close-knit family, and people came from everywhere it seemed to pay their respects to our little girl. When I whispered to Mother McKinnon about all the people, she squeezed my arm and told me that we have crawled into their hearts. Of course they would come to support us.

Right now, I just want to crawl into a hole and pull a stone over the top, but Davey must be tended to. If it wasn't for your son right now, Mary, I don't think I could go on living. Thank you.

May 27th

Dear Mary,

Spring in Ireland came softly this year. I still miss Elyssa terribly, but I think I am coming up out of the black hole I was in.

Marc has had a slew of offers since his debut with the New York Met. He is booked for two, nearly three years solid. He is to perform in New York in June, in Texas in July and in London again in October. He has been asked to sing in Paris also in October, but it depends on the terrorist situation.

We wondered why he hadn't received any roles for the first part of this year. Now we know. Performing after losing his daughter would have been too devastating.

Shannon will be sharing the stage with Marc in New York singing her favorite role in *The Barber of Seville*. It is her New York debut, and she is thrilled. I am so happy for her.

It is hard to believe that Davey is more than three and a half years now. He misses Elyssa too, but seems to be rather more resilient. When he is too quiet, I have learned to patiently ask questions until he opens up his heart.

We have had some interesting talks. Elyssa's death has refocused my attention on my beliefs in God. I know some people think it is just a crutch, but I was the one who watched my cherished, infant daughter die in my arms, and I choose to believe in a Hereafter and a God Who, though He is not responsible for bad things happening, allows all things to happen for a purpose.

It gives dignity to death, a reason to live, and hope for eternity. It is also comfort to a little boy who misses his sister, but is reassured by believing that God is taking care of her in heaven.

July 26th

Dear Mary,

Shannon's debut in New York was an astounding success! I knew it would be. She is a hard worker as well as a perfectionist and, of course, I am her teacher! I should say that I was her teacher. She doesn't need me any longer.

That is good because I am dying. There. I actually wrote it. I haven't told anyone yet although I'm sure Donnie suspects. I went into Cork last week with Donnie chauffeuring as usual. Even though this summer has been busy with plenty of tourists, I have been so very tired without my usual snap. Everyone attributes it to my continuing grief over Elyssa, but I knew it was something else.

Dr Kilpatrick was kind enough to refer me to an oncologist who specializes in cancer treatment. Today we drove back to Cork. The specialist, Dr. Campbell, says the cancer appears to have progressed rapidly throughout my lymph system and I only have a few months to live.

I feel numb, but mostly I am worried about the effect on Marc and Davey. I don't want to be the cause of more suffering for them. Marc is not back yet from Texas. How can I give him more bad news?

September 16th

Dear Mary,

I finally told them. Mother McKinnon began to suspect, and Donnie found out through sources only he knows. Actually, he was the one to tell his mother, she told Janice, Jenny, and Alice, giving them time to adjust to the news. Then all the men folk found out except for Marc, and Mother McKinnon helped me tell Marc.

Donnie took him on a long ride so Marc could ask questions and get some of his anger out of his system. He is mostly angry right now and feels as if God has given him too much to bear.

September 30th
Dear Mary,

Marc is still fighting it, but I think he is finally coming to terms with losing me. We had a long discussion last night while sitting on the love seat in front of the fireplace.

He wanted to know why I am so resigned. I told him that I'm not resigned at all; I want to go on living with the rest of them. Besides, I'm scared to face the end. But more important, I've realized that instead of wasting my time fighting this, I want to make each day count even if it's in a small way since I'm so tired.

The doctors say that there is nothing they can do when cancer spreads through the lymphatic system. If there was, I would pursue it mightily. What I don't want is to waste the precious time I have left being sick from treatment. Instead, give me pain killers, and let me spend as much time with the people I love as possible.

Marc wants to cancel all of his engagements, but I told him I won't die while he's gone to London, and London is not really that far away. I am selfish enough to want him to cancel the Paris engagement even though several more terrorists have been caught. Two of the leaders are still at large, and their followers are everywhere. Until they are apprehended, Marc is not safe.

November 9th

Dear Mary,

The end is near. The McKinnons moved us into the main house so they can help and so I can bask by the fire all day. I cannot move around much without considerable pain. My greatest joys are hearing what Davey has been doing with his cousins, being held in Marc's arms, and listening to the McKinnons sing evenings.

Isn't it interesting that when all is said and done, the most enjoyable things in life can't be bought and can't be earned. They are simply given out of love.

Mary, I have been so blessed. Though I would love to live another ten years, at least I feel as if I have been some use in this world, protecting Davey, loving and helping Marc, and teaching Shannon. But in truth, I receive so much more than I have been given.

Davey knows that I am going up to Heaven to help God take care of Elyssa. I told him that I will be looking down on him, watching him and taking care of him in ways he can't see. He can even talk to me any time he needs to talk to someone. I also told him that Marc is going to help him find his real Mommy and Daddy, but that Marc and I will always be his Maman and Papa.

I also think that God is going to give him a new Maman. Mother McKinnon and I talked about it a few days ago. I have thought for some time now that Shannon cares very deeply for Marc, but she would never betray our friendship by even dreaming something could develop. I have absolutely no problem with it, should Marc ever return her love, and I told Mother McKinnon so.

God is good to give me a glimpse into the future. If only I knew more about you. But I guess I will just have to trust you into God's hands where you will be safest after all. I love you, Sis.

*****

Those were the last words that my sister penned. Tears streamed down my face as I finished her journal, tears that were as cleansing as an Irish rain.

Chapter Thirty-Seven

My sister's journal and the letter from Marc gave me much to think about and, after my tears had been spent, filled me with restless energy. Somewhere, probably in Paris, was my son. And also in Paris was a mystery that needed a proper resolution.

But how could I possibly find my son and uncover the secrets behind Marc's whereabouts with him? I had few funds left, certainly not enough to gallivant over to Europe. For several weeks I meditated and agitated about what to do. At last I decided that I would have to talk to Mother Sebastiani and ask to be released from my duties at the convent to finish my education.

My plan was to obtain my certification in teaching. I needed very little for myself. I would pour most of earnings into a savings account until I had enough to travel to Paris, maybe even to live there for several months while locating my son and investigating Marc's whereabouts.

I had relinquished the wild fantasies of finding Will. Dreams of him still pervaded my sleep, but time had softened the sharply cutting edges of disappointment. No longer did I try to answer the question of why he had never returned for me. I knew he had intended to do so, but he had not for some inexplicable reason. He might be remarried by now, and I had no intention of embarrassing both him and myself by trying to find him.

I decided to leave the past in the past, cherishing only those memories that I could handle emotionally, that brought a tender smile to mind if not to face. Quite simply, my emotions were worn, and my tears were spent.

But Davey. Where was my son, Davey? He was mine, and my fiercely maternal instinct, so long suppressed, reasserted itself with renewed intensity. I must make all efforts to find him. How I dreaded talking to Mother Sebastiani aware as I was of my double-mindedness, of my treachery in stealing the boxes from my sister's coffin.

Mother Sebastiani, as always, was graciousness personified.

"Sit down, Mary, and tell me how I can help you," she said when I entered her office.

I sat, folding the edge of my sleeve in and out nervously. She crossed the small room to a tall, wooden filing cabinet and pulled out a file folder. Seating herself at the antique redwood desk, she folded her hands quietly in her lap and waited for me to begin.

"I-I stole some boxes out of one of the drawers in the mortuary a few months ago," I began baldly. Risking a glance at her face, I saw that her expression had not become stern as I had imagined it would, so I continued. "The dead person was my sister, Robyn, and the boxes were full of papers, mostly birth and death certificates, receipts, playbills, and a journal."

I continued painfully. "My-my son had gone to live with her when he was a baby, and I wanted to find out more about him. But my sister is dead, and her husband is in hiding; even their baby daughter is dead, and I need to find my son." The tears, all too readily, welled in my eyes once again. I started to speak again, but the impact of her words startled me into silence.

"I know."

I stared at her uncomprehendingly. How did she know? What did she know?

"I knew that your sister's body would be shipped here and that the boxes would be with it. They were intended for you all along, so I just made sure that you were the one who had them."

"But ..."

Mother Sebastiani raised her hand to silence me. "Your sister came to me while you were still in the hospital after delivering Davey. We spent some time together while she told me of her plans. She was so very worried about you, you see. She wanted me to watch out for you and your concerns from afar, and I have.

When you were younger, you and she had talked about coming to the convent here if either of you were in grave trouble. The idea, I believe, was planted in your minds by your mother."

I was astounded, but she was continuing.

"You see, your mother and I were very close friends in high school. She realized within several years of her marriage that she had made a grave mistake in marrying your father who not only was ten years her senior, but also had some disturbing problems."

Mother Sebastiani sighed and looked at me. "Am I
hurting you by speaking so familiarly of your family?"

I nodded my head no.

"By then, your sister had been born, and you came
soon after that. I went to visit your mother the day before she
passed away. She had written letters to you and your sister
that I was to give you at the appropriate time."

Letters from my mother?

"Your sister received her letter when she came to visit
me. I think it gave her the strength to do what she knew she
must do, but you must know that she was terribly anxious
about moving to Paris with your baby boy and the hardships
it could cause in her life as a new wife as well as the
heartbreak it was causing you."

She paused and toyed with a pen in front of her.
"Your mother had received a small inheritance from her
mother that your father never knew about. She left it in my
care for you and Robyn. Robyn and Marc decided to leave
her portion with me. We called in an old lawyer friend of
your mother's to write a will, explaining carefully how the
money was to be used."

She continued the saga while I sat still, trying to
absorb what she was saying. "When Marc and Robyn arrived
in Paris, they had their wills filed with attorneys there so
there would be no difficulties in transferring or using the
funds. Your sister was also concerned about your father
gaining knowledge of the will and trying to break it."

Leaning across her desk for emphasis, she said,
"Marc readily agreed to provide for Davey as if Davey was

his own son, but if any additional expenses arose, Robyn was free to use the money to care for Davey or herself."

"When Marc stumbled on information he was not supposed to be privy to," she continued, "he took his little family into hiding, fully cooperating with police. They had hoped that this little sabbatical would only last for six months at the most. But then Elyssa died and Robyn was struck with cancer."

"Robyn contacted me through the attorneys in France, and all of her monies were transferred to Paris for her use so her illness would not be a burden on the family finances. After her death, the Paris lawyers contacted me. It seems that there is still enough left for Davey's care."

Mother Sebastiani looked at me searchingly as if questioning my understanding of what she was telling me. She put on her reading glasses and slowly opened the folder on her desk.

"In this folder are records of all that has transpired. I also have the letter from your mother as well as one from your sister. Before I give you the records, before you make any decisions and before you even read your mother's letter, I think you need to read your sister's letter. I will leave you alone in here for thirty minutes while you read it, and then we will discuss your future plans."

She rose, handed me the letter, and quietly left the room.

I held the letter in my hand, considering its import. My sister had often alluded in the last several years of her time in the United States to more information about the family, especially my father.

A feeling of dread welled up inside of me, for I knew that I would discover the irrevocable truth in this letter. Surely though, my father's actions and their consequences would finally be put to rest. I had not seen him now for years, and I might as well confront the truth and put it behind me.

Restless, I stood and moved over to the small window that overlooked the lake, sparkling like a gem in its forest setting. Pulling the pages from the business-sized envelope, I began to read.

Dear Mary,

I am writing this letter and entrusting it to Mother Sebastiani's care so that if anything happens to me, you will know the full truth about Dad. Before I tell you, though, I want you to know that with Marc's help, I know I will overcome the problems Dad's abuse has caused me.

Marc is the most wonderful person I have ever met, and I truly believe that God created him especially for me. His mother is a doctor of psychology as well as a nurse, and because he is so close to his mother, he knows how to work with me.

If you think back, you will remember some very odd happenings in our house. It is still painful to write about this, so I won't go into details. Just suffice it to say that Dad abused me sexually. He started when I was ten with small things, but when I became a "woman," he forced me to do the unimaginable.

I think Mom suspected, but she never said anything. She was so frail emotionally that I truly believe she thought if she didn't acknowledge it, it wouldn't be true. I have been so angry with her for not protecting me. Marc is helping with that, too, and he says his Mom will help me even more.

Anyway, I found out that I was not the first one he had abused. It seems there have been two or three others, most of them girls, but one was a boy. I found this out from Will's mom. Will's father found out about it from a detective doing work for his company. The detective told him because he knew Will and you were dating.

Mom Merrill was the one who helped me to start the process of breaking away from the abuse. Before I went to college, I confronted Dad with what I knew, and told him he'd better not bother you or continue coming after me, or I'd expose the truth.

He was extremely irate, but it worked. He left you alone. But then I found him trying to kill Davey in the hospital. I won't let him kill my nephew, nor will I let him practice his evil on his first grandson.

What happens with his new wife's boys is their business. Marjorie has always treated me in a disdainful, haughty fashion, and I have not felt comfortable talking to her, so I decided that their welfare is not my responsibility.

I also found out that Dad suffers a form of dementia. His behavior certainly corroborates this. He could take medication for it, but he won't. If he did, it would probably destroy the delusions he has built in his mind about himself.

Taking your baby with me to Paris is the hardest thing I'll ever do. I know you think I'm an interfering busybody, but I know what Dad is like. I just hope that you will someday learn to forgive me.

We have always been so close, especially since losing Mom, and it is hard to leave the United States knowing I may never see you again. If only you could come with us, but I know your hopes of seeing Will again hold you back.

My first inclination was to convince you to come with us anyway, but one night, Marc asked me how I'd feel if I lost him. So I want you to know that I understand how you feel, and I hope it works out for you two. Once you two get back together, you had better come see us in Paris!

Davey is a special child, and I truly believe that God has surrounded him with people to take care of him and us. Mother Sebastiani has been an unlimited source of encouragement, the lawyer, Mr. Winsapple has been helpful and kind (he used to date Mom), and Marc's family is committed to helping us care for Davey.

I know that right now you are hurting, but I hope that eventually you will find the good in all of this. Mother Sebastiani keeps telling me that there is always a purpose for the things that happen in our lives, and we have to learn to see things from God's perspective and not from our own finite and limited human vision.

I love you, Sis. Nothing will ever change that.

Robyn Johnson Montaigne

I stood a long time at the window after reading her letter. The tears flowed again, but this time they were for a sister of whom I could no longer ask forgiveness. She had thought I was strong when she was the strong, courageous one.

The tears spent themselves, and I began musing over what she had written. It was true. God had surrounded us with people to care for us even when our parents could and would not: the Merrills, the Montaignes, the McKinnons, Mother Sebastiani, and even the lawyer I had never met, Mr. Winsapple.

Robyn's letter extended her love far past her grave, enveloping me with the special warmth and caring we had always shared as sisters. It also renewed my hope that I could reunite with my son.

When Mother Sebastiani returned, I was smiling through a soft rain of tears.

She smiled understandingly and said, "Your sister was a very thoughtful person. She tried to provide for an uncertain future in the best way she knew how. The attorneys were all impressed with her level-headedness for someone so young." She sighed. "I suppose the abuse she suffered caused her to grow up fast, but it also forged a strength in her that was uncommon for someone her age."

She sat at her desk again, and I followed to my chair. Handing me the folder she said, "The Paris attorneys recommend that you do not look for your son at this time. They are quietly closing in on the terrorist organization your brother-in-law inadvertently stumbled upon, and they feel that if someone from America began asking questions, it could put your son's life in danger. Their address is in this folder," she handed it to me, "and they want you to advise them of any change of address."

"But why can't my son join me here in America?" I asked.

Mother Sebastiani considered her words. "I don't know the full ramifications of what is happening over there, nor do I know exactly where your son is. All I know is that Marc and his family are taking care of him," she said slowly.

"I don't like to give advice without knowing the full situation," she continued, "but think about your son. He is with people he knows, and he is safe. For you to appear right now could seriously disrupt the flow of his life. He knows that Robyn and Marc are not his real parents, and I think that when the time is right for him, the Montaignes will encourage him to find you."

She continued, speaking slowly, consideringly. "It seems to me that your responsibility right now is to finish your education, and put yourself in a position to care for Davey. You do have some money left to you by your mother, but you are young and healthy. With the dedication you have shown and the experience you have gained here teaching music, you certainly have the ability to become a fine music teacher."

"Get the education you need, and you will have a high recommendation from me," she added. "Invest wisely the money your mother left you, and you should be able to retire early with a comfortable financial cushion. That will provide you with the resources you need to find your son if he doesn't find you first."

Her advice was sound, but oh, it was a bitter pill to swallow. I had come so close to my son only to lose him again.

Chapter Thirty-Eight

Taking Mother Sebastiani's advice, I had finished my education at the Conservatory and had taken a job teaching elementary school music. My stamina returned, but within a year of graduating from the Conservatory and during a routine doctor visit, I had been diagnosed with breast cancer.

Radiation treatments took care of the cancer, but dipping into my carefully hoarded funds to pay what insurance wouldn't cover, left me in a slough of depression. The one bright ray of sunshine in my life was Rosalie, my nursing friend.

Rosalie had been my favorite nurse from my very first visit at Hope Treatment Center. She was tender and compassionate, but she allowed me the dignity of doing things for myself, patiently waiting for me even though she could have completed the small tasks in a much shorter amount of time. I grew to love her as a dear friend. Her disarming personality and bright chatter would open doors for her that a more sober and analytical demeanor would not.

One evening over a steak dinner—"To bolster your energy for your treatment tomorrow," she said—I confided my story to her.

"And you've never tried to look Will up?" Her mouth gaped in amazement. "Mary, you're turning your back on the love of your life. You've given up on both him and yourself. Shame on you."

My face flamed, and I started to protest.

"Okay, okay. I know. You don't want to intrude on his life if he's married or whatever it is you're telling yourself, but I'll just bet he hasn't remarried. Not if he cared for you that much. Something had to have happened. I'll find out." She put on the sunglasses she was rarely without off-duty. "Just call me Detective Robbins."

Her pose was so exaggerated, her air so mysterious, that I had to laugh.

"But how will you find out?" I asked apprehensively.

She pushed her hands together, cracking her knuckles suggestively. "We're living in the 60's now, Darling," she said with a fake accent. "I have ways of finding out these things!"

"I'll just bet you do," I retorted. Then I really thought about what she was saying. "You won't do anything, uh, obvious, will you?" I asked nervously.

"The soul of discretion. That's me," she said. "Seriously, Mary. I'd never do anything to hurt you. It just sounds as if you need a third party to do some behind the scenes, undercover investigating. No one knows who I am, and I'll be careful not to arouse any suspicion."

I had to admire her determination to help.

Two weeks later, she popped over with some news. "I've found them! I've found the Merrills," she said exultantly. "They live in a town called Walterboro, about thirty miles from Charleston. And guess, just guess when they moved there?"

I couldn't venture a guess; I was rooted to the place I was standing, flooded with memories.

"The seventeenth of May, 1960," she continued, not waiting for me to answer. "Didn't you say that your sister was married on the twentieth? When Will left, I bet he didn't know they had moved, or maybe he forgot since he was so upset."

"I found out something else. Mr. Merrill suffered a heart attack on May twenty-first and both Will Merrill and his father were in the same hospital at the same time although Will remained in the hospital much longer than his father."

Astonishment flooded me at all she had learned. Will in the hospital? What had happened to him? Had he been in a car accident? And I had selfishly thought only of my need of him without a care that he might have needed me.

"Mary! Are you alright? You look like a cat caught in the flour. You'd better sit down."

I sat, a million thoughts chasing in and out of my mind.

"Oh. By the way, I also found out that Will has never remarried. And no one I talked to knows that it is his wife in California asking about him."

My hands began shaking when she used the word, "wife." I could only stare at her in dumb astonishment and wonder at what she had discovered in such a short amount of time.

On the heels of this news came a letter from Mother Sebastiani.

352

Dear Mary,
The people who were a threat to Marc and his
Family have been captured. Before Marc's
return to the opera stage, he is bringing Davey
to the United States, and is requesting that
your meeting take place here in two weeks.
Could you come a day early, my dear?

He has sent a letter ahead with ideas to
make the transition for Davey easier, and I
would like to discuss these ideas with you.

Yours truly,
Mother Sebastiani

Rosalie agreed to come with me, and so, twelve days later, on a crisp autumn morning, we wended our way from Sacramento to the Lake District of Lucerne.

Mother Sebastiani embraced me warmly. She held Rosalie's face between her hands, and I knew she saw the sweet spirit, the kindred spirit in Rosalie that I saw.

She invited us into her office to read Marc's letter.

In it, Marc expressed his concern about the coming reunion and the impact on Davey. He proposed that I come over to Ireland and Paris for several months so I could learn more of Davey's background.

That would be no problem. What had I been saving my money for but to spend it to be with my son?

Marc also wanted me to know ahead of time that he had married Robyn's friend, Shannon from Ireland. In fact, his letter informed me of what I already knew, that they had stayed with Shannon's family when Marc had uncovered information about the terrorist ring. Robyn had spent her last days there being made comfortable by Shannon's warm and caring family, and Davey had many close friends among Shannon's nieces and nephews.

Rosalie and I spent the afternoon helping in the kitchen. It brought back some warm memories of earlier times spent there.

The next morning we waited in the large oak-beamed room in the main hall. We could see a mist arising from the lake through the large front windows. The fire in the large stone fireplace took the chill off the morning.

And now Davey was on his way! I leaned my head back and let the excitement course through me. He would be close to eight. Closing my eyes, I took a deep stabilizing breath, and instead of focusing on the questions, I focused on the lessons I had learned.

I had finally let go of all the bitterness toward my sister. It was more difficult to let go of the anger I felt toward my father. He should have been the one protecting and nurturing us; instead, his mental instability had changed the whole tenor of family life, crippling each of us in different ways with a peculiar vulnerability in our relationships with others.

Age brought the realization that visiting a shrink no longer carried a stigma. The Christian psychologist I had chosen to see helped me to once again refocus. Instead of questioning God's wisdom in allowing me to have such a father, she helped me to focus on God's goodness in bringing people into my life who could combat the insane existence in my dad's world with the joie de vivre with which life can truly be lived.

Once again I remembered all the good times my sister, my mother, and I had enjoyed with the Merrill family. At first the memories hurt, but it was as if God massaged the tenderness away until I could view my memories objectively and without pain.

As footsteps echoed in the hall announcing Davey's arrival, I gripped Rosalie's hand. And then I saw his face. He had my dark hair, but his beautiful eyes, his nose and his mouth were all Will's. He was holding the hand of a tall man, tall with silver edging at the temple of the dark hair. It was Marc. Behind them I saw two dim shadows of a man and a woman, but my eyes were all for the boy beside Marc.

"Hello, Mama," he said engulfing me in a long hug. And then the tears flowed. I stood, rocking back and forth in his embrace for a long, long time. When my tears abated, he tugged my hand, leading me to Marc.

I grasped Marc's hand. "Thanks so much for your wonderful care and concern for Davey over the years. I don't think I have fathomed yet the cost of the commitment you and Robyn made in taking Davey with you and protecting him. I don't want to pull him away from you and what he's comfortable with, and I'd be glad to come over to Europe for a while."

He grasped my hands with one of his, pulling the woman behind him toward me. "I'd like you to know Shannon. We married a year ago. Your sister was the one to suggest it and give her blessing for it the month before she died."

"I'm so glad to meet Robyn's sister," Shannon said in her delightful Irish accent. "She was an angel for all of us, I think," she said thoughtfully.

My eyes moistened again, but my mind was whirling. If this was Marc and Robyn's Shannon, who was this man waiting patiently behind them? I looked beyond them, searching his face, and sucked in my breath as I realized I was looking into the face of the only man I could ever love.

"Will?"

"Mary!" Those were the only words we spoke. He enfolded me in his arms and I knew we had finally come full circle.

Over lunch that Mother Sebastiani and her staff thoughtfully provided, we kept coming back to the one person who had done so much for all of us: Robyn.

"Toward the end of her life, your sister encouraged me to look for Will and find out what had happened," Marc said. She said that the love you two had was so real, so unshakeable, that she knew it would have taken a lot more than Davey's grandfather to keep Will away. When Shannon and I came to the States, we began our search for Will. It began and ended in the outskirts of Charleston, South Carolina."

Will took up the story. "When I left that May day, all I could think about was talking to my mom and dad to get some wisdom on how to handle the situation. My idea was to fly you back to Charleston to live with us. But I fell asleep at the wheel on a mountainous road in North Carolina. I kept talking about Charleston, so I was taken to a hospital there. It was just by chance that one of my brothers who had come to visit my father saw my name on a hospital chart."

"I could remember California, and I kept having dreams of you begging for my help, but I couldn't remember any names or circumstances."

"My parents were in the middle of moving, and didn't even think to call; when Mom did, following Dad's heart attack, there was no answer. They finally nursed me back to health and my memory returned, but then I was called to do a stint in Vietnam. I couldn't go overseas, so they used me at the base in Charleston. I built a life there, but so much time had gone by, that I didn't want to bother you by showing up on your doorstep. I really was afraid you had remarried," he confessed.

"That's the same way I felt, why I never tried to find you," I gasped, tears smarting my eyes at our foolishness.

At Mother Sebastiani's insistence, we all spent the night at the convent. We put Davey in a room between us and Shannon and Marc. Rosalie agreed to sleep in the second twin bed in Davey's room since rooming was tight. Davey, the angel that he was, had no problem with his "big sister" Rosalie.

Our first night together in over twelve years. For a moment, I stopped to remember the people who, out of simple kindness, had done so much for me.

There were many, but Robyn was at the top of the list. In spite of her pain, in spite of her death, she lived on in all of our lives, not just in memory but in the essence of her spirit in each of our lives. She had lived her life so conscientiously, trying to do the best for all of us. In living her life to help those she loved, she had truly found the love she was so richly entitled to receive. I bowed my head in thankfulness.

When I raised my head, my heart beat unsteadily as I met the warm, calm gaze of the silvery blond headed man who I had loved so long ago and who I still continued to love. I stood and turned once again into his strong embrace. He bent his head to claim my lips with his, and it was as if the years slunk away leaving us with a love forged true by the fires of testing and time.

"I can't believe you are really here. It's really you. You truly are an angel," he said placing another kiss on my smooth cheek.

"It's really me, and believe me, I'm no angel" I said, breathless from his nearness. Without warning, happiness, a rare emotion, flooded and warmed my heart, and I knew, once and for all, that I was truly blessed with those simple yet profound things that can't be bought, purchased or priced.

THE END

Nell's Famous Coconut Cream Pie

Baked, single-crust pie shell	4 eggs
1 c. sugar	3 T. butter
½ c. cornstarch	1 t. vanilla
¼ t. salt	1 ½ c. flaked coconut
3 c. milk	Meringue

In saucepan, combine sugar, cornstarch, and salt, gradually stirring in milk. On medium/low heat, cook mixture until thickened and bubbly, being careful to keep stirring. Reduce heat, and cook for 2 more minutes. Remove pan from heat source.

Separate egg yolks from whites, setting whites aside for the meringue. Beat egg yolks with a fork. Gradually stir in 1 cup of the hot mixture (be careful that it's not so hot you create scrambled eggs!) Return egg mixture to the saucepan and bring to a gentle boil. Cook and stir 2 more minutes. Remove from heat source. Stir in butter and vanilla plus 1 cup of the coconut. Pour into baked pie shell.

Make the meringue using the reserved egg whites, 1 t. cream of tartar, ½ c. of sugar, 1 t. vanilla, and a pinch of salt. Whip until meringue forms stiff peaks.

Spread the meringue over the filling, sealing to edge. Sprinkle meringue with remaining coconut. Bake in 350° oven for 10-12 minutes or until meringue is golden. Cool.

Mom Merrill's Lemon-Poppy Seed Sour Cream Cake

3 c. sugar
3 c. flour
¼ t. salt
¼ t. baking soda
1 c. softened butter
Lemon Glaze

1 8-oz. container of sour cream
6 large eggs
2 T. lemon juice
1 t. vanilla extract
2 t. poppy seeds

Place first 9 ingredients in a 4-quart mixing bowl. Beat at low speed with a heavy-duty mixer 1 minute. Beat at medium speed 2 minutes. Pour mixture into a greased and floured 10-inch tube pan. Bake at 325° for 1 ½ minutes or until long toothpick in middle comes out clean. Cool cake pan for 10 minutes; remove from pan. Drizzle evenly with Lemon Glaze.

Lemon Glaze

1 c. powdered sugar
2 T. fresh lemon juice

½ t. vanilla extract
1 t. grated lemon rind
(optional)

Stir together first 3 ingredients until glaze is smooth. Add lemon rind, if desired.

A Preview of *A Secret Place*

In *A Secret Place*, Lawton and Lanie prepare for their wedding. But Lawton is becoming more involved in politics and the Merrill family property rights case, and finding time away from crowds of people is becoming rare.

Meantime, Blake is asked to help a cousin with a top-secret assignment on the Indian reservation. Tempers flare as younger members of the tribe want to bring in high-tech jobs, upsetting older members who believe in respecting the land. Outsiders also want to stop the techies, and they will do anything to prevent the tribe from joining the 21st century.

Add a cousin going through EMT training and a mayor who favors tax-rich properties over proper equipment, and the mix is positively charged to explode!

Everyone needs a secret place, but will they find it in time?